002

REKI KAWAHARA   ABEC   bee-pee

SWORD ART ONLINE
AINCRAD

SWORD ART ONLINE

"...No...It's my fault...
Thank you...for saving me..."

Silica § A beast-tamer with a
Feathery Dragon familiar

"...Sorry I couldn't save your friend..."

Kirito § A solo player aiming to beat the top floor of Aincrad. AKA "The Black Swordsman"

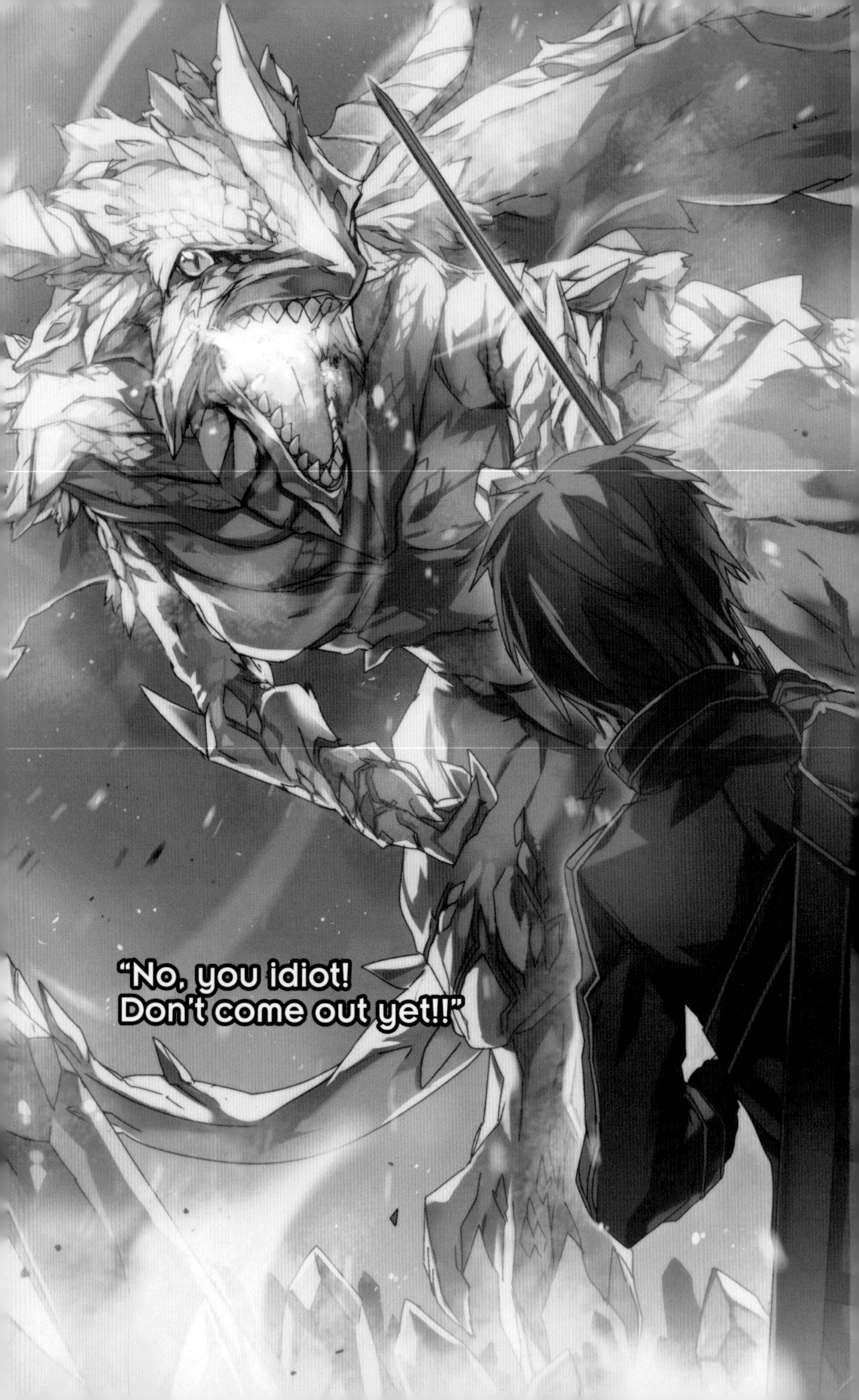
"No, you idiot!
Don't come out yet!!"

"The, uh, the dragon's attack pattern is: claws from left and right, ice breath, then a wind gale! B-be careful!"

Lisbeth § A blacksmith based in the town of Lindarth, on the forty-eighth floor

"Will you run away with me, Kirito?"

Sachi § A member of the Moonlit Black Cats, a guild in Aincrad

"Papa, carry me."

Yui § A mysterious girl found collapsed in the forest of the twenty-second floor of Aincrad

Floating Castle

Aincrad

A castle of rock and iron comprising one hundred floors. Inside are countless cities, towns, villages, forests, plains and lakes. Only one staircase connects each floor to its adjacents, and these staircases are located within dangerous mazes filled with monsters. The players within must navigate their way through these floors to the top, defeating powerful boss monsters with nothing more than the weapons in their hands. Outside of combat, there are also crafting disciplines like blacksmithing, leatherworking and tailoring; productive endeavors such as fishing and cooking; and even creative pursuits such as playing musical instruments. Players are not limited to adventuring within this vast, virtual world—they can literally choose their own lifestyles within the game.

Aincrad is the setting of Sword Art Online, the very first example of the VRMMO genre.

VOLUME 2

Reki Kawahara

abec

bee-pee

NEW YORK

SWORD ART ONLINE 2: Aincrad
REKI KAWAHARA

Translation: Stephen Paul

SWORD ART ONLINE
© REKI KAWAHARA 2009
All rights reserved.
Edited by ASCII MEDIA WORKS
First published in Japan in 2009 by
KADOKAWA CORPORATION, Tokyo.
English translation rights arranged with
KADOKAWA CORPORATION, Tokyo,
through Tuttle-Mori Agency, Inc., Tokyo.

English translation © 2014 by Hachette Book Group, Inc.

"Rudolph the Red-Nosed Reindeer" © 1949 St. Nicholas Music Inc. (renewed). All rights reserved.

Yen On
Hachette Book Group
1290 Avenue of the Americas, New York, NY 10104

www.HachetteBookGroup.com
www.YenPress.com

Yen On is an imprint of Hachette Book Group, Inc.
The Yen On name and logo are trademarks of Hachette Book Group, Inc.

First Yen On Edition: August 2014

Library of Congress Cataloging-in-Publication Data

Kawahara, Reki.
  Sword art online. 2, Aincrad / Reki Kawahara ; translation, Stephen Paul. — First Yen Press edition.
    pages cm
  "First published in Japan in 2009 by KADOKAWA CORPORATION, Tokyo."
  Summary: "Linked up and logged into the deadly VMMORPG "Sword Art Online" in both the real and virtual worlds, Kirito is stuck in a hell of one man's making, and like everyone else, unable to escape until the game is beaten"— Provided by publisher.
    ISBN 978-0-316-37681-5 (paperback) [1. Fantasy games—Fiction. 2. Virtual reality—Fiction. 3. Internet games—Fiction. 4. Science fiction.] I. Title.
  PZ7.K1755Swc 2014
  [Fic]—dc23
                                        2014011408

10 9 8 7 6 5 4

RRD-C

Printed in the United States of America

"THIS MIGHT BE A GAME, BUT IT'S NOT SOMETHING YOU PLAY."

—Akihiko Kayaba, *Sword Art Online* programmer

SWORD ART Online AINCRAD

Reki Kawahara

abec

bee-pee

An impossibly huge castle of rock and iron, floating in an endless expanse of sky.

That is the entirety of this world.

A tireless, month-long survey by a team of fanatical experts found that the base floor of the fortress was more than six miles in diameter, just large enough to fit the entirety of Tokyo's Setagaya ward inside. And considering the one hundred floors stacked one atop the other, the sheer vastness of the structure beggared the imagination. It was impossible to estimate the total amount of data it all represented.

Inside the castle were several bustling cities, countless smaller towns and villages, forests, plains, and lakes. Only one staircase connected each floor to those adjacent, and these staircases were located within dangerous labyrinths filled with monsters. It was difficult just to find them, much less reach them, but once some-one had cleared the stairs and arrived at a major city on the next floor up, a teleport gate linking to the new floor would open in every city below, allowing all players instantaneous travel among the various tiers of the castle.

It was thus that over two long years, its inhabitants slowly but steadily conquered this giant fortress.

The castle's name is Aincrad, a floating world of blade and battle with about six thousand human beings trapped within. Otherwise known as—

Sword Art Online.

002-01

The Black Swordsman

§ 35th floor of Aincrad
February 2024

"Please...don't leave me here all alone, Pina..."

Two tears trickled down Silica's cheeks, dripped, and landed on the large feather lying on the ground. The drops sprinkled into tiny motes of light.

That pale blue feather was the only remaining memento of her familiar Pina, the only friend and partner she'd known for many months. Just a few minutes ago, Pina had died, bravely protecting her master. The monster's weapon had delivered the final blow, and Pina had given a single, lonely cry, then shattered like ice. Just one long feather remained, the feather she so cheerily flapped whenever called...

1

Silica was a beast-tamer, a class not often seen in Aincrad. Past tense "*was*" being the key word. The familiar that served as proof of her occupation was now gone.

Even the term "beast-tamer" was not an official class or skill within the game, merely a nickname thrown around by the player population.

It is possible, if extremely rare, for the monsters of the game to display friendly curiosity in battle, rather than open aggression. With a quick offering of bait, you can successfully tame the monster, turning it into a very helpful familiar. Those lucky players who managed to snag their own familiars were called "beast-tamers" out of both admiration and jealousy.

Of course, you can't tame every single monster in the game. Only a few species of small-animal types are eligible. There are other factors involved that no one is entirely sure of, but one thing seems clear: You can't tame a monster if you've killed too many of its kind.

Upon examination, this makes the process extraordinarily difficult. If you specifically seek out a species for taming, they'll typically be antagonistic, which makes battle unavoidable. In other words, being a successful beast-tamer means encountering many individual monsters but running away at the very first sign of aggression. It's hard to imagine how tricky and tiresome that can get.

In that sense, Silica was unbelievably lucky.

Without any preparation or knowledge of the system, she'd descended on a random floor, wandered into a forest without a particular reason, and found that the very first monster she happened across was friendly. When she pulled out a bag of nuts she'd bought the previous day and tossed it to the creature, it just so happened to be its favorite food.

It was a Feathery Dragon, a tiny species covered in a down-like pale blue fur, with two large feathers in place of a tail. This type of monster was already quite rare. Silica was apparently the first to ever tame one, and she caused quite a stir when she walked back into Frieven, her hometown on the eighth floor, with the dragon perched upon her shoulder. Numerous players headed out in search of Feathery Dragons of their own based on her information, but no reports ever surfaced of another successful taming.

Silica named the little dragon Pina, after her cat back in the real world.

Familiars were typically not very powerful fighters, and Pina did not stray from the standard, but she did have several other useful abilities. She could search for monsters in the vicinity and heal small amounts of her master's HP, which immediately made hunting dramatically much easier. But most delightful of all to Silica was the warmth and comfort Pina brought to life in Aincrad.

The AI routines for familiars were not particularly advanced. They couldn't speak, of course, and only understood about ten different commands. But the salvation Pina gave to Silica— trapped in the closed world of Sword Art Online at just age twelve, crushed with fear and loneliness—was impossible to put into words. Only with her new partner was Silica ready to begin her adventure—to begin her life itself in SAO.

In the year since then, Silica and Pina had both grown in experience. Silica learned to use daggers and even gained some notoriety as a high-level player in the middle floors of Aincrad.

She was still inferior to the top fighters working at the front line, but out of the seven thousand surviving players, the few hundred "clearers" working the highest floors were a rare sight, even rarer than a beast-tamer. So it came to be that among the crowded middle floors, Silica earned a spot as one of the famed celebrities of the game.

Given the major lack of female players and her surprisingly young age, it didn't take long for "Silica the Dragonmaster" to make a legion of fans. It's hard to blame a thirteen-year-old girl for getting a little carried away, what with the never-ending stream of invitations from parties and guilds hoping to capitalize on her fame. But ultimately, that pride led her to commit a terrible mistake, one that no amount of regret could undo.

It started with a simple argument.

Silica joined a party she'd been invited to two weeks earlier, to adventure into a wooded region on the thirty-fifth floor known as the "Forest of Wandering." The actual frontier at this point was far above, on the fifty-fifth floor, so this region had been cleared long ago. But the top swordsmen only had eyes for the labyrinth of each floor, and thus the sub-dungeons such as the Forest of Wandering were left untouched for the mid-level players to tackle.

Silica's six-man party was full of experienced fighters, and their daylong expedition was a fruitful one. Monsters were slain, treasure chests found, and many col looted from the forest. As the first signs of evening settled in, the group was running low on healing potions, so they decided to call it a day and head back to town. The other female in the group, who brandished a long, thin spear, gave Silica what seemed to be a competitive admonishment.

"When we get back, we'll split up the items we found. But since your lizard heals you already, you don't need any heal crystals, I assume."

Silica immediately snapped back, on the defensive.

"And you were just wandering around on the back line not doing anything, so you don't have any use for crystals, anyway."

The argument only got worse, and the leader's attempts to intervene were sadly futile. Silica finally reached her breaking point and snapped, "I don't need your stupid items. I'm not working with you anymore. There are plenty of other parties who want me there!"

And ignoring the leader's pleas for her to stick with the group until they'd at least left the forest and returned to town, Silica stomped off down a different path, steaming in anger.

Having mastered about 70 percent of the Dagger skills and bolstered by Pina's help, Silica wasn't particularly troubled with the monsters of the thirty-fifth floor, even working alone. It shouldn't have been hard for her to dispatch any foes on her way back to town...if she hadn't gotten lost.

The Forest of Wandering wasn't named without reason, after all.

The dungeon was split into several hundred minor areas like a board game, massive trees towering on all sides. One minute after someone entered a new area, the exits to the adjacent areas—north, south, east, west—would switch to a random configuration. Therefore, traversing the forest meant zipping through each area in less than a minute or buying an expensive map item in town that showed the proper route.

Only the sword-and-shield-bearing leader of the group had a map, and within the Forest of Wandering, teleport crystals would take you not back to town but to a random area within the forest. This meant that Silica's only option was to try dashing through the dungeon as quickly as possible. What she didn't count on was how difficult it actually was to speed down the path as it twisted and curved, tree roots leaning out to trip passersby.

She should have been going straight north. But after a few instances of the clock hitting time just before she left an area, sending her in a totally different direction, Silica began to grow weary. The sunset was a deeper shade of red, and the more she hurried to escape the growing dusk, the worse her progress.

Eventually, Silica gave up on running and clung to the hope that her path would take her to the edge of the forest at some point. But Lady Luck was not kind to her. Monsters closed in on her as she traveled, and although she was well equipped for them in terms of level, the darkening surroundings made her footing unsteady. Even with Pina's help, it was impossible to escape battle unharmed, and soon she was out of both healing potions and her emergency healing crystals.

Pina seemed to sense Silica's unease and lighted on her shoulder with a trilling *krururu*, rubbing Silica's cheek with her tiny head. As she stroked her partner's long neck, Silica regretted the anger and impatience that had put her into this predicament.

She began to silently pray to God as she walked.

I'm so sorry. I'll never think of myself as special again. Please, just let the next warp take me outside of the forest.

She stepped into the wavering teleport zone as she prayed. After a brief bout of dizziness, she saw…the same old forest, deep and foreboding. It was dark beyond the trees, and there was no sign of the meadow that surrounded the forest.

Disappointed, she began to walk again—when Pina suddenly raised her head.

Kyuru!

It was a warning. Silica quickly drew her short sword from its scabbard, readying herself in the direction Pina was looking.

A few seconds later, a deep growl emerged from the shadows of a large, mossy tree. Silica focused on the spot, and a yellow cursor popped into being. It was more than one. Two…no, three. They were Drunk Apes, some of the strongest monsters to be found in the Forest of Wandering. Silica bit her lip.

Still…

In terms of her level, it shouldn't have been that difficult.

When mid-level players like Silica took to the wilderness, they typically played it cautious, leaving themselves a wide safety margin. They wanted to be strong enough that even if surrounded by five monsters, they could handle them all without needing healing items.

The mid-level players had different reasons for adventuring than the top fighters who strove to complete the game. They did it to raise the col necessary to lead their daily lives, to level enough to maintain their status as middle-class players, and to stave off boredom. None of those reasons was important enough to risk dying in real life. In fact, there were still more than a thousand people down in the Town of Beginnings who had never left, because they refused to expose themselves to any amount of danger that might raise their chances of dying.

On the other hand, periodic income was required to afford meals and a bed to sleep in, and there was the chronic unease that all MMO players felt when they sensed they were distinctly below average within the game. So after a year and a half in SAO, it was now common practice for a majority of the players to venture out into the wilderness here and there and enjoy a good adventure, albeit under very safe conditions.

Because of that, Silica the Dragonmaster shouldn't have had any difficulty with three Drunk Apes, even if they were the most powerful monsters on the thirty-fifth floor. *Shouldn't have.*

Silica lashed her tired mind into alertness and readied her blade. Pina floated off of her shoulder and took a battle position.

The large ape-men emerged from the shadow of the trees, covered in dark red fur. They held crude clubs and jugs that looked like gourds wrapped with rope.

The apes raised their clubs and roared, displaying their canines, but Silica darted first, determined to seize the initiative. She started with Rapid Bite, a mid-level charging Dagger skill, then led into a rapid combination attack that overwhelmed her target.

The Drunk Apes could only use low-level Mace skills, and while they hit hard, the speed and complexity of their combos were trivial. Silica struck quickly and precisely, then leaped aside to dodge the return blows. After several rounds of this hit-and-run tactic, the first ape's HP bar was significantly shorter. At regular intervals, Pina would breathe out bubbles that disoriented the foes.

But just before she was about to finish off the first ape-man with her fourth attack—the combo Fad Edge—a new enemy instantaneously switched in from her target's right. Silica was forced to change tactics, and she began work on this second ape. Her original target backed away and seemed to be drinking something from the gourd it held.

And then, out of the corner of her eye, Silica was shocked to notice the first Drunk Ape's HP bar refilling rapidly. Apparently, whatever the liquid contained within its gourd was, it had healing properties.

Silica had fought Drunk Apes once before on the thirty-fifth floor. There were two of them, and she'd had little trouble. She'd eliminated them before they could try switching out, so she'd never known about this particular ability of theirs. She gritted her teeth and reapplied herself to the second ape, determined to finish this one before it could escape.

But after a fierce rush that sent the monster's HP bar into the red zone, she stepped back in preparation for her finishing blow, and the third ape stepped into the gap. At this point, the first ape was practically back to full health.

This wasn't going well. The taste of impatience flooded her mouth.

Silica actually had very little experience fighting monsters solo. The level-based safety margin was just a numerical buffer, but a player's actual skill was a different matter altogether. Silica's impatience slowly began to transform into panic. Her attacks missed more and more, opening the door for enemy counters.

When she had beaten the third ape down to half health, Silica overreached, trying to string too many combos together. The ape did not miss her brief period of paralysis and connected with a critical blow.

The club was a crude tool of carved wood, but its weight and the Drunk Ape's strength stat augmented the damage done, carving away nearly a third of her HP in a single shot. A chill ran down her back.

The fact that she was out of healing potions only made Silica's panic worse. Pina could only recover a tenth of Silica's total HP with her healing breath, and it wasn't an ability Pina could use often. Even accounting for that healing, another three hits like that would kill her.

Death. Once that specter loomed over her mind, Silica couldn't help but falter. She couldn't raise her arms. She couldn't move her legs.

Until this point, battle had been a thrilling experience, something far removed from any real danger. It had never truly occurred to her that actual death could result from it.

As she helplessly watched the Drunk Ape tower over her, roaring with its club brandished high, Silica finally came to understand battle against the monsters of SAO. The truth behind the paradox: This might be a game, but it's not something you play.

With a low growl, the ape dropped its club onto Silica, who was standing stock-still. She fell to the ground, unable to withstand the shock. Her HP bar shot sideways, plunging into the yellow warning zone.

She couldn't summon a single thought. Get up and run away. Use a teleport crystal. Silica had a number of options, but she couldn't bring herself to do anything but watch as the club approached for a third time.

The clumsy weapon glowed red, and just as she was about to reflexively close her eyes . . .

A small shadow leaped in front of the club in midair. There was a heavy, percussive *thud*. Visual effects and blue feathers flew outward, and a tiny HP bar shrank to its left edge.

Pina was crushed on the ground. She raised her head, looking up at Silica with round blue eyes. She let out a small *kyuru* . . . and exploded into glittering polygonal shards. One of her long tail feathers floated through the air to settle on the ground.

Something within Silica audibly snapped. The invisible threads that held her captive were gone. Before the sadness, she felt rage. Rage at herself for letting a single blow drive her to panic and paralysis. But more importantly, rage at herself for throwing a fit over a silly fight, and being arrogant enough to think she could escape the forest on her own.

Silica nimbly leaped backward, evaded the monster's next swipe, then tore into the beast with a roar of her own. Her dagger flashed again and again, tearing into the ape-man.

Upon seeing its fellow taking critical damage, the first Drunk Ape tried to butt in again. Silica stopped its club with her left hand, not bothering to evade. Her HP did drop, but not as much as if it had hit her directly. Silica ignored the ape. She only had eyes for the third, the one who'd killed Pina.

She used her small size to slip inside the enemy's defense, driving her dagger into the ape-man's chest with all of her strength. With a splashy effect signaling a critical hit, the enemy's hit points were gone. It screamed, exploded.

As the shards flew around her, Silica turned and silently charged her new target. Her health gauge was already in the red danger zone, but she wasn't even cognizant of it anymore. Only the enemy she needed to kill filled her narrowing vision.

Just as she was engaging in a reckless charge beneath the downward trajectory of a club, all thoughts of death forgotten—

A horizontal white light lashed out and struck the two Drunk Apes from behind.

Instantly, their bodies were split into upper and lower halves. First one, then the other, burst into flying fragments.

Silica stood in disbelief, then saw that a single man was standing behind the evaporating pieces. His hair and coat were black. He wasn't all that tall, but his entire body seemed to emit a predatory intensity. Silica stumbled backward in instinctive fear. Their eyes met.

But his gaze was gentle, and as deep as the night. He slid his sword into the scabbard over his back with an audible *ching*, then opened his mouth to speak.

"...Sorry I couldn't save your friend..."

At the tremor of his voice, the last strength from Silica slipped away. The tears flooded out one after the other, unstoppable. Her dagger fell out of her hand, clattering on the ground. But Silica worried only for the unmoving blue feather and fell to her knees before it.

As the white-hot rage that had gripped her faded away, sadness and loss filled its place deep in her chest. That in turn led to tears, which spilled down her cheeks without end.

The AI programming for familiars wasn't supposed to contain routines in which the creature actively attacked enemy monsters. Which meant that when Pina darted into the path of the oncoming club, it was an act of personal will, a sign of the friendship that had built up between the two over the last year.

Her hands on the ground, Silica choked out the words between sobs.

"Please...don't leave me all alone, Pina..."

But the pale blue feather gave no response.

2

"I'm sorry," the swordsman in black said again. Silica desperately blinked back tears and shook her head.

"...No...It's my fault...I was stupid. Thank you...for saving me..."

She had to squeeze out the words between stifled sobs. The man slowly approached, knelt before Silica, and spoke hesitantly.

"About that feather...Does it have a designated item name?"

Silica raised her head, confused by this unexpected question. She rubbed the tears away and looked at the pale blue feather again, concentrating hard.

Now that she thought about it, it seemed strange that just one feather was left behind. When things died in SAO, whether monsters or players, they disappeared entirely, from equipment to items. Silica extended a trembling hand, then tapped the feather with her pointer finger, like clicking a mouse. A translucent window appeared, listing the weight and name of the item.

PINA'S HEART.

Just before Silica could burst into tears again, the man hurriedly butted in.

"W-wait, wait. If her heart item is left behind, there's a possibility you can revive her."

"Huh?"

Silica snapped to attention. She looked up into his face, mouth half open.

"It's not common knowledge, since it was only just recently discovered. On the south end of the forty-seventh floor, there's an outdoor dungeon called the Hill of Memories. It's actually pretty difficult for a pleasant name like that, though...Anyway, there's a flower that grows on the top of the hill, and it's supposed to resurrect famil—"

"R-really?!" Silica shrieked, hopping to her feet before he could finish. A light of hope was shining on her heart once again, which moments ago had been plunged into mourning. But...

"...The forty-seventh floor..."

Her shoulders slumped. That was twelve floors above, well out of her safe range. Just as she looked back to the ground dejectedly, the man murmured and put a hand to his head.

"Hmm...For travel cost and a bit extra, I could go get it for you. The problem is, I hear the flower won't bloom unless the beast-tamer who's lost her familiar goes there herself..."

Silica smiled at the surprising kindness of his words.

"It's okay. I'm grateful for the information. As long as I work hard and level up, I'm sure someday..."

"It's not that easy. You only get three days after the familiar has died to bring it back. Once you reach that point, the item name goes from Heart to Memento..."

"What? No!" Silica shouted.

Her current level was 44. If SAO was a typical RPG, it would be balanced so that the floor number corresponded with the player level best suited for it. But given the permanent consequences for dying, you wanted to be a good ten levels above your current floor.

Which meant that if she was going to the forty-seventh floor, she'd need to be level 55 at the lowest. But it was simply impossible to gain more than ten levels in three days—two, if she was giving herself enough time to actually get to the hill with the flower. Silica was very diligent in her adventuring, and it had taken her an entire year to reach her current state.

Silica slumped to the ground in despair once again. She picked up Pina's feather and with both hands, she cradled it to her chest. She rued her stupidity and helplessness, and the tears came again.

Somewhere above, she heard the man rising to his feet. She wanted to thank him again before he left but didn't have the willpower to open her mouth.

Instead, a shining, translucent system window popped into view: a trade prompt. She looked up to see that he was manipulating the same window above. Various items were appearing in the trading list: Silverthread Armor, Ebon Dagger...She had never seen any of them before.

"Um—" she started, but the man cut her off bluntly.

"This equipment should give you a boost worth five or six levels. If I go with you, we'll probably manage."

"Wha..."

Silica just stood there, mouth open. She stared at him, uncertain of his intentions. The system recognized her focus and brought up a green cursor to the upper right of his face, but in typical SAO fashion, it only displayed a simple HP bar—no name or level.

It was hard to guess his age. The commanding presence of his trim blacks, coupled with a relaxed manner, spoke of someone much older, but the eyes hidden behind his long bangs were naive, and the feminine roundness of his face suggested adolescence. Silica summoned the courage to ask.

"Why...are you doing all of this for me...?"

She was wary above all else. Much older men had approached Silica on several occasions, and one had even proposed to her. At age thirteen, this meant nothing but terror to Silica. She'd never even gotten a love letter from a classmate at school.

Eventually, Silica learned to avoid male players who seemed to have ulterior motives, and it was common knowledge that any deal in Aincrad that appeared too good to be true, probably was.

He scratched his head again, searching for the right answer. He opened his mouth to speak, then shut it again. Looking away, he finally muttered, "Well, this isn't some comic book...so if you promise not to laugh, I'll tell you why."

"I won't laugh."

"You look...like my little sister."

It was such a silly reason that Silica couldn't help but burst into giggles. She tried to cover her mouth, but it wasn't enough to stop them from escaping.

"Y-you said you wouldn't laugh..."

He slumped his shoulders and sulked, a pained expression on his face. That just made her laugh harder.

He's not a bad person after all...

It was while Silica was stifling her giggling that she decided it was worth a shot to trust the man's good intentions. She was already prepared to die. She had nothing else to lose, and this was her only chance to revive Pina.

She gave him a slight incline of the head and said, "Thank you for your help. First you saved my life, and now this..."

Silica looked down at the window and entered all of her col into the trade margin. There were more than ten pieces of equipment on his side, and they all seemed to be rare items you couldn't buy elsewhere.

"Um, I realize this is nowhere near enough for all of those..."

"Nah, I don't need the money. These are all leftovers, and it sort of fits the reason I came here, anyway," he muttered mysteriously. He hit the OK button without accepting the gold.

"Thank you... This is all too much. Um, my name is Silica."

Just a little bit, she was expecting him to be surprised at the name—"You're *that* Silica?!"—but it seemed he hadn't heard of her. For a second she was disappointed, and then she reminded

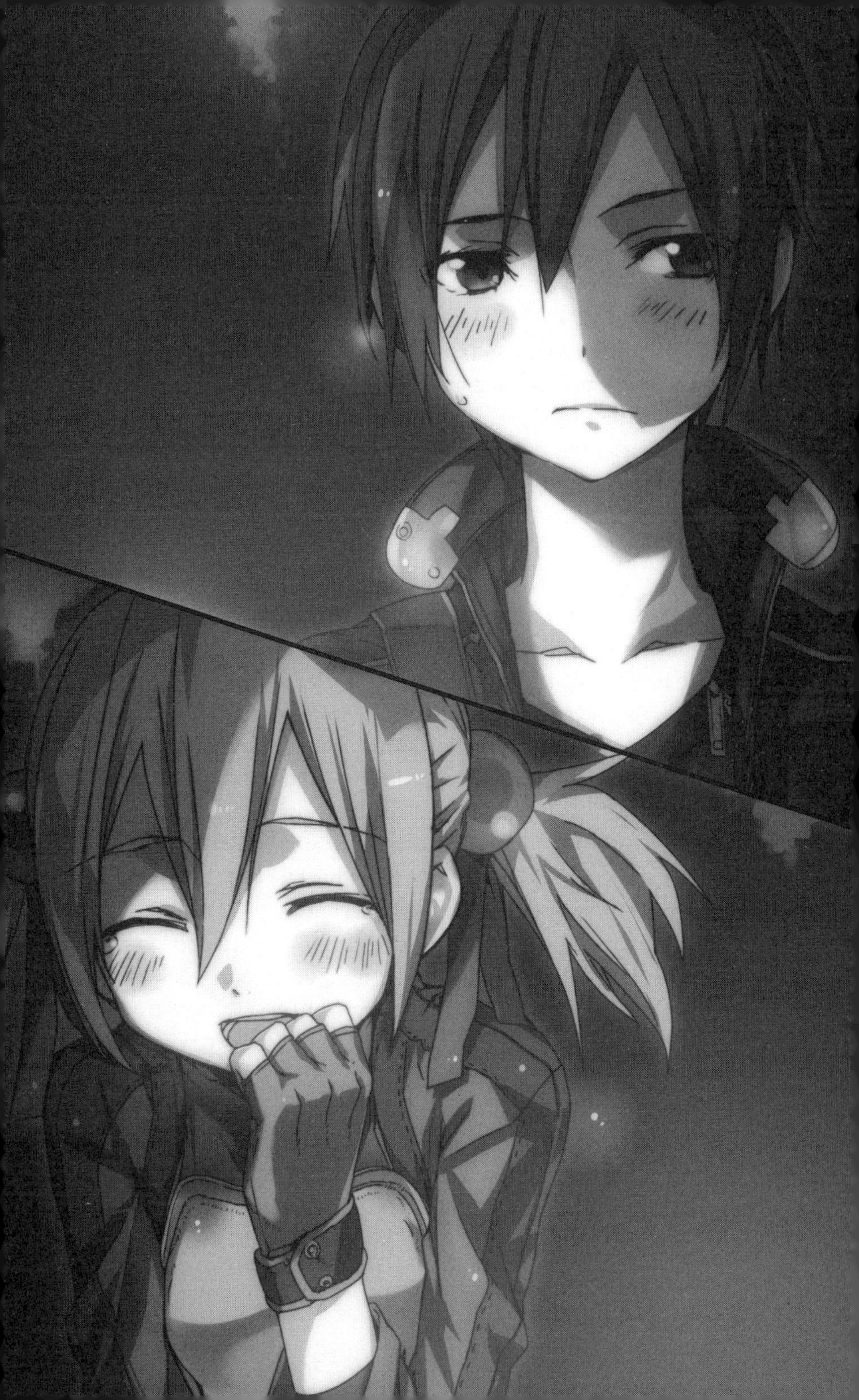

herself that being conceited was what had gotten her into this mess.

The man nodded, then extended a hand.

"I'm Kirito. Guess we're working together for a bit."

She grabbed his hand, and they shook.

The man named Kirito pulled a map of the Forest of Wandering out of the pouch hanging off his waist, checked to see which direction the exit of the forest was, and started walking. Silica trotted after him, putting Pina's feather to her lips and silently reassuring it.

Just wait, Pina. I'll bring you back, I swear…

The main city of the thirty-fifth floor was a pastoral farm town, full of houses with white walls and red roofs. It wasn't that large of a place, but it was currently a hotbed of mid-level player activity, so it was swarming with people.

Silica considered Frieven to be her hometown, down on the eighth floor. But since she didn't have the money to actually buy a home there, it was really no different from buying inn rooms on any other floor. The biggest difference was the taste of the food served by the NPC proprietors, and Silica found this cook's cheesecake to her liking. She'd been in town for two weeks before finally starting on the Forest of Wandering.

Silica walked down the large avenue to the teleport square with Kirito in tow, looking around curiously. Soon, players she recognized began calling out to her. Word had gotten around that she was unaffiliated again, and the party invitations were flowing.

"U-um, I appreciate the interest, but…" Silica did her best to politely decline the offers, then glanced to the side at Kirito. "I'll be in a party with him for a little while."

The disgruntled crowd protested, then shot suspicious looks at her new partner.

Silica had seen his ability for herself, but his unassuming

looks and reserved manner did not currently project an aura of strength to the crowd.

He wasn't even equipped with any expensive-looking gear—he wore no visible armor, just an old, faded leather coat over his shirt. A single sword was slung over his back. Not even a shield.

"Hey, you." A tall man with a greatsword who was the most persistent of her suitors approached Kirito and looked down on him. "I haven't seen you around before, and I don't appreciate your cutting in line. We've been after her for ages."

"That said...that's just the way the cards fall sometimes, you know...?"

Kirito scratched his head, uncomfortable with the attention. Silica turned to the accoster, slightly disappointed that Kirito hadn't given him more of an argument.

"Um, I asked him to join me. Sorry!"

She bowed deeply one more time, then grabbed the sleeve of Kirito's coat and walked away briskly. The men waved longingly after her, announcing they'd send more messages. She cut across the teleport square and down the main street, which stretched northward.

Once the crowd of players was no longer in sight, Silica gave a sigh of relief and looked up at Kirito.

"I-I'm sorry about all of that."

"No worries." Kirito grinned at her, as if to show it didn't bother him in the least. "I didn't realize you were so popular, Miss Silica."

"Just call me Silica. And I'm not...They're just inviting me to be their mascot, to make them look better. And...I let that attention get to my head...and wound up alone in the forest...and that's when..."

Thoughts of Pina brought back the tears.

"It'll be all right," Kirito said, perfectly calm. "We're going to bring Pina back. Don't worry about it."

Silica wiped away her tears and smiled at him. Oddly enough, she couldn't help but believe him.

Eventually, a two-story building much larger than the others came into view on the right side of the street. It was the Weathervane, Silica's inn of choice. Suddenly, she realized that she'd brought Kirito here without checking with him first.

"Oh, um…where is your home, Kirito?"

"I always stay on the fiftieth floor…but it'd be a pain to go back, so I'll just stay here for the night."

"Great!" Silica clapped her hands. "The cheesecake here is fantastic."

But just as she was pulling Kirito into the inn, a group of four or five people emerged from the item shop next door. It was the party she'd been working with for the previous two weeks. The men in front headed toward the square, oblivious, but the woman in the back just happened to turn around, and Silica looked straight into her eyes out of reflex.

"…!"

It was the very last person she wanted to see: the spearwoman she'd squabbled with, leading to her breakup with the party in the Forest of Wandering. She hid her face and tried to sneak into the inn without comment.

"Oh, is that Silica?"

She had no choice but to stop now.

"…Hello again."

"Well well, you made it out of the forest. How fortunate of you."

The woman with flashy red curls of hair, whose name was something like Rosalia, chuckled with a sneer.

"No use crawling back to us now, though. We already divvied up the items."

"I told you I didn't want any! Excuse me, I'm busy."

She tried to cut the conversation off short, but the woman wouldn't let her go. When she noticed the empty space on Silica's shoulder, a nasty leer crossed her lips.

"Oh? What happened to your little lizard?"

Silica bit her lip. A familiar couldn't be placed in item storage or kept elsewhere. If she didn't see Silica's friend around, there was only one explanation. Rosalia knew that, of course, but she played dumb, a smile sneaking across her lips.

"Uh-oh, does that mean what I think it does...?"

"She died...but—!" Silica glared at the spearwoman. "I'm going to bring Pina back to life!"

Rosalia's smug eyes widened slightly. She gave a soft whistle.

"Oh, so you're going to visit the Hill of Memories. Can you actually handle it at your level?"

"She can," Kirito cut in. He stepped forward, swinging his coat in front of Silica. "It's not that hard of a dungeon."

Rosalia gave Kirito an appraising look, and her red lips twisted into another sneer.

"Oh, did she lure you into working with her, too? You don't look all that tough."

Silica was shaking with helpless anger. She hung her head, trying to fight back tears.

"Let's go." Kirito put a hand on her shoulder and guided her into the inn.

"Good luck, I guess." Rosalia chuckled after them, but they didn't turn around.

The first floor of the Weathervane was one large restaurant. Kirito sat Silica at a table in the back, then went up to the NPC at the desk. He checked them in, clicking the menu above the counter, then returned.

When he sat back down across from her, Silica prepared to apologize for that bit of unpleasantness, too. But Kirito held up a hand to stop her, and he was smiling.

"Let's get something to eat first."

The waiter came by at that moment with two steaming mugs. They were filled with a curiously scented red liquid.

Kirito gave a toast to the formation of their new party, and Silica took a sip of the hot beverage.

"...Tasty..."

The spiced scent and sweetly sour flavor reminded her of the hot wine her father had let her taste ages ago. But Silica had tried every drink on the menu during her two-week stay and didn't remember this particular flavor.

"What is this?"

Kirito gave her a wry smile. "NPC restaurants let you bring in your own bottles. This is an item of mine called Ruby Ichor. A cup of it will raise your agility stat by one."

"B-but that must be so valuable..."

"Hey, keeping liquor stuffed in your inventory doesn't make it taste better with age. Besides, I don't know many people, so there are few occasions to open it up..."

He shrugged theatrically. Silica giggled and took another sip. The strangely familiar flavor seemed to loosen her heart, shrunken and hard after a day of much sadness.

Even after the cup was empty, she kept it clutched to her chest, trying to savor its warmth. She looked down at the table and muttered, "Why... would she say such awful things...?"

Kirito's face turned serious. He put down his cup.

"Have you played any other MMOs aside from SAO?"

"It's my first."

"I see. Well, lots of people change personalities when they take on a new character in an online game. Some turn good, some turn evil... That's the basis for the term *role-playing game*, see. But I think things are different with SAO."

His eyes hardened for an instant.

"I mean, even trapped here... I do realize it's impossible for every single player in the game to work together toward the goal of clearing. But even then, there are far too many who delight in the misfortunate of others, those who steal... even those who kill others."

Kirito stared right into Silica's eyes. Within the rage, she could see the color of an intense sadness.

"I think those who commit evil here are the ones who are truly sick in real life," he spat. But then he noticed the intimidated look on Silica's face and apologized with a smile.

"Then again, I don't have much room to talk. I'm not out there saving people left and right. I've even abandoned my partners to die before…"

"Kirito…"

Silica realized dimly that the black swordsman before her had to be harboring some incredible anguish. She wanted to share her sympathy but cursed her shallow vocabulary for not having the words she sought. Instead, she found herself grabbing his fist on top of the table with both hands.

"You *are* a good person, Kirito. You saved me."

He tried to pull his hands back briefly, surprised, but stopped just as quickly. A gentle grin tugged at the corner of his mouth.

"And now I'm the one being cheered up. Thanks, Silica."

In that instant, Silica felt a painful throb deep in her chest. Her heart began beating faster for no apparent reason. Her face was hot. She hastily let go of Kirito's hand, then clutched hers to her breast. But that deep ache would not disperse.

"Is something wrong?" he asked, leaning over the table. She shook her head vigorously, trying to summon a smile.

"I-it's nothing! I'm just hungry."

Once they'd finished dining on stew and black bread with cheese-cake for dessert, it was already past eight o'clock. They decided it was best to get an early rest before tomorrow's visit to the forty-seventh floor, so they headed up the Weathervane's stairs. A long procession of doors lined the wide hallway.

Kirito's room just happened to be next to Silica's. They looked to each other once more in tandem, and, laughing, said good night.

Before she changed into her nightwear, Silica decided to practice some combos with the new dagger Kirito had given her.

She tried to focus solely on the extra weight of this unfamiliar weapon, but the throbbing pulse in her chest wouldn't leave her alone.

Despite the distraction, she eventually managed to pull off a five-hit combo without a mistake. Silica opened her window and unequipped her gear, then flopped into the bed in just her underwear. She smacked the wall to call the pop-up menu, then turned out the lights.

She thought she'd sink right to sleep, given her fatigue, but for some reason, that relief did not come.

Every night since she'd become friends with Pina, she'd slept cradling that warm, fluffy body. Now her bed felt large and empty. After endless rolling back and forth, Silica finally gave up and rose to a sitting position. She looked at the wall on the left that separated her room from Kirito's.

I want to talk to him some more.

She was slightly alarmed at the realization. She'd only known him for half a day, and he was a boy. She'd always been careful not to get too close to them, so what made this enigmatic swordsman any different? Silica couldn't explain how her own mind worked.

She glanced at the lower right-hand corner of her vision to see that it was nearly ten o'clock now. The footsteps of players passing through the street below her window had died out, and the only sound from outside was the distant howling of a dog.

That would be silly. I should just go to sleep.

But contrary to her thought process, Silica silently slipped out of her bed. *I'll just knock real quietly*, she told herself. She checked her equipment menu and put on the cutest tunic she owned.

A few steps into the candle-lit hallway, she hesitated before his door. Many moments later, Silica finally raised her right hand and gave two hesitant knocks.

By default, all doors in the game are completely soundproof and do not let voices in or out. The only exception is within thirty seconds of a knock, and Kirito's response came almost immediately. The door opened.

Kirito had taken off his equipment and was wearing a simple shirt. His eyes grew wide when he saw her.

"Is something wrong?"

"Um…"

Silica panicked, just now realizing that she had no good excuse for coming over. Saying that she "wanted to talk" was just too childish to admit.

"Um, well, uhh…you see…I w-wanted to ask about the forty-seventh floor!"

Fortunately, he accepted her reason without further question.

"Oh, sure. Want to go downstairs, then?"

"Well, actually, I was hoping to talk in your room," she answered automatically, then hastily added, "b-because we wouldn't want anyone overhearing that valuable information!"

"Uh…well…that's true, but…"

Kirito scratched his head uncomfortably but finally muttered, "Okay then," and opened the door wide to let her in.

His room was exactly the same as hers: The bed was on the right, and a single tea table and chair were on the other side of it. There were no other fixtures in the room. The lantern built into the left-hand wall was giving off an orange light.

Kirito gave Silica the chair and sat on the bed, then opened his menu. He produced a small box with familiar ease.

The box contained a small crystal ball. It glinted with the light of the lantern.

"It's so pretty…what is it?"

"It's called a Mirage Sphere."

Kirito clicked the sphere with his finger to bring up another menu. He hit some buttons and pressed OK.

The orb began glowing blue, and a holographic image appeared above it. The picture seemed to be of an entire floor of Aincrad. The towns and forests were depicted in fine detail, down to the individual trees. It was nothing like the simple maps you could view from your system menu.

"Wow…"

Silica was spellbound by the transparent blue terrain. She felt that if she squinted hard enough, she might even be able to make out tiny people traveling the roads.

"This is the main town, and here's the Hill of Memories. We take this path here... but there are some tricky monsters around this area..."

Kirito pointed out the various features of the forty-seventh floor with his finger, easily recalling all the pertinent information. His calm, steady voice filled Silica with a gentle warmth.

"...and once we cross this bridge, the hill will be in sight—"

Suddenly, his voice cut off.

"...?"

"Shh..."

Kirito had a finger to his lips, his face stern. He cast a sharp glance at the door.

Like a bolt of lightning, he burst off the bed and to the door, wrenching it open.

"*Who's there?!*"

Silica heard thumping footsteps racing away. She hurried to the doorway, sticking her face around the frame beneath Kirito's body, and saw a figure just before it rushed down the staircase at the far end of the hall.

"Wh-what...?"

"I think we were overheard..."

"B-but... I thought you couldn't hear voices through doors..."

"If your Eavesdropping skill is good enough, you can. But few people bother to level it up that high..."

Kirito walked back inside and closed the door. He sat down on the bed, lost in thought. Silica seated herself next to him, her arms wrapped around her body. She was plagued by looming unease.

"But why would someone eavesdrop on—"

"I think we'll find out soon enough. Hang on, I'm going to write a message."

He gave her a dry grin, put away the crystal map, then opened a message window. His fingers flew over the holo-keyboard.

Silica curled into a ball on the bed behind him. Memories from her long-lost real life were flooding back. Her father was a freelance news writer. He was always hunched over an ancient computer, tapping the keys with a grimace on his face. She had always liked watching his working form from behind.

Her fear was gone now. As she gazed at the side of Kirito's face, Silica was wrapped in a long-forgotten warmth and was asleep before she knew it.

3

Silica slowly opened her eyes at the sound of the ringing chime in her ears. The morning alarm was only audible to her. It was seven o'clock AM.

She pushed the covers off and sat up. Silica was not a morning person, but she was in a surprisingly good mood today. Her mind felt cleansed and clear in the way that only a good, deep sleep could provide.

Yawning widely, she turned to step out of the bed, then stopped with a jolt.

The morning light streaming through the window illuminated a sleeping figure, seated on the ground with his top half propped up against the bed. She was about to scream, thinking it was an intruder, only to remember where she had fallen asleep last night.

I dozed off in Kirito's room and never left...

With that realization, her face grew as hot as though a monster were blowing fire breath on it. Knowing the graphical engine of SAO tended to exaggerate facial emotions, she wouldn't be surprised if actual steam was coming off of her. Kirito must have left her in the bed as she slept, then decided to take the floor instead. Silica covered her face with both hands and writhed in embarrassment and guilt.

After half a minute, she collected her thoughts and slipped out of the bed. Tiptoeing around to the other side, she bent down to look at him.

The dark swordsman's sleeping face was so unexpectedly cherubic that Silica had to stifle a giggle. His hard glare made him seem much older when awake, but right now he didn't look that far off from her own age.

It was fun to sit there spying on her oblivious prey, but Silica knew they had more important things to do and gently prodded his shoulder.

"Kirito, it's morning."

His eyes instantly snapped open, then blinked rapidly for several seconds as he stared at her. His dazed expression suddenly turned to alarm.

"Oh…s-sorry!" He bowed. "I was going to wake you up, but you were sleeping so peacefully. I tried to carry you back to your room, but the door was locked, so…"

The game ensured that it was impossible to break into a room rented out by another player, so if you weren't on the guest's friend list, there was no way to force your way inside. Silica hurriedly waved her hands.

"N-no, it's my fault! I'm sorry, I shouldn't have hogged your bed…"

"Don't worry about it. You don't wake up with aches and pains here, no matter how you fall asleep." Kirito rose to his feet, cracking his neck in seeming contradiction to what he'd just said. He raised his hands and stretched, then looked down at Silica as though remembering something.

"Well, first off…good morning."

"Oh! Good morning."

Together, they laughed.

The pair went downstairs to eat a hearty breakfast in preparation for the Hill of Memories on the forty-seventh floor, then walked out into the bright sunlight of early morning. The daytime players who were just getting their daily adventures started and the nighttime players who were coming home from a long hunt crossed paths in the street with very different expressions.

They stocked up on potions and the like from the item shop next to the inn before heading for the teleport gate. Fortunately, they were able to get there without the pushy suitors from yesterday harassing them. Silica stopped short just before jumping into the glowing blue portal.

"Oh...I don't know the name of the town on the forty-seventh floor..."

She was about to bring up her map to recall it when Kirito held out his hand.

"Don't worry, I'll lead the way."

Hesitantly, she took his hand.

"Teleport: Floria!"

A bright light flashed and swallowed them both. After a momentary tugging sensation, the visual effect wore off, and Silica's vision was filled with a different explosion of color.

"Wow!" she exclaimed with delight.

The teleport square of the forty-seventh floor was full of countless flowers. Narrow lanes in four directions framed the open space, and the rest of the curved plaza was walled off into large brick flowerbeds overflowing with an infinite array of unfamiliar flora.

"This is incredible..."

"Most people call this floor the Flower Garden. The whole forty-seventh floor is covered with flowers, not just the town. If you've got time, there's even the Forest of Giant Flowers on the north edge."

"Maybe some other time."

Silica smiled at Kirito and bent over a nearby flowerbed. She stuck her face into a pale flower that resembled a bluebottle and breathed in its scent.

The flower was exquisitely rendered, with five delicately veined petals, white stamens, and a light green stalk.

Of course, not every flower in this very flowerbed was so lovingly detailed, to say nothing of the countless plants and buildings that existed throughout Aincrad. The system simply didn't have the sheer resources required to handle so much detail, no matter how high-functioning the SAO mainframe was.

To avoid this overload but still provide its players with a feeling of realism, SAO employed a feature called the Detail Focusing System. If a player showed interest in an object and looked at it closely, the game would automatically adjust and render the object in finer detail.

When Silica had first heard about that capability, she actually held herself back from squinting at everything in sight, feeling guilty about causing extra stress on the system. But here, she was unable to stop herself, flitting from flower to flower like a bee, adoring each one in turn.

Once she'd had her fill of the sweet scent, Silica finally stood up and looked around the plaza again. Most of the people strolling the narrow paths among the flowerbeds were couples, hand-in-hand or arm-in-arm, chatting delightedly. So it was one of *those* spots. Silica snuck a glance at Kirito, who was standing idly at her side.

Do we look like the others? she thought, then felt her face explode with heat. Silica tried to hide her embarrassment with a rousing rallying cry.

"L-let's head out into the fields, then!"

"Uh, sure."

Kirito blinked once but quickly nodded and took off at her side.

Even past the teleport plaza, the streets of the town were filled with flowers. Silica thought about her meeting with Kirito yesterday as she strolled through the exploding color. It was impossible to think that it hadn't even been a full day ago—that's how important the black swordsman had become to her.

She threw a sidelong glance at him, wondering if he felt the same way, but his face was that same placid mask that defied any reading. Silica hesitated but eventually spoke.

"Um…do you mind if I ask about your sister, Kirito?"

"Wh-why her, all of a sudden?"

"Well, you said I reminded you of her. So I was curious…"

The topic of the real world was the greatest taboo in Aincrad, for several reasons. Primarily, there was the fear that if you reinforced the "falseness" of SAO by harkening to the real world, it might subconsciously loosen one's grasp of the true finality of death in this world.

But even then, Silica still wanted to know about this sister she resembled. She wanted to know what he sought from her in return, whether it was to be a surrogate family member or not.

"Well…we weren't really very close," he eventually mumbled. "She's actually not my sister, but my cousin. She was raised in our family from birth, for…certain reasons, but she probably doesn't know the truth. Maybe that's why I've always kind of kept my distance from her. I didn't even like coming face-to-face with her at home."

He sighed faintly.

"Plus, my grandfather's the strict type. He forced the both of us to start taking kendo lessons at a nearby dojo when I was eight, but I could never get into it; I quit after two years. Well, I got a good whupping for that one…My sister cried her eyes out and stuck up for me, saying she'd practice hard enough for both of us. After that I got heavily into computers, and she really did stick with kendo—she was placing highly in national tournaments right before Grandpa died. He must have been happy about that…Anyway, I've always felt inferior to her since then. That just made me more self-conscious around her…and here I am now."

Kirito stopped for a moment, then looked down at Silica.

"So maybe I helped you because I'm just satisfying my own needs. I guess I'm doing this out of the guilt I feel toward my sister. Sorry, I know it's weird."

Silica was an only child. She didn't entirely understand the feelings Kirito mentioned, but she felt she could understand a bit of what his sister was going through, for some reason.

"I don't think your sister blamed you for what happened. I mean, you can't work that hard at something without enjoying it. She must really love kendo," she said, trying to find the right words as she went along. Kirito grinned.

"All you do is cheer me up...Maybe you're right. I hope you are."

Silica felt the warmth in her chest begin to spread. She was delighted that he had opened up to her.

Eventually, they reached the southern gate of town. A silvery arch hung over the path, vines bursting with white flowers twined over the slender metal frame. The main street continued through it, into the green hills to the south before vanishing in the spring haze.

"Well...here's where our adventure starts."

"Yep."

Silica let go of Kirito's arm and pulled herself together before nodding.

"Between your level and that equipment, none of the monsters here should be unmanageable for you. But..."

He rummaged in the small pouch fixed to his belt, pulling out a sky-blue crystal and dropping it in Silica's palm. It was a teleport crystal.

"You never know what might happen out there. If something unexpected occurs, and I tell you to get out of there, use this crystal to jump back to this town. Got that? Don't worry about me."

"B-but—"

"Just promise me that. I've...lost an entire party before. I don't want to make that mistake again."

Kirito's face stayed hard, and Silica had no choice but to nod. He repeated his demand for a promise, then smiled to put her at ease.

"All right, let's go!"

"Okay!"

Silica grabbed the dagger on her waist and swore inwardly that she wouldn't panic like she had yesterday. She was going to use all of her strength to fight.

However...

"Aaaaagh! Wh-what *is* that?! It's so creepy!!"

Just a few minutes after they'd headed south into the forty-seventh-floor wilderness, they had their first encounter with a monster.

"Eeeek! Get away from meee!"

A simple description for the unsettling thing that pushed its way through the tall grass might be a "walking flower." Its dark green stem was as thick as a human arm, and the countless roots that split off from the base gripped the ground firmly. Atop the stem—or torso, if you wanted to call it that—was a huge yellow sunflower-like head with a gaping, toothy mouth in the middle, the interior a poisonous shade of red.

Two meaty-looking vines snaked out of the middle of the stem, suggesting that the monster attacked with its arms and mouth. The man-eating flower leered widely and lunged at Silica, brandishing its tentacle-like arms. Silica's love of flowers only made her recoil harder in disgust at the delicate plant's grotesque caricature.

"I said, go *away!*" She swung her dagger wildly, eyes mostly closed. Kirito's exasperated assurance soon followed.

"Don't worry, it's super weak. Just aim for the whitish part right beneath the flower, and—"

"B-but it's so grooooss!"

"You're never going to last if you can't handle this. Some monsters have multiple flowers, some are like giant flytraps, some have a million slimy tentacles..."

"Yeeeeek!!"

Kirito's descriptions were giving Silica goose bumps. Her panicked sword skill was predictably, woefully inaccurate. In the momentary pause after she unleashed the skill, the flower slipped in close, wrapping its two vines around her legs and lifting her up into the air with surprising strength.

"Wu-hah!"

Silica's vision spun upside down, and the system's virtual gravity callously did its work, sliding her skirt downward over her belly.

"Gwaaaa!"

She shrieked, extending her left hand to hold the skirt in place while she swiped out with the right, trying to sever the vine. Her unfamiliar position made that difficult. Face red with frustration, Silica finally shrieked for assistance.

"H-help me, Kirito! Don't look, but help me!"

"That's...kind of impossible," he murmured, covering his eyes with one hand. The giant flower shook her left and right in apparent entertainment.

"W-would you...just...knock it off?!"

Silica removed her hand from her skirt to grab the vine, then severed it with a slash. She felt herself fall, but the flower's neck was now in range, so she tried another sword skill. It struck true this time, and the giant flower head rolled away before the entire creature exploded. Silica plopped to the ground amid the flying polygons, then turned to Kirito.

"...Did you see them?"

The swordsman in black peeked at Silica through his fingers.

"...No, ma'am."

After another five encounters, Silica was getting used to the appearance of the monsters, and their progress was much faster. She *did* think she was going to pass out when the urchin-like monster slimed her from head to toe with its tentacles, though.

For the most part, Kirito stayed out of the battles, only stepping in to deflect blows with his sword when Silica was in trouble. Experience was awarded in proportion to the damage dealt when fighting with a party. By fighting these high-level monsters

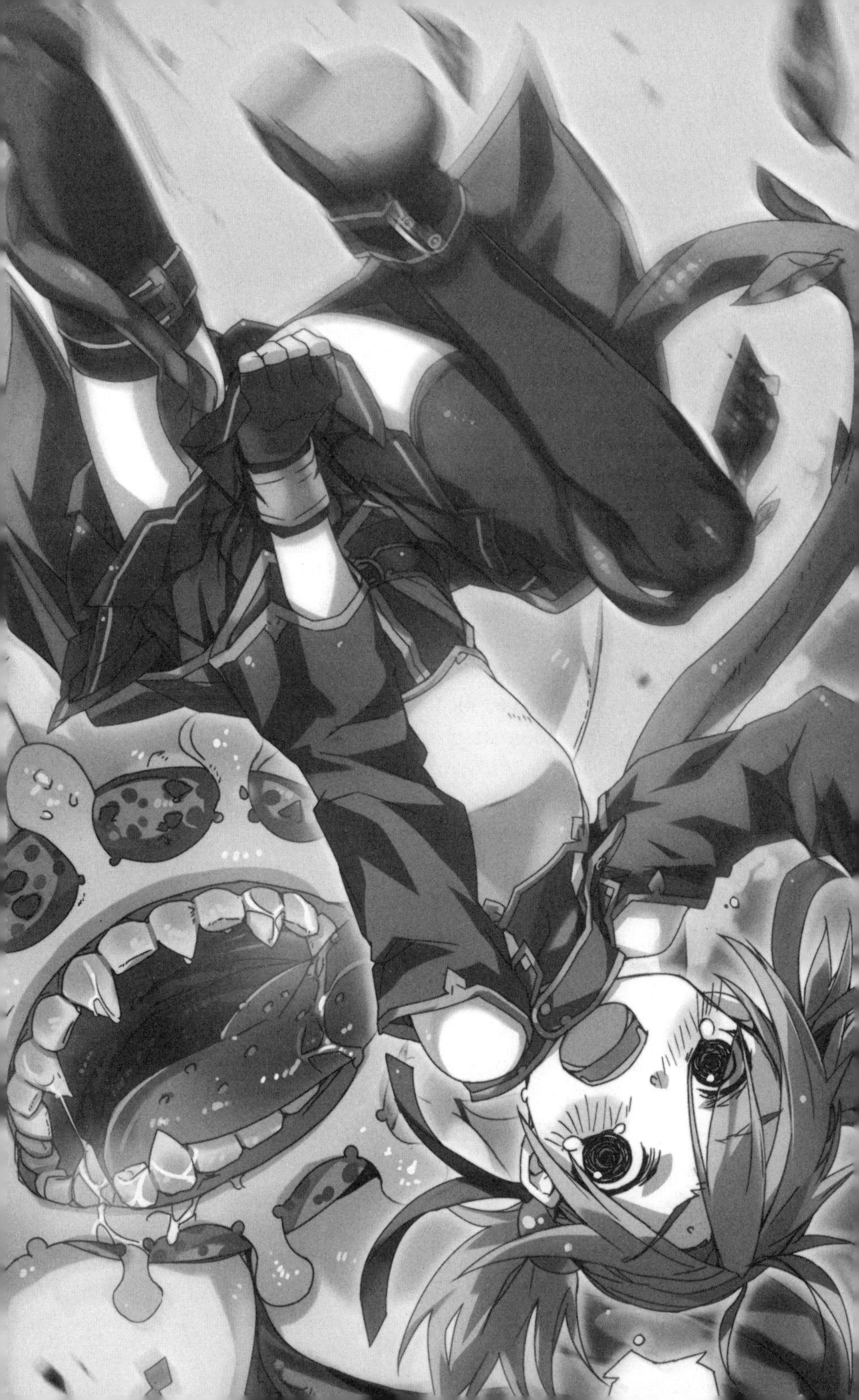

and doing nearly all the work, Silica was gaining EXP at a rapid rate, and she had already leveled up once.

A ways down the red brick path, they came to a little bridge over a running brook. On the other side of the bridge was a much larger hill than the others, and the path wound up it to the top.

"That's the Hill of Memories."

"It doesn't seem to have any branching paths from here, does it?"

"Nope. Just one straight trail all the way to the top, but they say you have to fight a considerable number of monsters. Let's be cautious."

"Got it!"

Soon. Soon Pina would be alive again. Her pace quickened.

As Kirito warned, the encounter rate rose rapidly as they made their way through the wildly colored flowers up the hill. The plantlike monsters were bigger than before, but the black dagger that Kirito gave Silica was stronger than it looked, and one good combination attack was enough to take down most of their foes.

Speaking of surprises, Kirito also proved to be far more powerful than she'd realized.

She knew that he was at a high level when she first saw him dispatch two Drunk Apes with a single blow, but they were now twelve floors higher in Aincrad and he still wasn't breaking a sweat. When they ran across multiple monsters, he would leave one and blast the others, returning to supervise Silica seconds later.

But the stronger he proved to be, the more suspicious she became. What had such a powerful swordsman been doing down on the thirty-fifth floor? He made it sound like he had some business in the Forest of Wandering, but she'd never heard of any particularly rare items or monsters emerging from its shadows. She vowed to ask him when this adventure was over.

The incline grew steeper as they made their way up the hill.

They fought off ever-fiercer foes and wound their way through a copse of tall trees to see the top of the hill ahead.

"Wowww…"

Without thinking, she rushed forward several steps and raised a joyous shout.

It was like a field of flowers in the sky. Trees surrounded the vicinity, but the entirety of the open space was completely full of beautiful flowers.

"We finally made it, huh," Kirito said as he approached from the rear, sheathing his sword in the scabbard on his back.

"And is this where… the special flower is…?"

"Yeah. There's a big rock in the middle somewhere, and the flower's on top of—"

Silica took off running before he could finish. Sure enough, she could see a shining white boulder in the center of the field. When she reached the chest-high rock, her breath ragged, she peered over to see what was on top.

"Huh…?"

There was nothing there. A few small blades of grass peppered the hollowed-out top of the rock like strings, but there was no flower to be seen.

"It's not here… Kirito, there's nothing here!" she called out to him as he reached the rock. The tears came welling up again, unstoppable.

"That can't be right… There, see?"

Silica followed his glance back to the rock to see…

"Ah."

A new bud was stretching upward from the tender grass even now. The focus system kicked in at her gaze, and the bud sharpened into much finer detail. Two pure white leaves opened like a clam, and a thin, sharp stem sprouted out from between them.

The plant grew thicker and taller before her eyes like a time-lapse video she once watched in science class, and eventually a large bulb formed at the end. Bizarrely enough, the sparkling white tear-shaped bulb was emitting a crimson light from within.

As Silica and Kirito held their breaths, the tip of the growth bulged—and with the chime of a bell, it popped open. Motes of light danced in the air.

The two were frozen still for a moment, content to gaze upon the tiny white flower, a delicate miracle unfolding before their eyes. Seven thin petals opened like starlight, and the gentle glow from within the flower spilled out, to melt into the air.

Silica looked up at Kirito, unsure if she should really touch such a beautiful thing. He flashed her an encouraging smile and nodded slowly.

She returned the gesture and reached out to the flower. The instant she touched the threadlike stalk, it crumbled as if made of the thinnest ice, leaving only the glowing flower in her palm. Holding her breath, she traced the surface with a finger. Silently, the info window popped open: PNEUMA FLOWER.

"With this...I can bring back Pina..."

"Yep. You just have to sprinkle the dew that builds up inside the flower onto the heart item. But there are lots of tough monsters around here, so we should probably head back to town before that. Just a bit more patience, and we'll be back before you know it. Let's go!"

"Okay!"

She opened her inventory and placed the flower on top. Once it had shown up in the list, she closed the window.

Silica was dying to use the teleport crystal to return instantly, but she stifled her impatience and started walking. That crystal was exorbitantly expensive and for emergencies only.

Fortunately, they met far fewer monsters on the return trip. Combined with the increased pace of the downward slope, they were back at the foot of the hill in no time at all.

Another hour on the road to town, and I'll see Pina again...

But just as she was crossing the bridge over the brook for the second time, her heart leaping in her chest, Kirito's hand came down on her shoulder from behind. She turned around with a start to see a stern glare on his face, pointed toward the grove of trees surrounding the path on the other side of the bridge. He called out a command in a low, menacing voice.

"Whoever's lying in wait over there, show yourself."

"Huh...?"

Silica hurriedly focused on the grove, but she couldn't see anyone. After a few tense seconds, the leaves rustled. A player cursor sprang into being—green, so it wasn't a criminal.

To her shock, Silica recognized the figure that appeared.

Hair as red as fire, lips the same shade, black leather armor that gleamed like enamel, and a thin cross-shaped spear in her hand—

"R...Rosalia? What're you doing here?!"

Rosalia ignored Silica's bewilderment and simply smirked.

"Your Search skill must be pretty impressive to see through my Hiding attempt, swordsman. Have I underestimated you?"

It was then that she at last turned to Silica.

"I'm guessing that you succeeded in procuring the Pneuma Flower, Silica. Congratulations."

Silica took several steps backward, suspicious of Rosalia's motive. She had a bad feeling about this, and a second later, that fear was confirmed.

"And now, I need you to hand over that flower."

"Wh...what for...?"

Now Kirito stepped forward to speak again. "That's not going to happen, Rosalia. Or perhaps I should refer to you by your proper title: leader of the orange guild, Titan's Hand."

Her eyebrows shot upward and the smirk disappeared.

In SAO, players who the system recognized as committing certain crimes—theft, assault, murder—were branded with an orange player cursor rather than green. Because of that, criminals were called "orange players" and their guilds "orange guilds." Silica was aware of this, but she'd never actually seen one for herself.

"Huh...? But...her cursor is...green..."

"Not everyone in an orange guild is actually orange. The green members identify their marks in town, slip into parties, then guide the victims to an ambush point. Our eavesdropper last night was one of her friends."

"But...oh my God..."

Silica looked at Rosalia, stunned.

"Th-then...the entire two weeks you were in our party, it was just..."

Rosalia flashed that venomous smile again.

"That's right. I was gauging the strength of the party, waiting for you to fatten your purses with more gold for the taking. Today was supposed to be my collection day, but"—she licked her lips—"I had to change my plans when the most promising part of the group dropped out, didn't I? And it seems I made the right call. The Pneuma Flower's quite a rare item, and demand is high. Good intelligence is worth its weight in gold!"

She stopped there, looking at Kirito, and shrugged.

"And knowing all that, you still went along with her little act. Are you really that dense? Or did she tempt you with that sweet young body?"

Silica saw red rage at Rosalia's insult. She was about to draw her dagger when Kirito grabbed her shoulder.

"Neither." He was still calm. "I've been looking for you, Rosalia."

"And what does that mean?"

"Ten days ago, you attacked the Silver Flags guild on the thirty-eighth floor. Four of them were killed; only the leader escaped."

"Oh...*that* penniless lot." She didn't even raise an eyebrow.

"Well, their leader hung around the teleport gate on the latest floor, tearfully begging anyone who came by to help him get revenge."

Kirito's voice was cold now, a sharpened blade of ice that threatened to cut anything it touched.

"But when I decided to take up his request, he didn't ask me to kill you. He wanted me to put you and your cohorts into the jail beneath Blackiron Palace. Can you understand what he's going through?"

"Not really," Rosalia said, uninterested. "What are you getting so worked up about, anyway? It's pathetic. There's no proof that the people you kill here are actually dead. Even if it's true, they can't try us in court when we get back. And don't get me started on how silly it is to preach about justice and laws when we don't even know if we *can* get back. People like you are the worst—the ones who bring all their logic with them into a world like this."

Her eyes flashed menacingly.

"So you took that weakling at his word and tracked us down, did you? You must not have anything better to do. Well, I'll admit that I took your bait…but what do you think you're going to accomplish, just the two of you?"

A sadistic leer spread across her lips. Twice, she waved her extended finger high in the air.

The next instant, the overgrowth at the sides of the path beyond the bridge rustled wildly as numerous figures emerged from hiding. Several cursors popped into Silica's view. Nearly all of them were glowing a malevolent orange. There were ten in all. If Kirito hadn't noticed the ambush, she would have skipped right over the bridge and into their trap. The only other green cursor among all that orange belonged to a man with the exact same spiky hair she'd seen vanishing around the corner of the inn hallway the previous night.

The ten new bandits were all men wearing outlandish clothes. They clinked and jangled with a variety of silver accessories. Most unpleasant of all, they were leering at Silica, their gazes lingering on her body.

Silica hid behind Kirito's coat, trying to swallow her disgust. She whispered to him, "There are too many of them, Kirito. We should teleport!"

"It's all right. Keep your crystal ready, but don't use it until I give the command," he said calmly, patted her on the head, then started walking across the bridge. Silica could only stand there. It was crazy. He was going to get himself killed.

"*Kirito!*" she shouted after him. The sound rang out across the field.

"Kirito?" muttered one of the bandits. He stopped smiling, his brows crinkling together as he looked around, trying to recall a fragment of information. "That outfit...a one-handed sword with no shield...the Black Swordsman?"

The man's face turned pale and he scrambled backward several steps.

"I-I-I don't think this is such a good idea, Rosalia. He's a beater...one of the old beta testers, and a front-line clearer, to boot..."

The rest of the group froze at that. Silica was just as shocked. She could only stare out at Kirito's back, which was hardly very big.

She'd had a suspicion from their fights that he was a very high-level player. But she could never have dreamed that he was a "clearer," one of the top swordsmen or women in the game who took it upon themselves to venture into unexplored labyrinths and beat boss monsters to advance the progress of the game. But she'd heard that clearers only used their strength to push the front line forward and were almost never seen on the mid-level floors...

Rosalia looked as stunned as the others, openmouthed for several seconds, before recovering and shrieking, "A clearer would never waste his time down here! He's just another one of those cosplay idiots who thinks he can scare us by dressing up as someone more powerful! And even if he *is* the Black Swordsman, what can one man do against all of us?!"

Emboldened by her argument, the large ax-wielder at the head of the orange players bellowed.

"Th-that's right! If he's a clearer, it means he's got tons of money and items! It just means he's an even juicier target!"

The rest of the bandits echoed his sentiments, drawing their weapons. The numerous blades glinted wickedly.

"We can't do this, Kirito...we've got to run!" Silica pleaded, squeezing her crystal. Rosalia was right; no matter how tough Kirito was, he couldn't beat a dozen opponents. But he didn't budge. He didn't even draw his sword.

Taking that as a sign of resignation, the nine orange players aside from Rosalia and the spiky-haired man plunged forward, screeching war cries. Their boots pounded on the bridge.

"Raaah!"

"Dieeee!!"

They formed a semicircle around the motionless Kirito, hacking and jabbing his body with their swords and spears all at once. He wobbled and lurched with the impact of nine weapons.

"Noooo!" Silica screamed, covering her face with her hands. "Stop! Stop it! He...he's going to die!!"

But of course the men were deaf to her pleas.

They were drunk with violence, some laughing maniacally, some jeering insults, but they all continued raining down blows on Kirito. Even Rosalia, who had walked up to the middle of the bridge, wore a look of unbridled glee, sucking on her finger as she took in the slaughter.

Silica wiped her tears and gripped the hilt of her dagger. She knew that jumping into the fight would do absolutely nothing, but she couldn't watch it any longer. But just as she was about to leap forward, she noticed something and pulled up short.

Kirito's HP bar hadn't moved a bit.

No, that wasn't quite accurate. The ceaseless blows were doing damage, but only a few tiny pixels were coming off his bar, and every few seconds, it would shoot back to full again.

Eventually, the bandits realized that their assault was having no effect and stopped, confused.

"What are you doing? Hurry up and kill him!"

At Rosalia's irritated order, the rain of blows began anew, but again there was no apparent effect.

"Wh...what's going on with this guy...?"

One of the bandits stumbled backward, his face twisted at the

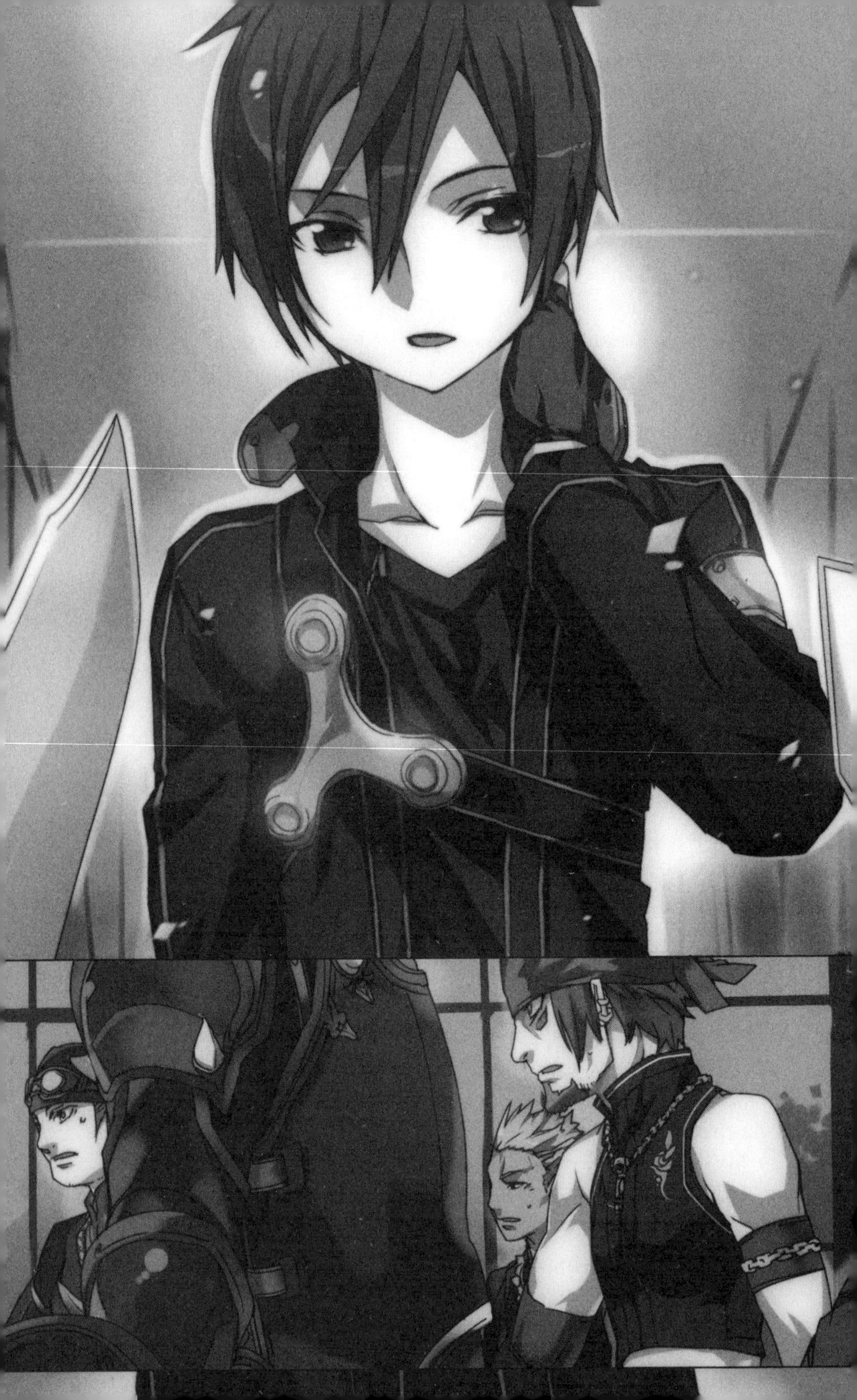

sight of something unnatural. The hesitation spread, and the other eight eventually stopped attacking and kept their distance.

A silence fell upon the bridge. At the center of it, Kirito slowly raised his head. His voice was soft.

"Four hundred points in ten seconds—that's the total damage the nine of you combined to inflict on me. My level is seventy-eight, and I have fourteen thousand, five hundred hit points. With my Battle Recovery skill, I automatically regain six hundred points every ten seconds. You could attack me for hours and never win."

The men looked on in stunned silence. Finally, the greatsword-wielder who seemed to lead the rest of them spoke, voice gravelly.

"That...that can't be possible...It's crazy..."

"Exactly," Kirito spat in reply. "But all it takes is an increase in certain numbers to make the crazy possible. That's the inherent unfairness of level-based MMOs at work!"

His voice, dark with some barely contained emotion, caused the men to falter. The looks on their faces went from shock to fear.

"Tsk!" Rosalia clicked her tongue and grabbed a teleport crystal from her waist. She held it high and said, "Teleport—"

But before she could finish, the air rippled audibly, and Kirito was standing right next to her.

"Aaah!"

He snatched the crystal out of her tensed fingers, grabbed her collar, and started dragging her back to the other side of the bridge.

"L-let me go! What the hell do you think you're doing?!"

Kirito silently tossed Rosalia into the midst of the frozen men, then jammed his hand into the pouch on his waist. He pulled out a blue crystal, but it was a much deeper color than the blue of a teleport crystal.

"This is a corridor crystal, which took all the money my client had. It's set to exit into the prison of Blackiron Palace. You're all going to jail. The Army will see to you once you're there."

Rosalia bit her lip for several seconds, then spoke up, a confident smirk on her red lips.

"And if I say no?"

"I'll kill every last one of you."

Her smile froze.

"At least, I'd want to... but in reality, I'll have to use this."

Kirito pulled a small dagger out from under his cloak. On closer look, it seemed to be coated in some light green substance.

"It's a paralysis poison. Level 5, so you won't be moving for quite some time. It'll certainly last long enough for me to toss every one of you into the corridor. So there's your choice: walk in on your own or get thrown in."

There was no bravado left in the group. They hung their heads silently, so Kirito put the dagger away and held up the deep blue crystal.

"Corridor open!"

The crystal shattered and a vortex of blue light appeared.

"Damn it..."

The tall ax-wielder slumped his shoulders and stepped in first. The remaining orange players followed him, some spitting a final curse before they went. The green eavesdropper walked in as well, leaving only Rosalia behind.

The redheaded thief still boldly refused to budge, even after all of her companions had disappeared into the portal. She sat cross-legged, glaring up at Kirito defiantly.

"If you're going to do it, do it. But if you attack a green player, you'll be oran—"

Before she could finish, Kirito grabbed her by the collar again.

"I'm a solo player, you know. One or two days of being orange means nothing to me."

And he yanked her up, dragging her toward the gate. Now Rosalia was struggling, flapping her limbs in vain.

"W-wait, stop, stop! Forgive me! Please! I... I know—why don't we team up? With your skill, we could take down any guild—"

But she never had the chance to finish. Kirito shoved her head-first into the corridor, and a few moments after she disappeared, the corridor flashed brighter and winked out of existence.

A lonely quiet arrived in their wake.

The birds twittered and streams burbled as though the raucous confrontation had never happened. But Silica couldn't move. She was filled with conflicting emotions—the shock at Kirito's identity, the relief that the bandits were gone—and she just couldn't open her mouth.

Kirito turned to look at her for several silent moments, then spoke in barely more than a whisper.

"I'm sorry, Silica. I used you like bait. I was thinking of telling you the truth about me . . . but I thought you'd be frightened."

Silica could only shake her head in vigorous denial. A whirl-wind of conflicting feelings was tearing up her insides.

"I'll take you back to town," he said, starting over the bridge. She called out to his back.

"I . . . I can't walk."

He turned around, laughing lightly, and offered a hand. Only when she squeezed it back did Silica find the strength to smile again.

They were silent nearly the entire way back to the Weathervane on the thirty-fifth floor. She had plenty of things to say, but Silica felt like her throat was stuffed with tiny pebbles.

When they reached Kirito's room on the second floor, the sun through the window was already red with dusk. When she gazed upon his silhouette, black against the sunset, she finally summoned a trembling voice.

"Are you really . . . going to leave, Kirito?"

There was silence. Eventually, the silhouette nodded.

"Yes . . . I've been away from the front line for five days now. I have to return to clearing the game . . ."

"Right . . . of course . . ."

What she really wanted to say was, *Take me with you!*
But she couldn't.

Kirito's level was 78. She was level 45. That was a 33-level gap. The distance that separated them was cruelly stark. If Kirito took her to where he was fighting, she'd be slaughtered by the first monster they met. The wall that separated them in this game was taller and thicker than any found in the real world.

"...I..."

Silica bit her lip, trying desperately to hold back the emotions that threatened to burst out of her. That turned into a pair of tears that trailed down her cheeks.

Suddenly, she felt Kirito's hands on her shoulders. He whispered to her, calm and low.

"Level is just a number. The strength we gain here is only an illusion, Silica. There are things much more important to be found. The next time we meet, it'll be in the real world. We can be friends again there."

She wanted to throw herself against the black swordsman's chest. Yet Kirito's calming words soothed the painful wrenching of her heart somewhat. She told herself that she wouldn't ask for any more than this, and she closed her eyes.

"Yes. I'm sure we will—I'm sure we will."

She stepped back, looked up at him, and was finally able to give him a smile with all of her heart. He grinned in return and said, "C'mon, let's bring Pina back."

"Finally!"

Silica nodded and waved open her main window. She scrolled through her inventory, found Pina's Heart, and materialized it.

After placing the pale blue feather on top of the table, she produced the Pneuma Flower.

Crimson flower in hand, Silica looked up to Kirito.

"Just sprinkle the dew inside the flower, onto the feather. That will bring Pina back."

"Got it..."

She gazed at the long blue feather and gave a silent speech.

Pina...there are so, so many things to tell you. About my incredible adventure...and the man who saved me—my big brother for a day.

And with tears in her eyes, Silica tilted the flower over the feather.

(The End)

Warmth of the Heart

§ 48th floor of Aincrad
June 2024

The workshop was filled with a pleasing sound: the slow churning of a giant water wheel.

It was a modestly sized home for a crafter, but the water wheel made it expensive. When I first spotted the house in the initial rush into Lindarth, the main town of the forty-eighth floor, I thought, *This is the one!* Then I saw the price tag and my jaw dropped.

From that point on, I worked myself to the bone, even taking out multiple loans at once. In just two months, I raised the three million col I needed. If this were happening in real life, I'd be covered in muscles, and my right hand would have thick calluses from swinging a hammer so much.

But it was all worth it when I beat out my rivals to purchase the deed, turning this little watermill into Lisbeth's Armory. It all happened three months ago, on a chilly day for spring.

1

After a rushed morning coffee—thank goodness this exists in Aincrad—serenaded by the music of the water wheel's rhythmic thumping, I changed into my blacksmith's uniform, inspecting myself in the full-length mirror on the wall.

Though I considered it a uniform, it was closer to a waitress outfit than heavy smithing garb. There was a cypress-brown top with puffed sleeves and a flared skirt in the same tone. I wore a white apron over that, with a red ribbon on the chest.

The outfit wasn't my own design. A friend of mine had arranged it, another girl the same age who often visited the shop to buy equipment. She claimed that heavy clothes didn't suit my baby face, and while I'd originally wanted her to mind her own business, it was true that *my* business had doubled since I started wearing this. So while it wasn't really my first choice, I'd been using it ever since.

Her advice didn't stop at clothes. She fiddled with my hair at every opportunity—it was currently set to an aggressively pink color in a short cut. Once again, though, the reactions from others suggested that it was working for me.

I'm Lisbeth the blacksmith, and I was fifteen when I first logged in to SAO. People thought I was younger than I looked back in the real world, and that pattern only grew more pronounced here. What I saw in the mirror was pink hair, large eyes with dark blue irises, and a petite nose and mouth that, combined with the apron dress, made me look like a little doll.

I was a serious student in the real world with little interest in fashion, which only made the dichotomy stronger. Even though I've gotten used to my new look recently, my personality has always been the same. Every once in a while, I can't help but snap at a customer, which always elicits shock.

I double-checked my equipment and exited the store, flipping over the CLOSED sign. I flashed the players waiting for entrance a dazzling smile and said, "Good morning, and welcome!" This was another thing I'd only recently gotten used to doing.

It had always been a dream of mine to run my own business, but even inside a video game, dreams and reality are very different beasts. I'd had more than enough experience with the difficulty of meeting customer demand from the moment I started selling in the street and living out of an inn bedroom.

My first lesson: If you're not good at smiling, make up for it with quality. In retrospect, the decision to focus on raising my Weaponcrafting skill at the expense of everything else was a wise one, as many of my repeat customers vouched for the quality of my weapons, even after I moved into my permanent storefront.

After I greeted all the customers, I left the business end up to my NPC employee and retreated into the workshop behind the storefront. I had about ten orders for custom equipment that needed to be fulfilled within the day.

Pulling the lever on the wall activated the bellows hooked up to the water wheel. That sent air into the furnace and set the grindstone spinning. I pulled an expensive metal ingot out of my inventory and tossed it into the burning furnace. Once it had absorbed enough heat, I pulled it out with tongs and set it atop the anvil. I got down on one knee, favorite hammer in hand, and selected the item to be produced from a pop-up menu. After a specified number of whacks with the hammer, the metal would turn into the desired item. There wasn't really any technique to it; the quality of the finished weapon would vary at random, but I chose to believe that the concentration of the blacksmith during the process affected the result. So I focused all my nerves on the ingot as I slowly raised the hammer. Just as I was about to strike the very first blow—

"Morning, Liz!"

"Aaah!"

The door of the workshop slammed open and my swing went wide. Instead of the ingot, I hit the corner of the anvil. Sparks flew everywhere as a pathetic *clang* echoed throughout the room.

I looked up to see the surprise intruder scratching her head and sticking out her tongue in guilty embarrassment.

"Sorry! I'll be more careful about that."

"How many times have I heard that one before? At least it happened before I actually started working on anything this time."

I stood up with a sigh and tossed the metal back into the furnace. Turning around with my hands on my hips, I looked up at my visitor, who was just a bit taller than me.

"Good morning, Asuna."

Asuna the fencer was a good friend and loyal customer. She wound her way through the now-familiar workshop and plopped into a round chair of unfinished wood, then flicked her shoulder-length chestnut hair with her fingertips. Every motion was as pristine as a movie star's, and despite having known her for many months, I couldn't help but admire her grace each and every time.

I sat myself in the chair next to the anvil and hung my hammer on the wall.

"So what's happening today? You're here early."

"Oh, I need this done."

She pulled the rapier off her belt, scabbard and all, and tossed it to me. I caught it one-handed and drew it out enough to check the blade. Its typical sheen was dulled with use, but the edge was still sharp.

"This isn't that bad at all. Seems a bit early to have it sharpened."

"Yeah, I know, but I want it to be shiny."

"Oh?"

I looked at Asuna again. She was wearing the same old knight's uniform of white with red crosses and a miniskirt, but her boots looked shiny and new, and there were small silver earrings sparkling in her ears.

"Okay, something's weird. This is a normal weekday. What happened to your mandated guild activity quota? I thought you said progress was slow on the sixty-third floor."

She smiled shyly at my question. "Actually, I got the day off. I'm going to meet someone after this…"

"Ohh~?"

I dragged the chair several clattering steps closer to Asuna.

"Tell me more. Who are you meeting?"

"I-it's a secret!" she stammered, blushing slightly. I folded my arms and nodded.

"I see…No wonder you've been so cheerful lately. You've finally found a boyfriend."

"Th-that's not it at all!" Now her face was really red. She coughed and gave me a sidelong glance. "Am I…really that different from normal…?"

"Of course. When I first met you, all you cared about was labyrinths this, conquest that! I thought you were a bit obsessed, honestly, but you've changed since the spring. I mean, I could never imagine you skipping out on your game-clearing on a weekday before."

"I see…Maybe he *is* rubbing off on me…"

"So who is it? Someone I know?"

"I don't…think so…but maybe?"

"Bring him next time."

"I swear, it's not like that! I mean…it's totally one-sided…"

"Really!"

This time I was truly stunned. Asuna was the sub-leader of the strongest guild in the game, the Knights of the Blood, and one of the most beautiful women in Aincrad. There were as many men who courted her as stars in the sky, but I'd never imagined the opposite would happen.

"I don't know. He's very strange," she said, gazing into the distance. A slight smile played across her lips. If this were a manga for girls, there would be an explosion of roses in the background.

"It's really hard to get a handle on him. It's like he goes to the beat of his own drum…but he's incredibly powerful."

"Oh? More than you?"

"Way more. I wouldn't last for a minute in a head-to-head duel."

"Well, well. This narrows down the list of names."

I consulted my mental registry of famous clearers while Asuna hastily waved her hands.

"Y-you don't have to guess!"

"In that case, I'll just have to look forward to the day you show him to me. Feel free to put in a good word about me if he has any weapons needs!"

"You're always looking out for your business, Liz. I'll tell him about your work…Oh, crap! Can you sharpen that now?"

"Sure thing. Just give me a second."

I stood up with Asuna's rapier in hand and walked over to the grindstone in the corner of the room.

The thin blade was housed in a red scabbard. It was a rapier named Lambent Light and was among the greatest of all the weapons I'd handled in SAO. Even with the finest materials, the finest hammer, and the finest anvil I could find, the random nature of the crafting process ensured a range of potential quality. If I was lucky, I might craft a blade this fine once every three months.

I cradled the sword with both hands and lowered it to the slowly spinning grindstone. There was no real technique to sharpening a weapon—you simply held it to the stone long enough for the process to finish—but a masterpiece of this quality demanded to be handled with proper respect.

I slid the blade carefully across the stone from hilt to tip. The process produced a cool metallic noise and orange sparks, and the silver metal began to regain its former gleam. By the time I was finished honing it, the rapier was practically a translucent silver, glittering in the morning sunlight.

I popped the weapon into its sheath and tossed it back to Asuna, then caught between my fingertips the hundred-col coin that came flying back.

"Thanks, come again!"

"Next time I'll need you to do my armor, too. But I'm in a rush today, so this is all for now." Asuna stood up and hung the rapier from her sword belt.

"Now I'm really curious. Maybe I should tag along."

"What? N-no!"

"Ha-ha-ha, I'm just kidding. But you'll bring him here sometime, won't you?"

"S-sometime."

Asuna waved and darted out of the workshop as though fleeing. I heaved a sigh and sat back in my chair.

"...Lucky."

I was surprised at the word that escaped my lips.

I wasn't really one for moping. In the year and a half I'd spent here, I'd poured all of my enthusiasm into building this business out of nothing, but now that I'd practically mastered my Blacksmithing skill and set up my own shop, I was running out of personal goals and found myself lonely from time to time.

There are few girls in Aincrad, so I've received my share of suitors, but I never felt in the mood. I'd rather have someone who I loved myself. In that sense, I was jealous of Asuna.

"If only some kind of wonderful matchmaking event happened for me, too," I muttered, then shook my head to clear it. I stood up and retrieved the glowing red ingot from the furnace, placing it back on the anvil. *This is the only lover I need for now*, I told myself as I swung the hammer down.

Normally the rhythmic clanging echoing throughout the workshop cleared my head, but today it couldn't get rid of the cobwebs.

It was the next afternoon that the man came to my shop.

I'd stayed up too late trying to finish up all my orders the previous day, so I was napping in the large rocking chair on the porch of the store.

The dream was about elementary school. I was a good, hardworking student, but I always felt drowsy in the first class after lunch, and the teacher often had to snap me awake.

That teacher was a favorite of mine, a young man fresh out of college. I was embarrassed to be scolded for sleeping, but I kind of liked the way he woke me up. He'd place a gentle hand on my shoulder and in a low, calm voice—

"Uh, hey…"

"Y-yes! I'm sorry!"

"Whoa—?!"

I bolted upright as though on springs and shouted, only to find standing before me a male player with a startled expression on his face.

"Huh…?"

I looked around. It wasn't my classroom, packed with rows of desks. There was only a road lined with trees, a waterway surrounding the wide stone path, and a lawn of grass. It was Lindarth, my second home.

Apparently I'd drifted off to sleep for the first time in ages. I coughed to hide my embarrassment and turned to my potential customer.

"W-welcome to my store. Is there a particular weapon you're looking for today?"

"Uh, y-yeah," he replied, nodding.

At a glance, he didn't seem that powerful. He might have been slightly older than me. He had black hair and a monochrome outfit of a black shirt, black pants, black boots. A single sword was slung over his back. The weapons I sold required high attributes to wield, and I was concerned that he didn't have a high-enough level to wield them, but I showed him in anyway.

"My one-handed swords are over in this case."

I showed him the display containing all my pre-made models, but he smiled awkwardly and cut me off.

"Er, actually, I'm looking to do a custom order..."

Now I was really worried. Made-to-order weapons with special materials were exorbitantly priced. He was looking at a six-digit cost, at least. I never liked seeing people turn red or white after I showed them what their orders would cost, so I tried to head him off before we reached that uncomfortable point.

"The market for metals is rather pricy these days, so it will be a considerable cost," I began, but I was shocked by what the man in black said next.

"Don't worry about the budget. I just want the best sword you can possibly make."

"..."

I stared at him, stunned, but somehow or another managed to find my voice again.

"...All right, but...I need to know what properties, what stats you're looking for..."

My tone had lost a bit of its civility, but he didn't seem to mind.

"Oh, good point. In that case..."

He pulled the sword harness off his back entirely and handed it to me. "How about something at least as good as this?"

It didn't look all that fancy. It had a black leather hilt and a scabbard of the same color. But the instant I held it in my hand—

It's so heavy!!

—I nearly dropped the blade. This thing must have required a phenomenal amount of strength. As a blacksmith and mace-wielder, I'd built my strength stat up fairly high, but there was no way even I could swing this sword.

I pulled it out of the scabbard with hesitation and found a

thick, meaty blade nearly black in color. One look told me this was an extremely well-crafted weapon. I clicked the blade with a fingertip to bring up a menu. CATEGORY: LONG SWORD/ONE-HANDED, NAME: ELUCIDATOR. There was nothing listed in the "crafted by" field. A fellow player had not created this.

The weapons of Aincrad fall into two large categories.

One is the "player-made" weapons created by blacksmiths within the game. The other is "monster drops," weapons earned through adventuring. As you might imagine, we smiths don't think much of dropped weapons. Some of us even use the terms *off-brand* or *generic* to describe them.

But this was clearly very rare, even among dropped loot. Normally, player-made weapons were higher in average quality than those dropped by enemies, but every once in a while, you found a truly monstrous blade among them . . . or so I heard.

At any rate, this had certainly gotten my competitive juices flowing. If I was a master smith, I couldn't afford to be shown up by a stupid looted item.

I handed the heavy sword back to him, then pulled down the single longsword I had on display on the back wall. It was my greatest masterpiece to date, forged about two weeks earlier. The blade glowed a dull red, as though rippling with a gentle flame.

"This is my best sword so far. I doubt it's inferior to yours."

He took my crimson blade and swished it about in the air, then tilted his head in puzzlement.

"A bit on the light side."

". . . Well, the metal I used is meant for speed . . ."

"Hmmm."

He swung it a few more times, clearly unsure of it, then turned his gaze on me.

"Can I test it out?"

"Test it . . . ?"

"The durability."

He pulled out his own sword, then laid it flat on the shop counter. Standing still over it, he slowly lifted my glowing red blade . . .

I hurriedly called out when I realized what he was about to do.

"W-wait, don't! If you do that, you'll break your sword in two!!"

"And that'll prove it's inferior. If it happens, it happens."

"But…"

I swallowed my protest. There was a sharp light in his eyes as he held the blade overhead. The red sword suddenly glowed with a pale blue visual effect.

"*Seya!*"

He brought it down with a flash. Before I could blink, sword met sword, and the shop rattled with the shock. The explosion of light was so fierce, I had to narrow my eyes and take a step back.

The blade split cleanly down the middle and burst into pieces.

Not his sword. My masterpiece.

"Aaaaagh!!"

I screamed and leaped onto his arm, wrenching the lower half of the sword away from him and scrambling about for the pieces.

There's no fixing this.

I slumped my shoulders in despair, and a moment later, the half sword in my hand burst into polygons and vanished. After several seconds of silence, I looked up.

"*What,*" I snarled as I grabbed the collar of his shirt, "the *hell* was that?! You can't just go around breaking people's stuff!"

He jerked his face away in panic.

"S-sorry! I didn't think the sword I was *holding* would break…"

I snapped.

"Meaning my sword was even weaker than you thought it would be?!"

"Huh? Uh, um, well…yes."

"You admit it! You've got some nerve!!"

I put my hands on my hips and leaned forward.

"W-well, I'll have you know that if I get the right materials, I can make a sword that will crush *your* stupid sword like an insignificant *twig*!"

"Oh?" He grinned at the bravado. "Well, that's the one I want, then. A sword that will snap mine like a twig."

He grabbed the black sword off the counter and sheathed it. Now the blood was truly rushing to my head.

"Well, if we're really doing this, I'll be involved in every step! Starting with retrieving the metals!"

My brain was screaming at me to stop, but it was too late now. His eyebrows rose and he cast an openly appraising gaze at me.

"Well…I don't mind. But wouldn't it be better if I got them myself? I don't want anyone dragging me down."

"*Arrgh!!*"

Could anyone be more irritating? I waved my arms wildly, stomping like a child having a tantrum.

"D-don't you dare humiliate me! I'm a master weapons-crafter, I'll have you know!"

"You are?" He whistled, clearly enjoying himself. "In that case, I ought to observe a master at work. I'll start by paying you for the last sword."

"I don't need your sympathy! Once I make one better than yours, I'll make sure you pay through the nose for it!"

"And I'll do it gladly. My name's Kirito. Nice to meet you, at least until this sword is finished."

I folded my arms and turned my head in a huff.

"Likewise, Kirito."

"Really? Not even a 'Mr.'? Fine, *Lisbeth*."

"Argh!!"

It was the worst possible way to form a new party.

2

It was just ten days prior that word of the mysterious metal spread throughout the blacksmiths of SAO.

Reaching the top floor of Aincrad was the grand quest, the ultimate goal of all, but there was an unlimited array of other quests to be undertaken, big and small. NPCs needed errands run, or protective detail, or certain items tracked down, but the rewards were never more than middling, and once an individual quest was finished, there was a cooldown period before it was available again. On top of that, some quests could only ever be completed once, by a single person, and everyone was on the lookout for those.

One such unique quest was spotted in a small village tucked away in a corner of the fifty-fifth floor. According to the bearded old chieftain, a white dragon dwelt in the mountains to the west. The dragon fed on crystals, which coalesced into a valuable metal ore within its belly.

It was obviously a quest to obtain weaponcrafting materials. Eager players formed a large raiding party and easily vanquished the dragon in its mountain lair…

But nothing came of it. The beast dropped a paltry sum of col and a few weak loot items, not even enough to pay for the potions and healing crystals used in the battle.

The next assumption was that the metal must be a random drop, so numerous parties approached the elder to initiate the quest and vanquish the dragon in turn. But again, nothing. After a week, white dragons had been slain in the dozens, but no one ever came away with the elusive prize. The eventual consensus was that there must be some hidden condition that no one had yet successfully met during the quest.

The man named Kirito nodded, cross-legged in the workshop chair, sipping on the tea I'd reluctantly made for him.

"I've heard that story, too. It's supposed to be quite a promising material for crafting. But no one's been able to get their hands on it, right? What makes you think we can just waltz in and succeed where everyone else has failed?"

"Some people are guessing that it won't appear unless there's a master smith in the party. And very few blacksmiths bother to raise their combat skills."

"I see. Maybe that's worth trying, then. Well, we should get going."

"..."

I was slack-jawed in disbelief.

"I can't believe you've survived with that attitude. We're not going goblin hunting, you know! And we'll need a full party to—"

"But what if we actually get the stuff, and then have to draw straws to see who gets it? Which floor did you say the dragon's on?"

"The fifty-fifth."

"Hmm, well, I can probably handle it on my own. You just hide where it's safe."

"...You're either very, very good or very, very stupid. But all right—you're on. I suppose it'll be worth watching you cry and teleport out to safety."

Kirito only snorted confidently, then downed the rest of his tea and set the cup on the workbench.

"Well, I'm ready to go whenever you are. Lisbeth?"

"Look, if you're going to be so buddy-buddy, just call me Liz. The dragon's mountain isn't supposed to be that big, and I hear it's short enough that you can do it and come back within the day, so I'll be ready in a minute."

I opened my window and equipped some simple armor over my apron dress. My trusty mace was in my item screen, safe and sound, and I had an adequate supply of crystals and potions.

When my screens were closed and I gave the okay sign, Kirito stood up. We headed out the storefront—fortunately, there were no waiting customers. I flipped the sign on the door to read CLOSED.

The light streaming onto the porch from the outer perimeter of Aincrad was still bright. There was plenty of time until nightfall. Whether we succeeded or failed at acquiring the precious metal—and it would certainly be the latter—at least I'd be back before too late in the day.

Or so I thought.

As we left the shop and headed for the teleport square, I couldn't help but wonder, *What in the world have I gotten myself into?*

I didn't think much of the black-clad man strolling nonchalantly beside me. At least, I didn't *think* I did. His bold statements irritated me, he was grandiose and overconfident, and he'd smashed my greatest masterpiece to bits.

Yet here I was, walking next to him. Not only that, I'd agreed to be in his party and go questing on a distant floor. In fact, as far as life in Aincrad was concerned, this might as well be a da—

Better force that thought straight out of my mind. This had never happened before. I was reasonably friendly with a few male players, but I always had my reasons to avoid spending time with them alone. I was afraid of crossing that line with any specific man. I always told myself that if I was going to do it, it had to be with someone I knew I loved.

But now I was here, walking with this strange guy. How had it come to this?

Oblivious to my inner turmoil, Kirito noticed a food cart at the side of the teleport square and rushed over to it. When he turned around again, there was a large hot dog stuffed in his mouth.

"Whum fhum, Wiffbeff?"

My anxiety instantly vanished. Worrying about this seemed pointless.

"Sure!"

And before the heavy aftertaste of the crispy hot dog— technically, a mystery food that only loosely resembled one—had left my mouth, we finally came to stand in the tiny village on the north end of the fifty-fifth floor.

The monsters along the way were no big deal.

Considering that the current frontier was the sixty-third floor, the foes here should have been worrisome. But my level was in the mid-60s, and for all his bluster, Kirito was pretty tough himself, and we made it through a handful of encounters with hardly any damage.

My only mistake was not realizing this floor had an ice theme.

"Bwa-choo!"

The instant we stepped into the safe zone of the village and I let down my guard, a massive sneeze exploded from my nose. The other floors were in early summer, but here there was snow piled on the ground and large icicles hanging from the roofs.

As I stood shivering in the bone-chilling cold, Kirito looked on in exasperation.

"Don't you have any extra clothes?"

"...No."

Despite not being outfitted for winter weather himself, Kirito fiddled with his menu, materialized a large black leather coat, and tossed it over my head.

"Are you going to be able to handle the cold yourself?"

"Unlike you, I've got willpower."

He was *so* obnoxious. But the fur-lined coat was indeed warm, and I could not resist its comforting embrace. The chill disappeared at once, and I sighed in relief.

"Well, which house do you suppose is the chief's?" Kirito asked.

I looked around the small village and spotted one building across the way that had a higher roof than the others.

"Is that it?"

"Looks like it."

We nodded and set off.

Several minutes later, our suspicions correct, we'd found the NPC chieftain, outfitted with an impressive white beard, and heard his story. Unfortunately, the story began with the rigors of his childhood, proceeding through adolescence and adulthood until his twilight years, stopping for a brief non sequitur to remark that, why yes, there *was* a dragon on the mountain to the west. By the time he reached that crucial detail, the village outside was wreathed in twilight.

We left the chief's house, exhausted. The setting sun lit the blanket of snow adorning all the buildings orange, a truly beautiful sight. But...

"I really didn't think getting the quest started was going to take so long."

"Seriously... what should we do? Come back tomorrow?"

We traded glances.

"But he did say that the dragon was nocturnal. That's the mountain over there, right?"

I looked where he was pointing and saw a treacherous, white-capped peak not too far in the distance. Of course, due to the absolute physical limitations of each floor of Aincrad, the "peak" could not be more than a hundred meters tall. It wouldn't be all that difficult to scale.

"All right, let's go. Besides, I'd rather not wait to see you blubbering with fear."

"On the contrary, try not to have your mind blown by my graceful sword work."

We turned our faces away from each other with simultaneous *huffs*. But for some reason, our constant trading of insults was starting to excite me...

I shook my head to clear my mind of that pointless thought and started stalking my way through the heavy snow.

Although the mountain appeared steep from a distance, once we actually got there, we had little trouble reaching the top. In retrospect, countless parties had scaled the mountain in the course of attempting the quest, so it should have been obvious that it wasn't very grueling.

Perhaps because of the time of day, the toughest monsters we ran across were Frost Bones, an ice-type skeleton—but skeletons were the perfect target for my crushing mace. The undead foes fell apart with a satisfying clatter as I pounded them left and right.

After climbing for most of an hour, we saw the peak right as we circled around a particularly tall protrusion of ice.

The roof of the next floor up was just above our heads. All around us, massive pillars of crystal jutted out from underneath piles of snow. The last remains of purple light refracting into rainbows through the crystals was spectacular.

"Wow…!"

I couldn't help but marvel in wonder, but Kirito grabbed my collar from behind.

"Wghak! What was *that* for?"

"Get ready to use your teleport crystal, if necessary."

The look on his face was serious. I nodded automatically and materialized the crystal from my inventory, placing it in my apron pocket.

"I'll handle it from here on out—this will be dangerous. When the dragon shows up, stay behind one of those giant crystals. And don't come out."

"…What's the problem? I'm actually fairly high-level. I can fight!"

"No!"

His black pupils stared straight into me, and in that instant I understood that he was saying it for my sake. I held my breath and nodded.

He flashed me a quick grin and placed a hand on my head before saying, "Okay, let's go." All I could do was give him another nod.

It suddenly felt as though the air itself had changed color.

I'd come here with Kirito either in search of a change of pace or out of simple reckless abandon—but I hadn't honestly considered that I was getting myself into a battle of life and death.

Well over half the experience I'd gained in the course of leveling up was from crafting equipment, and I'd never been in a deadly battle.

But I could tell that Kirito was different. He had the eyes of someone who put his life in the balance each and every day.

Trying to bring order to the emotions tearing me in different directions, I walked behind him to the center of the mountaintop. A quick look around showed no dragon yet. Instead, sitting in the space between the ring of crystal pillars was…

"Whoa…"

An enormous hole. It had to be at least thirty feet across. The sides of the hole were glittering with slick ice, and they seemed to extend vertically into nothingness. It was too dark to see the bottom.

"Wow, that's deep…"

Kirito kicked a small piece of ice over the edge. I saw it flash as it fell into the abyss, but no sound came back.

"Don't fall in."

"I'm not going to fall!" I retorted. In the next instant, a birdlike screech rattled against the mountaintop, ripping through the air dyed with the final strains of navy light.

"Get in the shadows!" Kirito commanded, pointing to a large nearby crystal. I hurried to obey his command, turning to his back as I ran.

"The, uh, the dragon's attack pattern is: claws from left and right, ice breath, then a wind gale! B-be careful!"

I hurriedly tacked on that last part. Still facing away from me, Kirito waved his left fist, the thumb boldly extended. At nearly the same moment, the air before him rippled, a giant shape oozing out of the air.

Roughly rendered clumps of polygons materialized one after the other. As they connected together and grew more detailed, a giant body took shape—and unleashed another massive, rattling roar. Countless tiny pieces flew in all directions, glittering as they evaporated into nothingness.

The white dragon's scales shimmered like ice. It beat its enormous wings smoothly, hovering in the air. All in all, it was even more beautiful than it was terrifying. Its large, ruby-like eyes glared down at us from above.

Kirito calmly reached behind his back, loudly drawing his ebony sword. As though that were the signal to begin, the dragon opened its jaws wide and unleashed a blast of white with a roaring sound effect.

"Watch out, that's its breath attack!" I screamed, but Kirito did not move. He stood boldly, his sword extended vertically.

Just as I thought, *There's no way he can block that ice breath with such a thin sword*, the blade began spinning like a windmill in his hand. Based on the light green haze enveloping the sword, it must have been a skill. It was already too fast to see, like a round shield made of light.

The ice breath bore down directly on the sword. There was a white flash and I turned my eyes from it. But the cascade of freezing air simply bounced off of Kirito's erstwhile shield, dissipating away.

I cast a hurried glance at Kirito to check his HP bar. The right corner was steadily closing left, perhaps a sign that he wasn't blocking the effects of the ice breath entirely. But to my amazement, it was healing back to full every few seconds. Battle Healing was known as an ultra-high-level skill—and in order to increase your proficiency with it, you had to take massive damage in battle, meaning that it was virtually impossible to safely power up the skill.

Who is this guy…?

I wondered it once again. No one this powerful could not be a clearer. But his name didn't appear in the registry of any of the top guilds in the game, like the Knights of the Blood.

Suddenly, Kirito moved again as the breath attack tapered off. He leaped at the airborne dragon with an explosion of snow.

The orthodox strategy against flying enemies is to attack them with polearms or throwing weapons, forcing them to the ground, where melee attacks will be effective. Impossibly enough, Kirito jumped almost high enough to eclipse the dragon's head, launching into a one-handed combo in midair.

With high-pitched twanging noises, he spun into the dragon's body faster than the eye could follow. The beast tried to fight back with its claws, but the blows were simply too slow.

By the time Kirito finally landed back on the ground, the dragon had lost a full 30 percent of its health.

It was overwhelming. A shiver ran down my spine at the impossibility of what I'd witnessed.

The dragon shot more ice breath at Kirito on the ground, but this time he dashed to the side and leaped again. Instead of the high-pitched combo, he pounded the beast with single, hammering blows. Each one tore large chunks off the monster's HP bar.

It was moving past the yellow zone into red now. One or two more hits would finish the battle. I got to my feet, preparing to give Kirito the honest recognition he deserved.

Just as I took a step out from behind the crystal pillar, Kirito shouted, as though he had eyes in the back of his head.

"No, you idiot! Don't come out yet!!"

"Why not? It's all over. Just finish it—"

At that precise moment, the dragon beat its wings powerfully from above. They clapped together loudly in front of its body, sending the snow beneath the beast upward in a huge flurry.

"…?!"

A few yards in front of where I stood dumbfounded, Kirito stuck his sword into the ground and tried to say something. The next moment, he disappeared into the flurry and I was buffeted up into the air by a wall of wind.

Damn... a gale attack!

I belatedly remembered the attack pattern I'd just spoken aloud a minute ago as I spun through the air. Fortunately, the attack itself wasn't that strong, and I suffered very little damage. I spread my arms to maintain balance as my landing approached.

Except that when the snow cleared, there was no ground below.

It had knocked me directly over the gaping hole in the top of the mountain.

My mind stopped working. My body froze.

"No way..." I mumbled as I fell, helplessly extending my hand into space—

—only to have a black leather glove firmly snag my fingers.

I opened my eyes, dazed and unfocused.

"...!!"

Kirito had torn himself away from the distant battle with the dragon, dashed back without a moment's hesitation, and grabbed my hand in midair. I could feel him tug me up to his chest. His other arm circled around my back and drew me close.

"Hang on!!" he shouted into my ear, and I squeezed both arms around his torso. That was when we began to fall.

The two of us plunged straight down the center of the massive hole, holding each other tight. The wind screamed in my ears, the borrowed coat flapping around us.

If this hole extended all the way down to the lowest point of this floor of Aincrad, we would undoubtedly die. The thought did occur to me, but I couldn't feel it. I just stared upward, dazed, at the shrinking circle of light above us.

Suddenly, Kirito moved his right hand, still clutching his sword. He drew it back, then thrust forward. With a metallic *ga-shunk*, light exploded around us.

He was changing the angle of our fall by unleashing a heavy thrust attack, driving us toward the wall of the pit. The sheer face of blue ice grew closer. I gritted my teeth. *Here it comes!*

Before we crashed into the wall, Kirito swung again, jabbing the sword as hard as he could into the ice. The collision set off sparks like a weapon being touched to a grindstone. With a jolt, our fall slowed but did not stop.

Kirito's sword continued to grind into the ice wall with a screeching like the tearing of sheet metal. I craned my head to look down in the direction of our descent—there was the snow-piled bottom of the pit. It was visibly approaching. Seconds left before impact. I bit my lip to prevent myself from screaming and clung to his body.

He let go of the sword, wrapped both arms around me, and spun so that his back was facing downward. And then—

A shock. A blast.

The snow sent skyward by our landing drifted downward, melting as it hit my cheek. The chill pulled my reeling senses back. I opened my eyes—and there were Kirito's, black and deep at close range.

One of his cheeks twitched into a pained grin. He still clung tightly to me.

"...We survived."

I managed to nod. "Yeah...we survived."

We just lay there for several long moments—it could have been minutes, for all I knew. I didn't want to move. His weight and warmth made my head fuzzy.

But eventually he loosened his grip and slowly rose to a sitting position. He returned his sword to its scabbard, then produced two small bottles from the pouch on his waist and handed one to me.

"You should drink that, just in case."

"Mm..."

I grunted and sat up, taking the bottle. I still had a third of my health remaining, but Kirito, having taken the brunt of the fall, was down in the red zone.

I pulled out the stopper and downed the sweetly sour liquid

in one go before turning to Kirito. It was hard to find the right words to express myself.

"Um…th-thanks. For saving me…"

He gave me his usual wry, cynical smile.

"It's a little early to be saying that."

I looked upward.

"Well, we made it away from the dragon, at least, but how're we gonna get out of this hole?"

"Uh…we teleport, of course." I rummaged through my apron pockets for the blue crystal, then showed it to him. But…

"It's pointless. This was obviously built to be a fall-trap for players. They're not going to make it that easy for us to escape."

"But…"

I shot him a determined glance, then chanted the command, crystal in hand.

"Teleport: Lindarth!"

My order echoed weakly off the icy walls. The crystal's response was to sparkle silently. His expression unchanged, Kirito gave a helpless shrug.

"If I'd been sure the crystal would work, I'd have tried it while we were falling. I had a feeling this was an anti-crystal zone…"

"…"

I hung my head, then felt him plop a hand on it. He scrunched my hair vigorously.

"Look, don't get depressed. The fact that the crystal won't work is simply proof that there has to be a different way out."

"But you don't know that! It could be a trap designed so that the fall kills its victims. I mean, we *should* have died."

"Oh…good point."

I slumped my shoulders in exasperation.

"Oh, come on! You aren't even going to try to cheer me up?!"

He grinned in response to my flared anger. "That angry face suits you better, Liz. Keep it up."

"Wha—!"

He took his hand off my head and stood up, while I stiffened with anger and embarrassment.

"Well, guess it's time to start testing stuff out...Any ideas?"

"..."

At this point I had no choice but to laugh off his lackadaisical attitude. But doing so did make me feel a bit better, so I smacked my cheeks and got to my feet.

A flat ice floor lightly coated with snow was the bottom of our hole. The diameter of the hole was around ten meters, about the same width as it was near the top. There was a pitiful amount of light trickling down from a great distance above, reflecting off the ice walls as it traveled down. Within minutes, it would be pitch black.

There didn't seem to be anything like a passage out on either the walls or the floor. I put my hands on my hips and rolled my head around, desperately working my brain. I spoke the first idea that popped into my mind.

"Umm...what if we called for help?"

"Wouldn't this count as a dungeon?" Kirito asked dismissively.

A player can send a "friend message" to anyone registered on their friends list—for example, I could send one to Asuna—but that function doesn't work in dungeons. There's also no way to track location. I opened my messaging window just in case, but as Kirito suggested, it was inaccessible.

"What if we yelled for other players who went hunting the dragon?"

"We had to climb a good two hundred and fifty feet to get up here. I don't think our voices will carry..."

"I see...well, where are your ideas, genius?" I snapped, frustrated that all of my suggestions were being shot down. The next thing out of his mouth was preposterous.

"We'll run up the wall."

"...Are you stupid?"

"We won't know until we try..."

I watched, dumbfounded, as Kirito approached the wall, then took off at full speed toward the opposite side. The snow on the ground shot up in a flurry, his wind whipping into my face.

Just before he hit the wall, Kirito crouched, then exploded upward. He put his legs against the wall far above and started running on its surface, his body leaned forward at an incline.

"No...way..."

I stood stock-still, eyes and mouth agape, as Kirito ran around the walls of the hole in a spiral pattern, like a ninja in some bad American B-movie. He grew smaller and smaller—and then slipped and lost his footing, around a third of the way up the wall.

"Aaaahh!"

He came falling down directly over my head, his arms flapping uselessly.

"Whaaa—?!"

I leaped out of the way, and with a *smack*, there was suddenly a human-shaped hole in the snow where I'd just been standing.

Precisely one minute later: Kirito was slumped against the wall, his second potion stuck in his mouth. I sighed.

"You know, I always thought you were stupid, but this...?"

"I would have made it if I had a longer approach."

"No freakin' way," I muttered.

Kirito tossed his empty bottle back into his pouch, ignoring my barb and stretching.

"Well, at any rate, it's too dark to try anything now. We'll have to camp out. The one bright spot is that it doesn't look like any monsters pop into this area."

The dying light of the sun was long gone now, and the bottom of the hole was nearly entirely shrouded in darkness.

"Good point..."

"And on that note...." Kirito popped open his menu and started pulling items out of it. A large camping lantern. A cooking pot. Several mysterious bags. Two mugs.

"Do you always carry this stuff around?"

"I spend the night in dungeons all the time."

This was apparently not a joke. He clicked on the lantern to light it, absolutely straight-faced. With a faint *poof,* a bright orange light brightened the surroundings.

Kirito placed the small pot on top of the lantern, then shoveled up some snow and tossed it in. He opened the small bags, emptied them into the pot, then put a lid on top and double-clicked it. A cooking timer floated up.

The scent of herbs immediately tickled my nostrils. I hadn't eaten a thing since those bites of hot dog earlier today. My stomach suddenly growled to life, as though just realizing it was hungry.

The timer dinged and disappeared. Kirito lifted the pot and poured its contents into the two mugs.

"My Cooking skill is zero, so keep your expectations low."

"Thanks…"

I took the proffered cup and felt its warmth spread through my hands. The contents were a simple soup of herbs and dried meat, but they must have been high-quality ingredients, because it tasted good enough. The heat of the meal slowly spread through my chilled body.

"This is all…so weird. It's like it's not even real," I muttered into my soup. "I'm here in an unfamiliar place…with an unfamiliar person…just sipping on soup together."

"Well, you're a crafter, Liz. But when you do lots of dungeon-crawling, you often have to camp out in impromptu parties with people you meet along the way."

"Oh, really. Tell me about dungeons, then."

"W-well, um, I don't really have any great stories…Oh, but before that—"

He grabbed the empty cups and pot and shoved them back into his menu, then rummaged around some more. This time he produced two large bundles of cloth.

They appeared to be camping bedrolls. They resembled real-life sleeping bags but were much larger.

"These are high-class articles. They shut out the cold and have a hiding effect that protects you from active monsters." He grinned, tossing one to me. Laid out on the snow, it was large enough to fit three of me inside.

"Seriously, I can't believe you carry all these things around. And *two* of them..."

"Gotta make the most of your inventory space."

Kirito took off his equipment and dove into the left side of his bedroll. I followed his lead, removing my coat and mace and slipping into the bag like it was a glove.

His boast wasn't empty; the inside really was warm. And it was much softer than it looked.

We were facing each other a few feet apart, the lantern between us. I felt strangely shy about it. I decided to break the awkward silence.

"So, tell me a story."

"Uh, okay..."

Kirito folded his arms behind his head and began to speak.

There was the story of how he fell into an MPK trap—the act of luring powerful monsters into a confrontation with other players to kill them. There was also the tale of the boss monster with low attack but extremely high defense, requiring the group to take shifts sleeping while the others occupied the monster's attention, a battle that took two whole days. And the story of a party of a hundred fighters, who had to divvy up their spoils through a dice competition...

They were all thrilling tales with a touch of humor to them. And together, those tales told a story of their own: that Kirito was indeed one of the clearers, the very best players in the game.

But if that was the case, the fates and lives of thousands of players were resting on his shoulders from moment to moment. He shouldn't be risking his life looking after the likes of me. Who was I?

I rolled over to look at his face. His black eyes glittered with the light of the lantern as he gazed back.

"Hey, Kirito...can I ask you something?"

"So polite, suddenly...What's up?"

"Why did you save me? There was no guarantee you'd survive the fall. In fact, it was way more likely that we'd both die. So... why...?"

His mouth tightened for an instant but relaxed just as quickly.

"If I had to watch someone die, I'd rather die with them. Especially if it was a girl like you, Liz," he responded calmly.

"You really are an idiot. No one else would be like that."

But despite my bold words, I could feel the tears threatening to well up. Something twisted and pulled deep within my chest, and I fought to calm myself.

It was the first time I'd heard such honest, straightforward, heartwarming words since coming to this world.

In fact, I'd never even felt such kindness in the real world.

I could sense that pent-up longing for human contact, the loneliness that had built up for months, forming into massive waves that threatened to throw me off-balance. I wanted to sense Kirito's warmth up close, to touch it directly with my heart...

And before I knew it, the words spilled out.

"Here...hold my hand."

I tilted to my left and extended my hand out of the bedroll, reaching over to his side. Kirito stared for a moment with his obsidian eyes, then quietly agreed and echoed my action. Our fingertips touched, we both retracted, then clung tighter.

His hand was much warmer than the mug of soup I'd been holding just a few minutes earlier. The underside of my hand was resting on the icy floor, but I didn't even notice the cold.

The difference was human warmth.

In that moment, I finally understood the truth of the thirst that had wracked a part of my heart ever since I'd set foot in this world. I was afraid of thinking about the fact that this reality was virtual—that my true body was far, far away, impossible to reach. So instead, I found my own goals to pursue: to improve my crafting, to grow my business, telling myself that this *was* my real life.

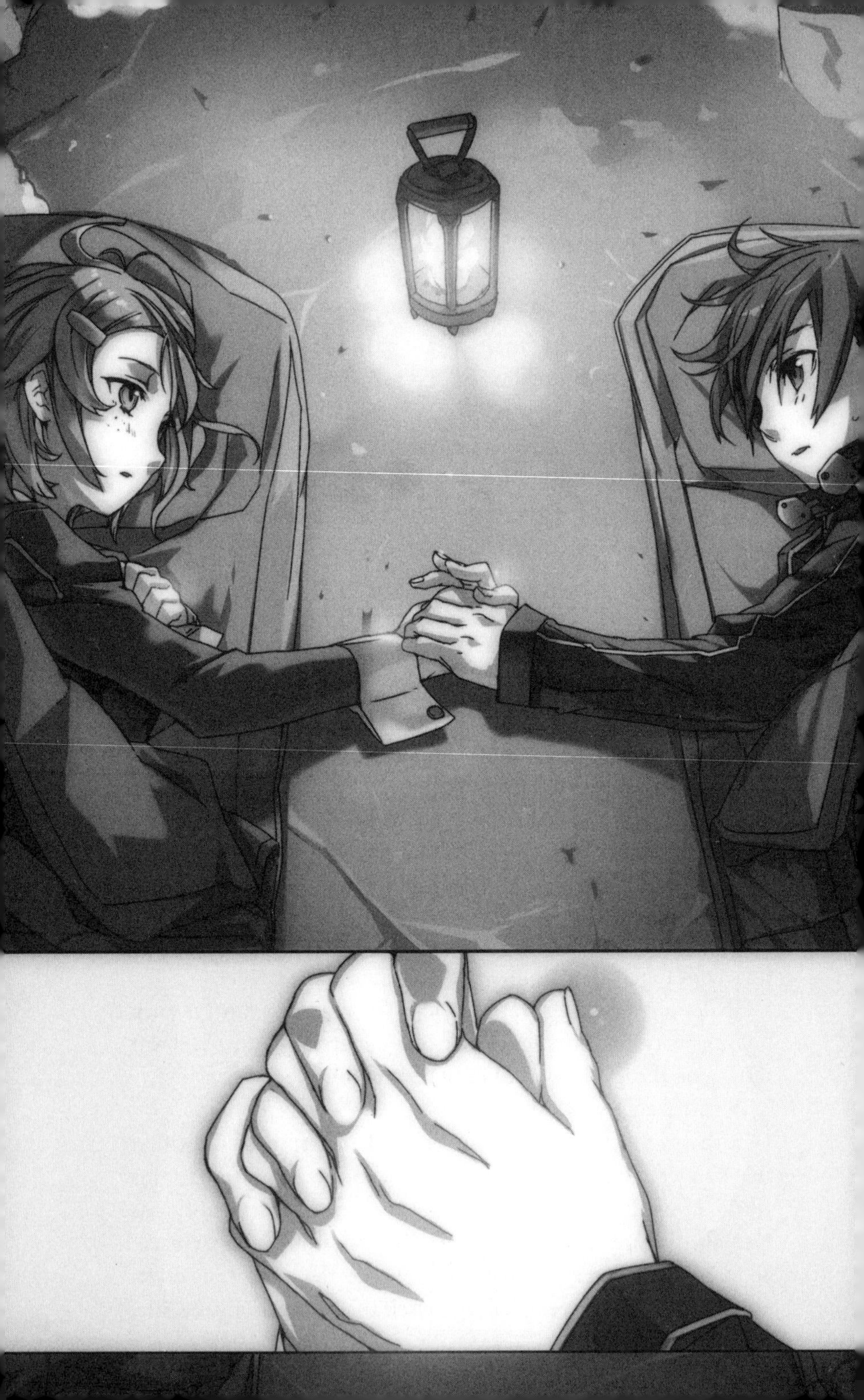

But deep in my heart, I always knew. That this was fake, that it was data. That I was starving for true human warmth.

Kirito's body was just a mass of data as well, of course. The warmth that enveloped me now was only an illusion, the product of electric signals stimulating my brain.

But at last I realized that this wasn't the problem. The only truth—in the real world or this virtual world—was what I felt in my heart.

I smiled and closed my eyes, still holding his hand tight.

Despite the quickened pace of my heartbeat, sleep found me disappointingly fast, pulling me down into a comforting darkness.

3

A pleasant scent tickled my nose. Slowly opening my eyes, I found the world to be full of white. The morning sun, bouncing endlessly off of the icy walls, set the snow pile into the vertical shaft a-shimmer.

Looking around, I noticed a steaming pot had been placed on top of the lantern. That was the source of the smell. In front of the lantern, facing sideways, was the man in black. The glimpse of him seemed to light a tiny fire within my breast.

Kirito turned to me and grinned.

"Morning."

"…Good morning."

Upon pushing myself up to a sitting position, I realized that the hand I'd fallen asleep extending had been tucked back underneath the bedroll. I touched it to my lips, imagining that the warmth was still saved in my palm, and hopped up to my feet.

Kirito handed me a steaming cup. I accepted it gratefully and plopped down next to him. The cup smelled like flowers and mint, a kind of tea I'd never tasted before. I took in a sip, then another, feeling the warmth spread through my heart.

I tilted sideways, leaning over to lean on Kirito. When I turned my head, our eyes met, and we both turned away immediately. For a minute, the only sound was the sipping of tea.

"Hey," I murmured into my mug.

"Yeah?"

"What if we never get out of here?"

"Then we'll need these sleeping bags."

"That was a quick answer. I was hoping for a bit more contemplation." I laughed, elbowing him. "But it wouldn't be the worst thing in the world, I guess…"

I tilted my head to rest on Kirito's shoulder, but he suddenly leaped upward with a cry, and I sprawled over onto the floor instead.

"Hey, what's the big idea?" I complained, but Kirito didn't turn back around. He started racing for the center of the large hole. Grumbling, I stood and followed.

"What is it?"

"Hang on…"

He knelt down and started scraping away the snow, digging out a hole in the layer that covered the ground.

"Wha—?"

A silver flash leaped across my face. Something under the snow was gleaming, reflecting the morning sunlight.

Kirito brushed away the snow, then grabbed the thing with both hands to lift it up. I bent over for a closer look, unable to suppress my curiosity.

It was a rectangular object, silver and translucent, just big enough to overflow both of Kirito's hands, if he held them together. An object of a very familiar size and shape to me—an ingot. But I'd never seen one this color.

I extended a finger and tapped on the surface of the block. A pop-up appeared, describing it as a CRYSTALLITE INGOT.

"Could this be…?"

I looked up at Kirito and he nodded hesitantly.

"Yeah…it's the metal we came here to find…I'm guessing."

"But why would it be buried down here?"

"Hmm…"

Kirito craned his neck, scrutinizing the ingot clamped in his fingers, then let out a brief exclamation of understanding.

"The dragon chews the crystals...and smelts them into the alloy in its belly...Ha-ha! That's neat."

He chuckled in appreciation and tossed the ingot to me. I hastily reached out to catch it with both hands, clutching it to my chest.

"Would you fill me in already? I'm tired of being left in the dark."

"This shaft isn't a trap. It's the dragon's nest."

"Wh-what?"

"That ingot is the dragon's waste product. It's poop."

"P..."

I looked down at the ingot held tightly to my chest, my cheek twitching.

"Eugh!" I tossed it back at Kirito.

"Whoa!"

He deftly bounced it back with his fingertips. We played a brief game of hot potato, tossing it back and forth like a pair of kids, until Kirito quickly opened his inventory and shoveled the ingot inside.

"Well, now we've got what we came for. The only thing left..."

"...is escaping."

We traded glances and sighed in unison.

"I guess we should just brainstorm and start testing our ideas."

"Yeah. If only we had wings like a dragon," I began to say, then realized something and stopped still, mouth agape.

"What is it, Liz?" Kirito peered into my face, puzzled.

"You just said this was a dragon's nest, right?"

"Yeah. I mean, there's poop here, so..."

"Enough about the poop already! If the dragon is nocturnal, doesn't that mean it'll come back to the nest in the morning...?"

"..."

We stared at each other for a moment, then turned to look upward at the aperture of the pit. The very next instant—

A black shadow bled into the white circle of light far, far above. It grew larger and larger. Within moments, I could make out two wings, a long tail, and four powerful limbs armed with claws.

"H...h..."

We both started backing away, not that there was anywhere to hide.

"Here it comes!" we cried in unison, drawing our weapons.

As the white dragon descended the shaft, it noticed us just before it reached the ground and gave a shrill, piercing cry, stopping in midair. Its red eyes and long, vertical pupils were glaring at us angrily, intruders in its sanctuary. But there was nowhere to hide in the narrow pit. I readied my mace, trying to stifle my nerves.

Kirito stepped in front of me, sword in hand, and rattled off some quick commands.

"Listen, don't step out from behind me. If your HP start to drop, drink a potion right away."

"O-okay." I nodded, determined to listen this time.

The dragon opened its maw wide for another screech. The beating of its wings sent the snow flying. It smacked its long, powerful tail against the ground repeatedly, carving deep furrows into the mounds of snow.

Kirito brandished his sword, preparing to charge and seize the initiative—when he stopped for some reason.

"...Wait...no way..." he murmured.

"Wh-what is it?"

"Um..."

He sheathed his sword without answering my question, then turned around and pulled me to his side.

"Huh?!"

Ignoring my panic, Kirito hoisted me up over his shoulder.

"H-hey, wait, what are you— Whoa!!"

The surroundings suddenly turned to a blur as a shock wave exploded around me—Kirito had started racing toward the wall. He leaped just before we hit it, then raced sideways along the curved walls, just as he'd attempted last night. Only this time, he stayed level rather than going up. The dragon's head craned as it tracked us, but Kirito hit his boosters, racing faster than the beast could follow.

A few seconds later, Kirito landed back on the ground as my eyes raced with dizziness. Once I blinked them into focus again, the dragon's backside came into view. It had lost sight of us and was searching left and right on the wrong side of the hole.

It seemed to me that Kirito was going to attack it from behind, but instead he approached it quietly, reached out, and grabbed it firmly by the tip of its tail.

In that instant, the dragon let out another screech. Was it just me, or did it sound like a scream of surprise? Now I was thoroughly confused as to Kirito's plan, and I let out a yell of my own, but the dragon beat its wings and began rising with terrifying speed.

"*Bfft!*"

Air beat my face. I felt myself flying through the air as though I'd been shot from a bow. We were rising quickly through the shaft, swaying left and right as the dragon's tail whipped back and forth. The floor of the circular pit grew smaller and smaller.

"Hang on tight, Liz!" Kirito bellowed, and I clung to his neck for dear life. The sunlight reflecting off the ice walls was getting lighter and lighter, and the pitch of the air whistling past my ears shifted subtly. There was an abrupt explosion of white, and then we were outside the hole.

When I opened my eyes again, I could see the entirety of the fifty-fifth floor laid out in front of me. Directly below was the snowy mountain, a pristine cone. Farther away was the tiny village. Beyond the vast snowfield and intricate forest was a procession of sloped roofs that marked the floor's main city. Everything I saw glittered brightly in the light of the morning. For a moment, I forgot my fear and exclaimed in wonder.

"Wow…"

"Yeaaaaah!!"

Kirito whooped and let go of the dragon's tail. He tightened his grip around my side and our momentum sent us spinning through the air.

The flight only lasted a few seconds, but it felt ten times that long. I think I was laughing. The overflowing light and wind cleansed my heart. My emotions were fit to burst.

"Hey, Kirito!!" I shouted at the top of my lungs.

"What?!"

"I really like you!!"

"What?! I can't hear you!!"

"Nothing!!"

I hugged his neck and laughed wildly. Our miraculous moment came to an end as the ground approached. Kirito took one last spin and braced himself for impact, his legs wide.

Bawoof! Snow shot upward. There was a long glide. We slowed down gradually while weaving through the white crystals like a snowplow, and finally we came to a halt at the edge of the peak.

"...Whew." Kirito sighed, plopping down on the snow. I reluctantly released my grip on his neck.

We turned around to look at the massive hole, while the dragon circled overhead, having apparently lost sight of us.

Kirito reached back to his sword and started to pull it out of its sheath, then shoved it back. A wry grin crossed his face as he murmured to the dragon.

"Sorry about all the hunting, day after day. Once word gets out on how to find the item, they won't be trying to kill you anymore. Live in peace."

Yesterday, I would have thought, *Are you crazy, talking to a monster that's just a series of algorithms?* But for some reason, my heart accepted Kirito's words as true and honest. I reached out and gently gripped his hand.

As we watched silently, the white dragon craned its head around; gave a crisp, clear screech; then descended back into the shaft. Silence returned.

Finally, Kirito turned to me and said, "Shall we go?"

"Yeah."

"Wanna take a crystal back?"

"No...let's walk."

I started walking forward with a smile on my face, still holding Kirito's hand. But then I remembered something and looked back to him.

"Oh...we left the lantern and sleeping bags down there."

"Now that you mention it...oh, well. Someone else might find them useful."

We grinned at each other and started hiking down the mountain, headed home for sure this time. The sky beyond the outer perimeter of Aincrad was a brilliant, unblemished blue.

"I'm home!"

I shoved open the familiar door of my shop.

"Welcome back," the NPC girl behind the counter returned politely. I waved to her and took a look around the shop. I'd only been gone for a single day, but somehow it all looked new and different.

Kirito followed me inside the door, another hot dog from that same street cart shoved into his mouth again.

"It's almost lunchtime; we should eat at a proper restaurant," I complained, but Kirito grinned and opened his item window instead.

"Before that, let's get this sword made."

He flipped through his inventory and materialized the platinum ingot, tossing it to me. I caught the metal—willfully ignoring the source of the substance—and nodded.

"Yeah, let's get it over with. Come back into the workshop."

We proceeded through the door in the back of the storefront, where the *thunk*ing of the waterwheel became much louder. I hit the switch on the wall, starting up the bellows to push air into the furnace. It began glowing red almost at once.

I placed the ingot into the opening, then turned to Kirito.

"You wanted a one-handed sword, right?"

"Yep. Thanks." He sat himself into the round guest chair.

"Coming right up. Just so you know, the quality will be affected by random variables, so keep your expectations reasonable."

"If it's a failure, we can always go get another ingot. We just need to remember a rope."

"A really, really long one."

I chuckled, thinking about the preposterous drop down that shaft. Inside the furnace, the ingot was getting good and cooked. I reached in with the tongs and pulled it out onto the anvil.

After grabbing my smithing hammer off the wall and configuring the menu, I gave Kirito one last glance. He nodded silently. I smiled in response and raised the hammer high over my head.

The powerful swing caught the glowing metal square, and a clear, pure *clang!* echoed off the walls, red sparks flying everywhere.

In the chapter of the game's reference materials dedicated to Blacksmithing, the only detail offered about this step is, "Strike the ingot a number of times, depending on the type of weapon being created and the rank of metal being used."

That could be interpreted to mean that the player's skill has no bearing on the act of hitting the metal with a hammer, but given the nonstop trading of whispered rumors and secret techniques in SAO, most people strongly believed that the precision of the crafter's rhythm and a strong will would indeed affect the final result.

I considered myself a rational, levelheaded person, but months and months of practice led me to give credence to this theory. When I made a weapon, I shut out all other information, focusing entirely on the hammer in my right hand, striking firmly with a mind free of all distractions.

But...

This time, amid the clanging of the metal, my mind was whirling with a number of conflicting thoughts.

If I performed this job properly and made a satisfactory weapon, Kirito would take it back to the front line, and it was unlikely I'd see him much after this. Even if he did come back for maintenance and sharpening, it would be once every ten days, at the most frequent.

But I don't want that, screamed a silent voice within me.

I'd been starving for human warmth—in fact, it was because I was lonely that I hesitated to get close to any specific male players. I was afraid of that loneliness turning into love. And it wouldn't be a real romance, just an illusion of chemicals and data created by this virtual world.

But when I felt the heat of Kirito's hand last night, I realized it was that hesitation itself that was this world's thorny trap. I am me. I'm Lisbeth the blacksmith, and also Rika Shinozaki. It's the same for Kirito. He's not a character in a game; he's a flesh-and-blood human being. Which means my burgeoning feeling of attraction to him must be real, too.

If I forge a sword that meets his satisfaction, I'll tell him how I feel. I'll tell him I want him to stick around, to come back to this house every day after his adventures in the labyrinths.

As the ingot was pounded into shape and took on a greater shine, the emotions within me solidified into certainty. My feelings spilled out through my right hand, flowing into my hammer, and from there, the sword that was taking shape before my eyes.

Finally, the moment came.

Somewhere between 200 and 250 strikes, the ingot suddenly emitted a much brighter shine than before. The glowing rectangular shape morphed before our eyes, lengthening from both ends and sprouting a protuberance that was likely to be the hilt.

"Whoa," Kirito murmured in wonder, hopping up from the chair to watch. Within a few seconds, the object was fully generated, and a new sword rested on the anvil.

It was a beautiful weapon, very beautiful. For a longsword, it seemed a bit on the fragile side. The blade was thin, but not as thin as a rapier. The entire thing seemed just a tiny bit translucent, as though it had inherited that characteristic from the ingot. The blade itself was a brilliant white, while the hilt was a bluish silver.

One of the sales pitches for SAO claimed that it was "a world in which a player's sword represents him," and indeed, there is a vast variety of weapons in the game. A list of the unique weapon names among all the categories would number several thousand.

Unlike in a normal RPG, the variety of different weapons grows as they rise in rank and power. Low-rank weapons might have bland names like "Bronze Sword" or "Steel Blade"—and there are countless examples of them scattered around SAO— but the finest weapons currently in use in the game, like Asuna's "Lambent Light," are one-of-a-kind.

Naturally, there are other rapiers with similar characteristics, whether player-made or dropped by monsters. But they'll all have different names and shapes. That's how high-level weapons bewitch their users—becoming trusted partners, a piece of one's soul.

The name and shape of a weapon is determined by the system itself, so even the one crafting it doesn't know what it will be ahead of time. I picked up the glittering sword with both hands—and was shocked by its surprising weight. This weapon would require a strength stat at least as high as Kirito's Elucidator. I put my knees into it and hefted the sword up to my chest.

With my right hand cradling the hilt of the sword, I awkwardly tapped it with a finger to bring up the pop-up menu.

"Let's see, it's called the Dark Repulser. I've never heard of it, so I'm sure it's not listed in any of the weapon indexes yet. Here, try it out."

"Thanks."

Kirito reached out and grabbed the hilt. He lifted the blade easily, as though it weighed nothing at all. He fiddled with the equipment mannequin inside his menu and targeted the white sword. This meant the system officially recognized the new blade as properly equipped, displaying the new parameters for the player's perusal.

But Kirito ignored the numbers and closed the menu. He took a few steps back and swung the blade back and forth.

"Well?" I asked, unable to wait. Kirito stared at the sword silently for a few moments—then broke out into a wide grin.

"It's heavy. Nice sword."

"Really? Hooray!"

I raised my fist in triumph. Kirito returned the salute and we bumped fists.

It had been a long time since I'd felt this way. It was the same way I had felt when customers praised the ramshackle weapons I had sold in my roadside display in my days down around the tenth floor—the moments that I'd been glad I was a blacksmith. It was a feeling that I'd gradually forgotten, when my skills became good enough that I began selling to high-level players.

"I guess it's all just a matter...of how you look at it..."

Kirito tilted his head, curious of my self-absorbed murmuring.

"Er, n-nothing. Anyway, shall we go somewhere to celebrate? I'm pretty hungry," I announced, loudly, to hide my nerves. I pushed Kirito's shoulders from behind, trying to guide him out of the workshop—when I was struck by a sudden doubt.

"...Hey."

"What?"

Kirito looked over his shoulder. His black sword was still slung over his back.

"You originally said you wanted something as good as this sword. I can tell the white sword is a very nice weapon, but it doesn't seem that different from your looted sword. Why do you need two similar swords?"

"Ahh..."

Kirito turned around to face me, clearly grappling with what to say.

"Well, I can't explain the full details. But I'll tell you if you promise not to ask any further questions."

"Why so cryptic?"

"Here, stand back."

He had me back up against the wall of the shop, then drew the black sword from its scabbard, still holding the white sword in his left hand.

"...?"

I couldn't tell what he was going to do. He'd been fiddling with his equipment screen, but the system only recognized the sword in his left hand as being his equipped weapon. Having another sword in his right hand wouldn't help him out in the least. In fact, it was more likely to disable his sword skills because the system would detect an irregularity in his active weapon.

Kirito spared a single glance at my baffled face, then took on a battle stance, right sword forward, left sword back. He crouched, and an instant later—

Red visual effects burst outward, coloring the entire workshop for a moment.

Kirito's swords shot forward in an alternating pattern faster than the eye could follow. *Shba-ba-ba-bam!* He didn't hit anything, but all the objects in the room trembled with the force of the air.

That was very clearly a Sword skill, recognized and aided by the game system. But...I'd never heard of any skills that used two swords!

Kirito stood up silently after he finished his combo, which seemed to have at least ten different blows. He snapped both of his wrists forward, returned his left sword to the sheath on his back, and then gazed at me. My breath hitched.

"That'll do. I need a sheath for this sword. Can you fashion something for me?"

"Uh...s-sure."

How many times had this Kirito managed to shock me? I should have been getting used to it by now. I decided to hold off on the questions and touched the wall to bring up my workshop's home menu.

The shop storage was full of various supplies, so I scrolled through the list until I found a bundle of scabbards I'd bought from a fellow craftsman. I picked out one finished with black

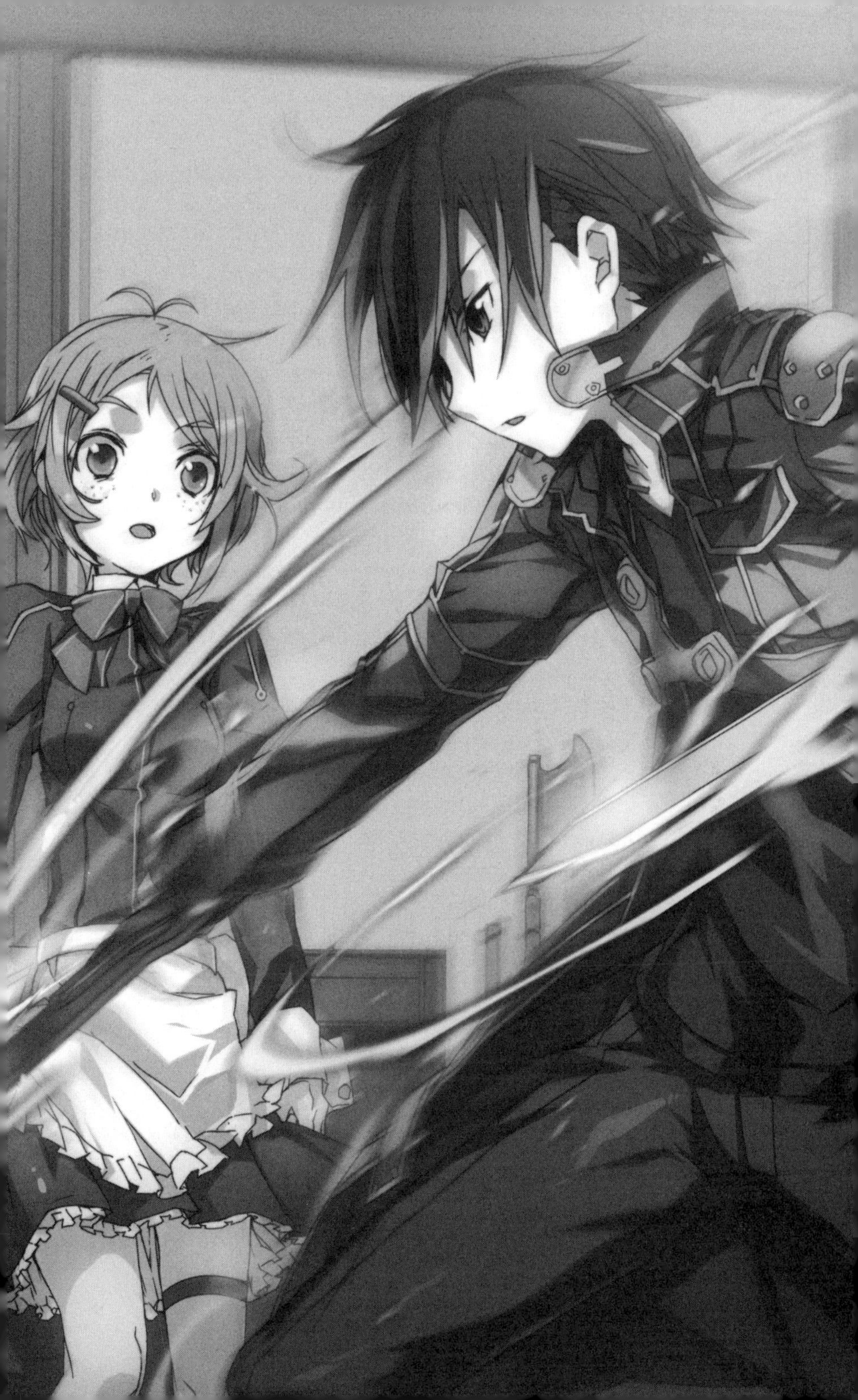

leather that seemed a good fit for the sword on Kirito's back, and
I pulled it out of the menu. My studio logo was printed on the
finish, nice and small. I handed it to him.

Kirito snapped the white blade into the sheath and placed the
entire thing in his window screen. I thought he might just leave
both of them equipped, but apparently not.

"Was that...a secret?"

"Yeah, kinda. It'd do me a solid if you didn't tell anyone."

"Aye-aye."

A player's skill information was his lifeline. If someone didn't
want you snooping, you had to obey. But more importantly, the
fact that he'd considered me worthy of seeing his secret in action
filled me with delight.

"So." Kirito placed his hands on his hips and looked at me.
"That finished up our deal. How much do I owe you?"

"Uhh, erm..."

I bit my lip for a moment—then spoke what I'd been feeling in
my heart.

"I don't need any money for it."

"...Pardon?"

"Instead, I want to be your personal blacksmith."

His eyes widened slightly.

"What...do you mean by that...?"

"When you're done with an adventure, come here for maintenance. Every day. From here on out."

My heartbeat was racing now. Was it just a virtual effect, or
was my real heart racing just as quickly? My cheeks were hot. My
entire face must have been bright red.

Even Kirito, he of the effortless poker face, blushed and looked
down when he realized what I meant. He'd always seemed older
than me, but that simple gesture made him feel the same age, or
perhaps even younger.

I summoned my courage and took a step forward, taking hold
of Kirito's hand.

"Kirito...I..."

I'd shouted the same words at the top of my lungs when we burst out of the dragon's lair, but now that I was saying them face-to-face, my tongue wouldn't move. I stared into Kirito's black eyes, willing myself to put the feelings into words, when...

The door of the workshop slammed open. I let go of Kirito and leaped away.

"Liz, I was so worried!!"

The visitor shouted and raced inside, barreling into me with a massive bear hug. Long chestnut-brown hair danced through the air.

"A-Asuna..."

She leaned in close to my stunned face, glaring, then proceeded to tear into me.

"None of my messages reached you, I couldn't find you on the map, none of the regulars knew where to find you—where the heck did you go last night? I even went to Blackiron Palace to make sure the worst hadn't happened!"

"S-sorry, sorry. I just got stuck in a dungeon..."

"A dungeon?! You?! By yourself?!"

"N-no, with him..."

I glanced over Asuna's shoulder. She spun around, saw the black swordsman standing there awkwardly, and froze in place, her eyes and mouth open wide. Then, her voice a full octave higher than usual—

"K-Kirito?"

"Yes?!"

Now it was my turn to be shocked. I turned to look at Kirito, who was just as stock-still as Asuna. He cleared his throat lightly and raised a hand in greeting.

"Hi, Asuna. It's been a while...if two days counts as a while, I guess."

"Y-yes...you startled me. So you decided to visit. If you'd just said something, I would have joined you."

She clasped her hands behind her and smiled shyly, the heels of her boots clicking on the floor. I noticed the spots of pink on her cheeks...

And understood everything.

It wasn't coincidence that Kirito came here. Asuna had recommended my shop to him, as she promised me she would. He was the boy she had a crush on.

Oh my God... What should I do?

The words spun in circles throughout my head. It felt like all the warmth of my body was flowing away, escaping out of my toes. I couldn't move. I couldn't breathe. I couldn't find the proper outlet for how I felt...

Asuna turned back to me and chirped, "He wasn't rude to you, was he, Liz? I bet he gave you some ridiculous request."

She looked briefly puzzled. "But, wait... does that mean you were with Kirito last night?"

"Um... listen..." I forced myself forward, grabbing Asuna's hand and pushing the door open. Before we walked out, I turned around and spoke quickly and professionally in Kirito's direction, careful not to look directly at him.

"Just a minute. I'll be right back..."

I pulled Asuna out into the storefront, shut the door behind us, and wove through the shelves of inventory to the front door.

"W-wait, Liz, what's going on?" Asuna asked, clearly baffled, but I kept heading for the main street, my pace quick. I couldn't be around Kirito another moment. If I didn't escape the workshop, I was afraid I'd take it out on him.

Asuna seemed to realize the gravity of the situation, as she followed without another word. Finally, I let go of her hand.

We went into the east-facing alley across the street, where there was a small open-air café, almost hidden beneath a tall stone wall. There were no other customers there. I picked out a table in the corner and sat down in the white chair.

Asuna took the seat across from me and peered into my face, clearly concerned.

"What's the matter, Liz...?"

I flashed her a big smile, trying to summon all of my energy. It was the same easy smile I always used when we chatted about silly rumors.

"That's him, isn't it?" I crossed my arms and glanced at her.

"H-huh?"

"The boy you like!"

"Oh…" She looked down, her shoulders hunching, then nodded. Her cheeks were pink again. "Yeah."

I widened my grin, trying to ignore the sudden lance of pain that shot through my chest.

"Well, he certainly is very strange."

"Did Kirito…do anything to you?" She looked worried. I gave her a hearty nod.

"He certainly did. Within two minutes, he'd broken the nicest sword in my shop."

"Oh no…I'm so sorry…"

"It's not like it's your fault, Asuna."

The sight of her apologizing, hands clasped together, only made the throbbing in my heart worse.

C'mon, Lisbeth. You can do this…just a bit more.

I did my best to keep my smile going.

"Well, anyway, the properties of the sword he wanted required a very rare type of metal, so we had to go to an upper floor to find it. When we got there, we fell into a trap that was pretty tricky to get out of, and that's why it took a while to get home."

"I see…So even if you'd tried to send me a message, it wouldn't have reached me…"

"We probably should have invited you along. I'm sorry."

"No, I was busy with guild work anyway…So did you make the sword?"

"Yep, all done. I never want to undertake such a bother of a job again, though."

"You'd better make sure you get a nice hefty price tag out of it!"

We laughed together. I wrung the final words out, still holding that smile.

"Well, he's kind of weird, but he's not a bad person. I hope it all goes well for you, Asuna."

It was as far as I could get. The last word trembled out of my lips.

"Um, yeah. Thanks…" Asuna nodded, peering into my face, her head tilted in curiosity. I vigorously stood up before she could see what was threatening to well up behind my eyelids.

"Ah, crap! I forgot that I promised to stock up on some stuff. I need to go down and pick it up!"

"Huh? What about the store… What about Kirito?"

"You handle him, Asuna! Thanks!"

I turned on my heel and dashed away, waving to Asuna over my shoulder. I couldn't turn around to face her.

Once I'd run far enough toward the teleport gate square that I couldn't be seen from the café, I turned the corner to the south. I ran straight for the corner of the town, in search of a place I could be alone, my mind in tumult. When my vision blurred, I wiped my eyes clean. Over and over.

The next thing I knew, I was standing before the wall that surrounded the town. There was a line of evenly spaced trees planted along the gentle curve of the wall. I stopped in the shade of one of them, clutching the branches to stay upright.

"Sng…sob…"

The sounds escaped from the depths of my throat. The tears I'd been trying hard to hold back spilled forth, forging lines down my cheeks.

It was the second time I'd cried since I came to this world. After the very first day, when I'd cried from a panic attack at that initial shock, I swore I would never cry again. I didn't want the game's emotion system to force virtual tears down my cheeks. But even in real life, I'd never felt hotter, more painful drops run across my face.

During our conversation, I'd failed to say the most important words to Asuna: "You know, I like him, too." I don't know how many times I'd gotten close. But I couldn't do it.

The instant I saw Kirito and Asuna next to each other in the workshop, I understood that my place was not at his side. I knew it because I had put his life in danger on that snowy mountaintop. Only someone with a heart as strong as his was meant to stand next to him. Someone...like Asuna...

There was a strong magnetism between the two of them, a fit as tight as a sword and its custom-made scabbard. I could feel it clear as day. Asuna had spent months pining after Kirito, slowly closing the distance between them—I couldn't possibly step in over the course of a single day and ruin all of that.

That's right...I've only known Kirito for twenty-four hours. My heart is simply shaken out of its usual pattern by going on an unusual adventure with a stranger. It isn't *real*. This feeling isn't *real*. If I'm going to fall in love, it has to be steadily, thoroughly, properly—that's what I always told myself.

So why are there so many tears?

Kirito's voice, mannerisms, expressions—everything I'd seen over those twenty-four hours floated up over my eyelids. The feeling of his palm, when he'd rubbed my head, grabbed my arm, held my outstretched hand. The warmth of him, of his heart. Each time my mind touched those memories, the pain jabbed deeper into my chest.

I have to forget. It was all a dream. Let the tears wash it away.

I dug my fingers into the branches of the tree, clinging to stay upright, sobbing. It was all I could do to keep my voice down. In the real world, you run out of tears at some point, but it seemed like the virtual teardrops would never dry up.

And then I heard a voice from behind.

"Lisbeth."

A jolt ran through my body. A gentle, soothing voice, high-pitched with youth.

It must be an illusion. He couldn't be here. I was so sure that I didn't even bother to wipe my tears before turning up to look.

There was Kirito. The eyes sheltered behind his black bangs told of his own troubles. I stared back into them for a few moments, then spoke in a trembling voice.

"...You shouldn't have come just now. In a few minutes, I'd be back to the usual, cheerful Lisbeth."

"..."

He took a step forward, reaching out a hand to me. I shook my head, refusing to give in.

"How did you know I'd be here?"

Kirito turned his head and pointed back toward the center of town.

"I went up there." His finger was pointing to the steeple of the church bordering the teleport plaza, towering over the other roofs in the far distance. "You can see the entire town from that point."

"Hah...hah." Despite the continual outpouring of tears, I couldn't help but let an involuntary chuckle leave my lips. "You never stop being ridiculous."

I like even that about you...unbearably so.

The wracking sobs were about to return. I desperately tried to stifle them.

"Sorry, I'm—I'm fine. Go back to Asuna."

Having squeezed out all that I could manage, I started to turn away, but Kirito continued.

"I...I wanted to thank you, Liz."

"Huh...?"

I spun back to him. This was not what I expected.

"You see...I used to be in a guild, and the other members all got wiped out because of me...Ever since, I swore that I would never let anyone get close to me again."

For a moment, his brows furrowed, and he bit his lip.

"So...normally, I avoid partying up with anyone. But yesterday, when you said we should do that quest together, I said yes for some reason. It was a mystery to me the entire time. 'Why am I walking with this person'?"

For an instant, I forgot about the pain in my chest.

That—that was how *I'd* felt...

"Every time someone gave me a party request, I refused them.

Watching people I knew—hell, even people I *didn't* know—fight just terrified me. All I could think of was running from battle and never looking back. That's why I hung out at the very farthest reaches of the frontier: to stay away from people. When we fell into that hole, and I said I'd rather die than be the only survivor, I wasn't lying."

He smiled weakly. I held my breath at the bottomless self-loathing I saw behind that expression.

"But we survived. Somehow we both made it, and that was such a joy to me. And that night, when you held out your hand to me, I understood. Your hand was so warm...I realized that you were truly alive. I understood that I, and everyone else here, aren't running out the days until we inevitably die. We're living in order to live. So...thanks, Liz."

"..."

Now a true smile radiated forward with all of my heart. I was gripped with some strange, indefinable feeling.

"You know...I've been searching for something, too. Something true in this world. And then I found it—the warmth of your hand."

It felt as though the dagger of ice stabbed into my heart was melting. My tears had stopped. We stood in silence for several moments, looking into each other's eyes. For a brief instant, I felt that same miraculous feeling that had occurred during our flight brush my heart.

I've been vindicated.

Kirito's words had scooped up the broken pieces of my brief love and kindly buried them someplace deep.

I blinked hard, brushing away the small remaining drops, and gave him a smile.

"You should tell Asuna the same things. She's in pain, too, you know. She wants your warmth."

"Liz..."

"I'll be fine." I nodded and crossed my hands over my chest. "The heat will stay here for a while yet. Please...you have to end this world. I can hang on until then. But when we get back to reality…"

I grinned devilishly.

"That's when Round Two begins."

" … "

He smiled back and nodded, then waved his hand to call up a window. Curious, I watched him remove Elucidator from his back and place it in his item list. Soon, a new sword took its place on his equipment mannequin. Dark Repulser: the white sword that contained so many of my emotions.

"Starting today, this sword will be my partner. I'll pay you back on the other side."

"I'm holding you to that. It'll cost ya!"

We laughed together and bumped fists.

"Let's go back to the shop. Asuna's got to be sick of waiting around…Plus, I'm getting hungry."

I started off, leading the way. One final brush of my eyes dislodged the last remaining tear. It fell away, glittered with light, and vanished.

4

The next morning was even colder than usual.

I was rubbing my hands together as I entered my workshop, and I wasted no time pulling the lever on the wall to stoke the fire. The water wheel thunked and clanked like always as I held my hands up to the warm furnace. Given the weather, I couldn't help but worry about what would happen if the creek outside ever froze solid.

After a minute, I came back to my senses with a start and checked my in-game scheduler. I had eight orders due today. I had to get working soon, or the day would be over before I knew it.

The first order was a lightweight longsword. I stared down my list of available ingots, found one that matched the budget and specs of the customer, and tossed it into the furnace opening.

My skills with the hammer and available selection of metals were so great these days that my work output was a constant stream of high-level weapons. Wait for the ingot to reach the right temperature, place it on the anvil. Select the hammer, swing it hard.

But when it came to one-handed longswords...nothing I'd made surpassed the sword I made back in early summer. This made me both frustrated and happy.

The sword I'd infused with all the pieces of my heart was likely on the front line today, cleaving foes left and right. Every once in a while, I got to hold it to the grindstone, and unlike normal weapons, it seemed to grow more translucent with use, not the other way around. It almost made me think that rather than losing numerical stats, it would eventually shatter like a crystal when it wore down.

But that was likely far off in the future. The current frontier was the seventy-fifth floor. That sword needed to last much longer in its rightful place: Kirito's right hand.

I only realized that I'd reached the necessary number of strokes when the ingot emitted a red glow and began to morph. Watching the magic moment with bated breath, I reached out to appraise the brand-new blade.

"It'll do, I suppose," I muttered, then placed it on the worktable. Time to find the right ingot for the next weapon. This one would be a two-handed ax with long reach...

Well after lunchtime, I finally finished the last of the orders and rose to my feet. I rolled my head slowly and let out a great big yawn. A small photograph hung on the wall caught my eye.

Me and Asuna, our shoulders touching, peace signs in the air. Next to Asuna and a half step behind was Kirito, smiling awkwardly. We'd taken the picture just outside this shop. About half a month ago—when they came to inform me of their marriage.

Anyone could see they were made for each other, but it had taken them six months to reach that point. It was irritating to watch them stumble, and I'd had to lend a helping hand at several points. So, I was overjoyed to finally hear of their union...along with just a little twinge of pain.

That night still pops up in my dreams all the time. That magical night, sparkling like a jewel amidst two years of doldrums. It was like an eternal fire keeping the warmth in my chest alive, even after five months.

"And despite myself..."

I muttered silently, tracing the photo with a finger. For considering myself such a pragmatic realist, I'd never realized what a romantic I was at heart.

"...I've been in love with you ever since."

I gave the photo one last tap and turned around. *It* happened just as I was leaving the studio, wondering if I should fix myself a late lunch or just eat out:

A sound effect I'd never heard before rang out far above my head, deafeningly loud. It was an alarm, ringing like a bell...I looked up at the ceiling first, but it seemed the sound was coming from much farther away, echoing down from the floor above.

I rushed outside to see what was happening and was awakened to something even more unexpected: The NPC helper that had been manning my desk every single day since I'd opened the store had vanished without a sound.

"...?"

I stared at the space she normally inhabited, wide-eyed, but she showed no sign of returning. Whatever was happening was serious business.

I fell out of the front door, only to be frozen in my tracks by something even more shocking.

The flat, metallic gray lid of the floor above, several hundred feet over my head, was completely covered in giant red words. I could make out a repeating pattern of two different pieces of English: WARNING and SYSTEM ANNOUNCEMENT.

"System...announcement..."

I recognized this sight. I would never forget it: It was the exact same scene we'd all witnessed two years ago, on the day that this became a game of death. It had been plastered behind that massive avatar as ten thousand helpless souls learned the rules that would become their new lives.

After a few seconds frozen still, I finally looked around and saw plenty of other players looking up at the warning in shock. Something about the sight struck me as off, and I quickly realized why.

There wasn't a single NPC walking the street or selling goods in the area. They must have all disappeared at the same time my storekeeper did…but why?

The blaring alarm suddenly stopped. After a brief silence, a soft female voice emerged, just as loud.

"This is an important message to all players."

Unlike the voice of Akihiko Kayaba two years ago, this voice was artificial, electronic. It was obviously a system announcement, but SAO seemed to be designed to remove all possible traces of human management, and this was the first time I'd ever heard it. I swallowed and listened up.

"The game is switching to forced management mode. All monsters and items will no longer spawn. All NPCs will be recalled. All players' HP will be fixed at maximum value."

Is it a system error? Some kind of fatal bug?

My heart was gripped by anxiety. But then—

"As of 14:55 on November Seventh, Aincrad Standard Time, the game has been cleared," the system proclaimed.

The game had been beaten.

For several seconds, I didn't understand what that meant. The other players around me were similarly baffled, their faces frozen. At the following words, they all leaped into the air.

"All players will now be logged out of the game. Please stop where you are. I repeat…"

An enormous cheer rose instantly. The ground—no, the entire castle of Aincrad—shook. Players embraced, rolled on the ground, thrust their fists into the air, and screamed.

I didn't move. I didn't speak. I just stood in front of my store. In time, I lifted my hands to cover my mouth.

He did it. Kirito did it. As crazy as he always was…

I was certain it was him. The front line was only the seventy-fifth floor, so only Kirito could do something as insane, reckless, and impossible as this.

Somehow, I thought I felt a whisper at my ear.

I kept my promise…

"Yes…yes…you finally did it…"

Hot tears sprang into my eyes at last. I didn't wipe them away. I lifted my right arm into the air and jumped up and down wildly.

"Heyyy!!" I cupped my hands to my mouth, shouting at the top of my lungs, as though to reach his ears many floors above.

"Let's meet up again sometime, Kirito!! I love you!!"

(The End)

The Girl in the Morning Dew

§ 22nd floor of Aincrad
October 2024

1

Asuna's alarm was set to go off at 7:50 every morning.

Why such an oddly specific time? Because Kirito's alarm went off at exactly 8:00. She liked to wake up ten minutes early and, in the comfort of the bed, lay gazing at the man sleeping next to her.

On this morning, too, after Asuna woke to the soft melody of woodwinds, she carefully rolled over and, her chin in her hands, considered Kirito's sleeping face.

She'd fallen in love half a year ago. They'd become adventuring partners two weeks ago. And they'd gotten married and moved into these woods on the twenty-second floor just six days ago. She loved him more than anyone in the world, but the truth was that Kirito still harbored many mysteries to her. This could even be said to include his sleeping face: the more she stared, the harder it was to tell his actual age.

Due to his off-kilter, aloof nature, she typically thought of him as being older than she was. But when he was fast asleep, like now, there was a youthful innocence to his face that made him appear like a little boy.

She knew she could just ask him how old he was. It might be taboo here to talk about real life, but they were husband and wife.

Forget ages—they ought to be trading real names and addresses, things that would help them meet again once this nightmare was over.

But Asuna was having trouble broaching the topic.

She was afraid that the instant she talked about real life, their married life—this wonderful dream—would become virtual, fake. This everyday life in the woods was her only reality—the thing she cared about most. Even if they never escaped this world and her body was doomed to waste away without her, she would have no regrets as long as they met the end together.

Which is why I want the dream to last a little longer... Asuna reached out and traced Kirito's cheek. *He really does look so young when he's sleeping.*

She had no doubts about his strength at this point. He'd been stockpiling an astronomical amount of experience since the beta test, earned massive stats through countless battles, and had the will and judgment to use them expertly. He'd lost in his duel against Heathcliff, the leader of the Knights of the Blood, but Kirito was still the strongest player in the game, Asuna knew. No matter how dreadful the challenge, she'd never been worried in battle at his side.

But gazing down at him sleeping beside her, she couldn't help but associate him with a fragile, naive younger brother. She had to protect him from harm.

She sighed softly, leaned over, and circled her arms around his body.

"I love you, Kirito...let's be together forever," she whispered.

He stirred and slowly opened his eyes. Their glances met at a close distance.

"Whoa!" Asuna leaped backward. She caught her balance kneeling on the covers, face bright red. "G-good morning, Kirito. Did you...hear that...?"

"Morning. Hear what?" he replied, stifling a yawn and waving to her.

"N-nothing, nothing!"

*   *   *

After their breakfast of eggs, black bread, salad, and coffee, it took only two seconds to clear off the table. Asuna clapped her hands together.

"Okay! Where are we going to hang out today?"

"Jeez." Kirito grimaced. "There's gotta be a better way to say that."

"But every day's so much fun!"

Asuna wasn't lying in the least.

Though it was painful to recall, until she'd fallen in love with Kirito, the first year and a half of being a prisoner inside SAO had left her heart frozen cold.

She'd cut down on her sleeping time to raise her skills and level. Once she'd reached the rank of sub-leader of the Knights of the Blood, she'd attacked the game's labyrinths at a pace that caused complaints from her guildmates. Her only purpose was beating the game and escaping. Everything else was meaningless to her.

In a way, Asuna had to curse her poor fortune that she hadn't met Kirito sooner. Ever since their first encounter, her days had been filled with more color and pleasant surprises than she'd ever experienced in real life. Only with him did she feel like her experiences here were actually worth remembering.

Which meant that every second they spent together was like a delicate jewel to Asuna. She wanted to visit every place she could, speak with him on every subject there was.

Asuna pouted, hands on her hips. "So you don't want to go out and have fun?"

Kirito grinned in response and pulled up his map. He set it to visible mode to show Asuna. The map showed the series of forests and lakes that made up the floor.

"This is the spot." He pointed to a stretch of woods slightly removed from their home.

Because the entirety of Aincrad was egg-shaped and the twenty-second floor was closer to the bottom, it was relatively spacious, a good eight kilometers in diameter. There was a massive lake in the middle of the floor, the southern shore of which seated the village of Coral, the floor's main settlement. The labyrinth was on the northern shore. Everything else was covered in beautiful conifer forests. Asuna and Kirito's home was close to the perimeter, nearly at the southern tip of the floor, and Kirito had singled out a location perhaps a mile and a half to the northeast.

"Yesterday, I heard a rumor in the village...about the depths of the forests here...and what might be lurking there."

"Huh?" Asuna responded to Kirito's enigmatic leer, confused. "What's there?"

"A ghost."

After a moment of silence, she hesitantly pressed him for more details.

"Meaning...like, astral-type monsters? Wraiths and banshees, that sort of thing?"

"No, no, the real thing. The ghost of a player...a human being. A little girl."

"Uh..."

Her faced ticked uncontrollably. She was more susceptible to ghost stories than the average person, she knew. The ancient castle labyrinths on the very spooky horror-themed sixty-fifth and sixty-sixth floors were so bad, she'd had to find excuses not to participate in their conquest.

"B-but this is a game; it's all digital. There can't possibly be ghosts here!" She forced herself to smile desperately.

"Are you sure about that?" Kirito knew about Asuna's fear of ghosts and gleefully piled on more pressure. "What if it's the vengeful spirit of a player who died and now haunts her still-active NerveGear? And logs in late at night to haunt the fields..."

"Stop!!"

"Ha-ha-ha, sorry. That one crossed the line. Look, I don't really think there'll be a ghost there, but if we're going to explore, why not pick a spot that might have something neat to find?"

"Aww..." Asuna pouted, looking out the window.

The weather was good for the season—rapidly approaching

winter. The warm sunlight was lighting up the grass in the yard. The physical nature of Aincrad meant that you never saw the sun directly except for early morning and sundown, but the game's lighting system ensured that everything was uniformly lit during the day. And at current, it might be the time of day that was least likely to feature any ghosts.

Asuna jutted her chin at her husband defiantly.

"Fine, let's go, then. But only to prove there's no such thing as ghosts."

"That settles it. And if we don't find it today, we'll have to go at night next time."

"Not on your life! And if you're going to be this mean, I won't fix you a lunch."

"Ugh! Forget what I just said, then."

She gave him one last glare, then smiled.

"C'mon, let's get ready. If you cut the bread, I'll cook the fish."

It was nine o'clock once they'd finished packing their fish burgers in their lunchboxes and headed out the door. Out on the front lawn, Asuna turned back to Kirito and said, "Let me ride piggyback."

"P-piggyback?" he yelped, stunned.

"Well, it's no fun always seeing things from the same elevation. It should be easy with your strength stat, right?"

"W-well, that's true, but…you're too old for this…"

"Age has nothing to do with it! Come on, it's not like anyone's going to see."

"Fine, fine! All right, then…"

He crouched down, shaking his head and presenting his back to Asuna. She rolled up her skirt and straddled his head, one leg on each shoulder.

"There we go. And if you try to turn around and look, I'll slap you."

"That seems a bit unfair, doesn't it?"

Kirito stood up easily as he grumbled, and she found her eye level delightfully higher than usual.

"Wow! Look, you can already see the lake from here!"

"*I* can't see it!"

"Okay, I'll give you a ride a little later."

"..."

Asuna placed her hands on his slumped head and commanded, "Forward march! Set course north-northeast!"

As Kirito started trekking away, Asuna laughed wholeheartedly from atop his shoulders, keenly aware of how much this time with him meant to her. Without a doubt, she was more alive now than she'd ever been before in her seventeen years of life.

When they had walked down the path—technically, when *Kirito* had walked—for a dozen or so minutes, they reached one of the many lakes on the twenty-second floor. There were a number of fishermen players with lines cast into the water already, perhaps due to the gentle weather. The path ran over the hills that surrounded the lake, and although there was still some distance to the shore on the left-hand side, the fishers noticed the pair and began waving. They all seemed to be smiling, some of them even laughing at the sight.

"You said no one was going to see us!"

"Ha-ha, I guess they did. Go on, Kirito, wave back."

"Absolutely not."

Kirito grumbled, but he didn't attempt to set her down. She could tell that he was secretly enjoying the fun.

Eventually the path made its way down a hill and deep into the forest; they made their way through massive pine trees that resembled Japanese cedars. The rustling of the needles, babbling of the brook, and twittering birdsong played beautiful accompaniment to the calming sight of a thick forest in late autumn.

Asuna cast a glance at the branches of the trees, which were much closer to her than usual.

"These trees sure are big. Do you think they're climbable?"

"Hmm," Kirito pondered. "I don't think the system limits you from climbing them... Wanna try?"

"No, we'll save that for the theme of our next adventure. Speaking of climbing—"

She straightened up as best she could from his shoulders and looked to the outer perimeter of Aincrad, through the trees ahead.

"There are those things like support pillars around the outer edge, going all the way up to the ceiling of this floor. What do you suppose happens if you climb all the way?"

"I've done that before."

"What?!" She leaned over to look at Kirito's face from above. "Why didn't you invite me along?"

"That was before we were as close as we are now."

"Oh, come on. You were avoiding me the whole time!"

"Uh...was I?"

"Yes, you were! I asked you out over and over, and you wouldn't even go out for tea."

"Th-that's because...Well, more to the point," Kirito said, trying to steer the conversation away from its current dubious course. "It basically didn't work. It wasn't that hard to climb, since the rock had all kinds of notches and handholds, but about eighty yards up I got yelled at by a system error saying, this is an off-limits zone!"

"Ha-ha-ha! See, you're not supposed to cheat."

"It's not funny. It startled me so much, I lost my grip and fell off..."

"Wait, what? That fall would be fatal."

"Yeah, I thought I was going to die. If I'd been just three seconds later in getting my teleport crystal, I'd be on the list of the fallen."

"Jeez, that's so dangerous. Don't ever try that again."

"You're the one who brought up the idea!"

The forest was getting deeper as they chattered on. It seemed as though the birdsong was growing scattered, and even the light through the branches was weaker than before.

Asuna took another look at the surroundings and asked, "So... where's the place we're supposed to be heading?"

"Let's see," Kirito said, checking their location on the map. "Ah, we're almost there. Just a few more minutes."

"All right ... So what exactly did the stories say?"

Asuna didn't really want to find out, but not knowing also made her uneasy.

"Apparently, about a week ago, a wood-crafting player came around this area to collect some timber. The wood from this forest is supposed to be pretty nice, and he was so focused on his task that he lost track of time. When he turned around to go home, he saw something white flit into the shadows of a nearby tree."

"..."

This was already too much for Asuna, but Kirito didn't stop.

"He panicked, thinking it was a monster at first, but he was wrong. He said it looked like a human being, a small girl. White clothes and long black hair. She was just slowly walking away into the woods. So he focused on her, thinking she must be a player rather than a monster."

"..."

"But there was no cursor."

"Eek...!"

A tiny, involuntary shriek caught in her throat.

"'That can't be right,' he thought, foolishly approaching the girl. Then he called out to her. The girl stopped where she was ... then slowly turned around to face him, and ..."

"S-s-st-st-stop ..."

"That's when the woodcrafter realized, under the light of the moon ... that he could see the tree through her white clothes."

"—!!"

Asuna trapped a silent scream and clenched Kirito's hair.

"That's when he took off running, knowing it was all over if she completely turned around. Once he was close enough to see the lights of the town, he thought he was safe. And when he turned back to look ..."

"—?!"

"There was nobody there. The end."

"...You...stupid...*jerk*!!"

Asuna jumped off his shoulders and prepared to punch him solidly in the back. But suddenly, something white caught the corner of her eye, far off in the dark conifer forest.

With unbearable foreboding, Asuna trained her vision on the thing. While not at Kirito's level, her Search skill was quite advanced. The skill's effect automatically kicked in, rendering the area of her focus in much sharper detail.

The white something appeared to be flowing in the breeze. It wasn't a plant. It wasn't a rock. It was cloth. In fact, it was a simple one-piece dress. There were two thin lines extending downward from the hem—legs.

It was a little girl. A young girl in a white dress, just like the one in Kirito's story, watching them in silence.

Asuna's consciousness was in danger of slipping away. She opened her mouth and managed to croak out a few words, barely louder than a breath.

"K-Kirito...there."

He followed her gaze, then froze just as solid as she was.

"Y-you've gotta be kidding me..."

The girl did not move. She stood where she was, perhaps a hundred feet away, staring at them. *If she starts to walk toward us, I'm going to faint*, Asuna felt certain.

The girl's body swayed. She fell to the ground in a strangely inorganic way, like an animatronic figure that had just run out of power. They heard a quiet *thump* as she landed.

"Wait a second." Kirito narrowed his eyes "That's not a ghost!"

He dashed off toward the girl.

"W-wait, Kirito!" Asuna shouted as he left her behind, but he continued dashing toward the fallen girl. "Oh, honestly!"

Asuna had no choice but to stand and follow. Her heart was still racing, but on the other hand, she'd never heard of ghosts fainting before. It simply *had* to be a player.

A couple seconds later, Asuna reached the foot of the pine tree

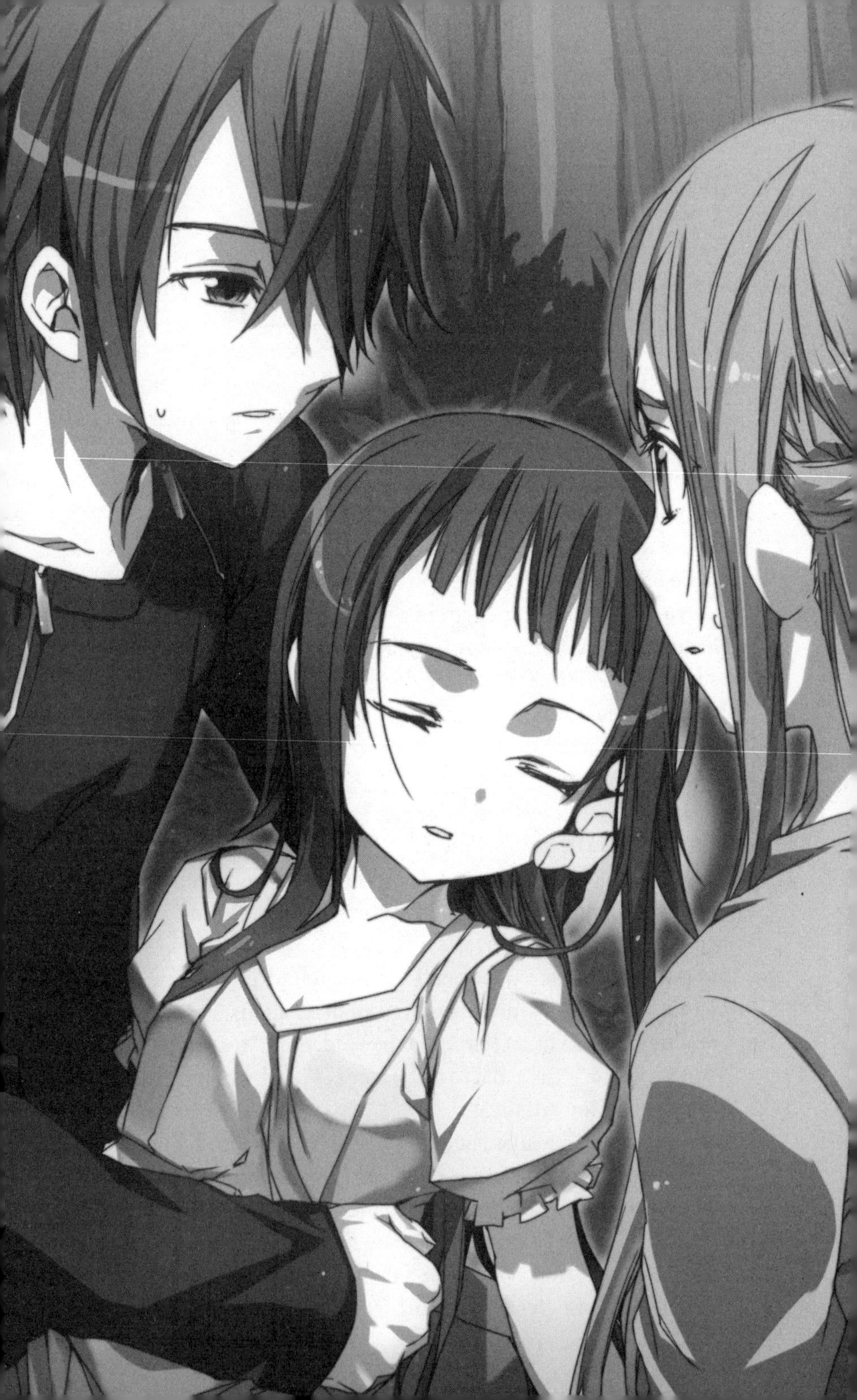

where Kirito was holding the tiny girl. She was still knocked out: Her long-lashed eyes were closed, her arms hanging limply at her sides. Asuna took a cautious glance at the girl's dress, but it wasn't see-through.

"D-do you think she's all right?"

"I think...so," Kirito mumbled, peering into the girl's face.

"Then again, nobody actually breathes or has a heartbeat here..."

Most basic human biological processes are omitted from SAO's simulation. You can actively breathe in and feel the sensation of air down your windpipe, but player avatars themselves do not engage in automatic respiration. When in a state of tension or excitement, you can feel your heart pounding, but it's impossible to actually pick up the pulse of another body.

"She hasn't disintegrated...which means she must be alive. But this is very strange..." He trailed off, uncertain.

"Strange how?"

"She can't be a ghost, because I can touch her. Yet there's no targeting cursor..."

"Oh..."

Asuna trained her gaze on the girl's body again. Any kind of living, moving object in SAO, whether player, monster, or even NPC, would always have its own color cursor, but this girl did not. She had never seen this phenomenon before.

"Maybe it's some kind of bug?"

"That's my guess. In a normal game, I'd call a GM about this, but there's obviously no GM here...Plus, it's not just the lack of a cursor. She's too young to be a player."

He was right. The body cradled in Kirito's arms was too tiny. She couldn't have yet been ten. The NerveGear had a cautionary age restriction, meaning that children under the age of thirteen could not use it.

Asuna felt the girl's forehead. It was chilly and smooth.

"But how did such a little girl get inside Sword Art Online?" she asked, biting her lip in concern. "We can't just leave her here.

I'm sure we'll find out more when she wakes up. Let's take her home with us."

"Yeah, good call."

Kirito stood up, still holding the girl. Asuna took another look at their surroundings, but the only thing of note was a dried-out old stump, and nothing that would suggest a reason for the girl to be there.

Even after they'd hurried out of the forest and back home, the girl did not wake. They placed her on Asuna's bed and pulled up the covers, then sat on Kirito's bed nearby and watched her.

After a length of silence, Kirito finally spoke in a soft voice.

"Well, the fact that we were able to carry her into our home means she's not an NPC."

"Yeah...that's true."

The system controlled NPCs, and players couldn't move them out of a certain fixed range of coordinates. If you tried to hold or grab them for more than a few seconds, a harassment warning would pop up, and you'd be buffeted away by an unpleasant shock.

Kirito continued his train of thought.

"And it's not an event that kicks off a quest. If that were the case, it would have updated our quest logs the moment we touched her. Which means the most likely explanation is that she is indeed a player and just happened to be lost in those woods."

He cast another glance at the bed.

"If she didn't have any crystals or know how to teleport, I think she would have stayed in the Town of Beginnings from the moment she logged in, rather than wandering out in the wilderness. I don't know why she'd have come all the way out here, but maybe someone in the Town of Beginnings knows who she is... Maybe we'll even find her parent or guardian there."

"I agree with that. I just can't imagine such a small child being able to log in on her own. She must have come here with her family...I just hope they're safe."

Before she voiced her last thought, she turned to Kirito and locked eyes with him.

"She will wake up, won't she?"

"Yeah. The fact that she hasn't disappeared yet means there are still signals going to and from her NerveGear. She must be closer to a state of sleep. So she'll wake up eventually... I believe."

He nodded firmly, a clear note of optimism in his voice.

Asuna got off the bed and knelt next to the sleeping girl. She reached out and rubbed the tiny head.

She was a very beautiful girl. She almost looked more like a fairy than a human. Her skin was a pale and delicate white, like alabaster. Her long black hair shone in the light, and her clear, vaguely foreign face seemed as though it would be bewitching, once she opened her eyes and smiled.

Kirito crouched down next to Asuna. He hesitantly reached out to brush the girl's hair.

"She can't be, what... more than ten? Eight, maybe?"

"That's what I'm guessing... She's easily the youngest player I've ever seen in the game."

"Definitely. I met a beast-tamer who was really young, but even she was at least thirteen or so."

Asuna abruptly spun around to Kirito, the information unfamiliar.

"I didn't realize you had such a cute young friend."

"Yeah, sometimes we trade messages... b-but that's not my point! There's nothing between us!"

"I wouldn't be so sure. You're awfully dense." She turned away in a huff.

Sensing that things were turning against him in a hurry, Kirito hastily stood up and said, "Oh, look at the time. We should eat lunch!"

"You're still going to tell me all about her later." Asuna glared at him, then grinned, deciding to let him off the hook for now. "C'mon, let's eat. I'll put on some tea."

*   *   *

As the late fall afternoon lazily passed and the red light from the outer perimeter vanished into darkness, the little girl kept sleeping soundly.

Asuna was closing the curtains and lighting the wall lamps when Kirito returned from the village. He shook his head without a word to show that he'd found no clues about the girl.

It was hard for them to enjoy a cheerful dinner given the situation, so they shared a brief meal of simple soup and bread, at which point Kirito opened up the newspapers he'd bought earlier.

The "newspapers" were not like the large sheaves of paper sold in the real world, but rather a single sheet of parchment the size of a magazine. The surface of the sheet was a screen, like a system window, its information fully scrollable as though it were a website.

The contents of the paper were just a wholesale copy of a player-run strategy site, complete with not just news but a simple manual, FAQ, lists of items and equipment, and so on. Among those lists was a wanted persons classified section, and that was what Kirito and Asuna were examining. Perhaps someone was searching for this girl. But...

"...Nothing..."

"Nothing."

After many minutes of searching, they gave up and slumped their shoulders. At this point, they had no choice but to wait for the girl to wake and tell them her story directly.

Normally, they spent their night hours on idle entertainment—chatting, simple games, even going on a nighttime stroll—but it was hard to get into the mood on this particular evening.

"Should we just go to bed?"

"Yeah." Kirito sighed.

They turned out the living room lights and headed into the bedroom. The little girl was using one of the beds, so they'd have to snuggle together in the other one—which they ended up doing every night anyway, as a matter of fact. They changed quickly into their nightclothes.

With the lamp extinguished, they slipped into bed.

Kirito had many odd skills, one of which was his ability to fall asleep instantly. When Asuna turned to her side to say something, his breath was already slow and steady with sleep.

"Sheesh," she muttered, then turned in the other direction, toward the girl's bed. In the pale blue darkness, the little black-haired girl was still fast asleep. Asuna had been avoiding thinking about the girl's past, but staring at her in the darkness like this, she inevitably began to ponder.

It was one thing if she'd been together with some kind of guardian, perhaps a parent or older sibling. But if she'd come to this world all alone and spent the last two years in fear and solitude, it would be a horrifying ordeal for an eight- or nine-year-old child. It was hard to imagine she could stay mentally healthy.

And what if...? Asuna imagined the worst. What if she'd been wandering around that forest and fallen into a coma because of some deep scarring to her mind? Aincrad had no psychological therapists, nor system managers to aid a person in need. It would be at least another six months until the game might be beaten, and it would take more than Kirito and Asuna's hard work to make that happen. In fact, one of the reasons they were taking this hiatus from the front line was that their levels were so much higher than the rest of the game population, it made it difficult to form a balanced party.

And no matter how deep the girl's suffering was, Asuna could not save her from it. That thought sent an unbearable pain through her heart. Before she knew it, she had left the bed and moved to the little girl's side.

Asuna brushed the girl's hair for a moment, then pulled back the covers and slipped in next to her. She hugged the tiny body close. The girl did not move, but Asuna felt as though she saw her expression ease.

"Good night. I hope you wake up tomorrow," she whispered.

2

A gentle melody flowed through Asuna's mind as she dozed in the white light of morning. It was her wake-up alarm, a soft oboe tune. She let herself drift through the familiar melody in the weightlessness of sleep. In time, light strings joined the song, clarinets echoed the primary melody, and a faint humming came in...

Humming?

It wasn't her singing along. Asuna opened her eyes.

The black-haired girl in her arms, eyes still closed, was humming along to the sound of Asuna's wake-up alarm.

She wasn't missing a beat. But that was impossible. Asuna had set her alarm to be audible to no one but herself, so it shouldn't be possible for anyone to hear the song playing inside her head.

But there was something more important than that at the moment.

"K-Kirito! Kirito, wake up!" Asuna called out to her husband, still sleeping in the other bed. Eventually, she heard him rise, murmuring sleepily.

"Morning... What's up?"

"Come quick!"

The floorboards creaked. Kirito craned over Asuna to peer into the bed. His eyes went wide.

"She's singing…?"

"Y-yeah."

Asuna gently rocked the girl in her arms. "Wake up, sweetie… Open your eyes."

The girl's lips stopped moving. Her long eyelashes fluttered, then her eyes slowly came to be fully open.

Wet black pupils trained directly on Asuna's at close range. After several blinks, the girl's pale lips began to open.

"Ah…uh…"

Her voice was fragile and pristine, like the ringing of delicate silverware. Asuna helped her up to a sitting position.

"Thank goodness you're awake! Do you know what happened to you?"

The girl clammed up for several seconds, then shook her head.

"I see… What's your name? Can you say it?"

"Na…me…My…name…" She tilted her head and a lock of that shining black hair fell over her cheek. "Yu…i. Yui. That's… my name."

"Yui! That's a nice name. I'm Asuna, and this is Kirito."

Asuna turned her head to indicate her partner, and Yui's eyes followed her lead. She flipped back and forth between Asuna and Kirito, who was leaning over to get a closer look.

"A…una. Ki…to."

Her lips moved hesitantly, struggling with the sounds. Asuna felt last night's anxiety return. The girl looked about eight years old, and based on the amount of time since she must have logged in, she would actually be closer to ten now. But the halting way she was speaking was more akin to a toddler learning how to talk.

"Yui, why were you all alone on the twenty-second floor? Is your daddy or mommy around?"

Yui cast her eyes down and said nothing. After a moment of silence, she shook her head.

"I don't…know. I don't…know anything…"

*　　*　　*

They carried her over to one of the chairs at the table and handed her a warm cup of sweetened milk, which she took in both hands and started to sip. Asuna pulled Kirito off to the side to confer, checking on Yui out of the corner of her eye.

"What do you think we should do, Kirito?"

He bit his lip, glaring as he thought, then eventually hung his head.

"Looks like she's lost her memory. But more worrying is the way she's acting. She might have suffered some brain damage…"

"Yeah…I was thinking the same thing."

"Dammit!" His face twisted, as though on the verge of tears. "I've seen a lot of awful things in this world…but this has to be the worst. It's so cruel…"

When she saw his eyes moistened, Asuna felt something rise into her chest. She put her arms around him.

"It'll be okay, Kirito. I'm sure we can do something to help her."

"…Yeah. Yeah, you're right…"

He looked up, placed his hands on her shoulders, then approached the table. Asuna followed him. Kirito rattled the other chair next to Yui and sat down.

"Hey, Yui, honey. Is it okay to call you Yui?" he asked brightly. She looked up from her cup and nodded.

"Good. Then you can call me Kirito."

"Ki…to."

"It's Kirito. Ki-ri-to."

"…"

Yui scrunched up her face in silent concentration.

"…Kiito."

He grinned and patted her on the head.

"I guess it's a bit too hard to say. You can call me anything you like. Whatever's easiest for you."

Yui sat in heavy thought. Asuna picked up her empty cup,

refilled it with more milk, and placed it back on the table, but Yui still hadn't moved.

In time, she slowly raised her head to look at Kirito, and spoke hesitantly.

"...Papa."

She turned to Asuna.

"Auna is...mama."

Asuna shivered unconsciously. It wasn't clear if Yui had confused them for her real parents or was simply seeking those roles from the closest thing she could find in Aincrad, but Asuna wasn't thinking about that. She desperately tried to hold back the emotions that were bursting upward through her.

"That's right...it's Mama, Yui-chan," she said, beaming.

Yui finally showed off the first smile of her own. Those expressionless eyes finally flashed beneath her even bangs, and for an instant, she was like a doll that had come to life.

"Mama!"

Asuna's heart throbbed when she saw the little hand extended toward her.

"*Uhk...*"

She barely stifled the sob that threatened to rip from her throat, but she did manage to keep her smile. Asuna lifted Yui from the chair and clutched the girl to her breast, feeling a tear of many mixed emotions welling up and falling down her cheek.

After another mug of hot milk and a little bread roll, Yui was apparently tired again. Her head began to sway wearily back and forth.

Asuna watched Yui from across the table, wiping her eyes. She turned to Kirito.

"I...I..."

She couldn't put her feelings into words.

"I'm sorry. I just...don't know what to do..."

Kirito gazed at her with sympathy for a time. Eventually, he said, "You want to stay here and take care of her until she regains her memory, right? I know how you feel—I feel the same way. But it's a real dilemma...It just means it'll be that much longer before we can return to advancing the game, which is that much longer before she's freed from this prison."

"Yeah...that's a good point."

Asuna's level was one thing, but Kirito was, without exaggeration, one of the most powerful forces advancing the game. As a solo player, he had contributed more labyrinth mapping than several major guilds combined. Their honeymoon was only meant to last a few weeks, but Asuna couldn't shake a feeling of guilt that she was monopolizing Kirito for such a long time.

"We should start by doing what we can," Kirito said, watching Yui as she began to snooze. "We'll go to the Town of Beginnings to see if her parents or siblings are around. She's obviously pretty unique within the game, so if anyone knows her, we should be able to find them."

"..."

His idea was sensible. But Asuna realized with a start that she did not want to leave this little girl. She'd dreamed of this life alone with Kirito for so long, but somehow, she had no resistance to growing that number to three. It was almost as though Yui was their daughter. When Asuna thought about what that meant, she turned red all the way to her ears.

"...? What's wrong?"

"N-nothing!!" She shook her head furiously. "A-anyway, we should visit the Town of Beginnings when Yui wakes up. We can take out a notice in the classified section of the newspaper, too."

Asuna spoke rapidly, clearing the table while pointedly avoiding looking at Kirito. Yui was now solidly asleep in her chair, but in comparison to last night, her sleeping face somehow seemed to be at peace.

They moved Yui to the bed, where she slept for the rest of the morning. Asuna began to worry that she might have fallen into another comatose state, but the little girl woke again just as lunch was being prepared.

Asuna baked a fruit pie—not one of her standard dishes—just for Yui, but she seemed more interested in the mustard-slathered sandwich that Kirito was chowing down.

"Are you sure, Yui? It's really spicy."

"Uhh! I want the same thing as Papa."

"Well, if you're ready for it, go ahead. It's important to experience new things."

Kirito handed Yui a sandwich, and she opened her tiny mouth as wide as possible to take a huge bite. They watched her closely. Yui chewed, a look of stern concentration on her face, then swallowed and smiled.

"Yummy."

"You've got guts!" Kirito laughed and rubbed her head. "We'll have to go with an ultra-spicy entree for dinner tonight."

"Let's not get carried away! That's not on the menu."

But if they found Yui's guardian in the Town of Beginnings, they'd be alone again when they returned. Asuna felt loneliness brush her heart once more.

Yui had helped finish the rest of the sandwiches and was happily sipping milk tea when Asuna asked her, "Want to take a trip outside this afternoon, Yui?"

"Trip?"

She looked confused. Kirito considered how best to explain it.

"We're going to look for your friends, Yui."

"What is…friends?"

Kirito and Asuna looked at each other. Many things about Yui's "condition" were a mystery. It wasn't so much that her mental age had somehow regressed, but that her memory had vanished in places.

In order to fix that, the best solution would be to find her true guardian, someone who could watch over her, Asuna told herself.

"A friend is someone who will help you, Yui. C'mon, let's get ready."

Yui looked skeptical, but she nodded and stood obediently.

The white, puffy-sleeved dress she wore was made of sheer

material, nowhere near proper for the early winter weather outside. Being cold wouldn't cause you to catch the flu or take damage—though there were no guarantees if you went streaking through the snow—but it was certainly unpleasant.

Asuna scrolled through her inventory and pulled out items of thick clothing, then found a sweater that suited the little girl. Suddenly, she stopped still.

In order to put on equipment and clothing, you needed to attach it on the mannequin in your status menu. SAO had difficulty modeling soft objects like cloth and liquids, so clothes were treated less like distinct objects to be interacted with, and more like an extension of the player's body.

Kirito picked up on Asuna's hesitation and asked Yui directly.

"Can you open your window, Yui?"

As they suspected, she only looked at them, uncomprehending.

"Okay, just trace your finger down in the air. Like this." Kirito swung his finger, and a rectangular purple window appeared beneath his hand. Yui clumsily mimicked his action, but nothing happened.

"That's what I was afraid of. The system must be bugged somehow. And what a horribly fatal bug to have, not being able to check your status. You can't do *anything*."

Kirito bit his lip. Yui had been waving her right index finger to no avail, so she tried it with her left hand. A glowing purple window popped up immediately.

"There!"

Yui giggled in delight, while Asuna and Kirito shared a shocked look over her head. What was going on?

"Can I take a look, Yui?"

Asuna crouched over to look at her window, but the status screen was only visible to the player herself by default, so there was nothing but a blank purple slate there.

"Here, let me see your hand." Asuna took Yui's little hand and moved her pointer finger over the spot where she thought she remembered the visibility mode checkbox would be.

Her aim was true, as familiar-looking information abruptly sprang onto the window with a beep. Despite the situation, it was incredibly rude to sneak a peek at another person's status screen, so Asuna did her best to avoid looking at anything but Yui's item list.

"Wh-what is this?!" she exclaimed in surprise as her eyes moved over the window.

The top screen of a player's menu in SAO is divided into three basic areas. At the top is the player's name in the English alphabet and two thin bars representing HP and EXP. The right half of the screen below that is the mannequin displaying the player's equipment. The left half of the screen is a list of command buttons. The icons can be customized from countless sample designs, but the basic layout is unchangeable.

But for some reason, the top of Yui's menu just featured the eerie name "Yui-MHCP001," with no indicators for HP, EXP, or even level. There was an equipment mannequin but only two buttons on the left side: ITEMS and OPTIONS.

Kirito noticed Asuna freeze and came over to see for himself, then held his breath. Yui seemed to have no idea of the significance of her menu, and she stared up at the two quizzically.

"Could this be...another system bug?" Asuna wondered, but Kirito grunted deep in his throat.

"I don't know... This looks less like a bug than it does something that was designed to be this way. Damn! I don't think I've ever been this frustrated that there are no GMs around."

"I've never even thought about wanting a GM, since SAO barely even has any lag, much less major bugs. I guess there's no use wracking our brains over this..."

Asuna gave up and moved Yui's finger to touch the ITEMS button. She placed the sweater on the surface of the window and it glowed for a second before vanishing into the inventory list. Once it showed up there, Asuna dragged the name onto the equipment figure in the window.

With a chime, Yui's body flashed for an instant, and she was suddenly wearing a light pink sweater.

"Wow!"

Her face shone. She held out her arms and examined herself. Asuna then added a skirt in the same color, black tights, and red shoes, before returning Yui's original one-piece to the window.

Yui was giddy over her new outfit, rubbing her cheek on the soft fabric of the sweater and pulling on her skirt hem.

"Well, shall we go?"

"Papa, carry me."

She held up her hands, and Kirito picked her up with one arm around her side, smiling shyly. He looked to his wife.

"Asuna, make sure you're prepared with your regular equipment in case anything happens. We'll be staying in town, but it is the Army's territory."

"Yeah... we can't be too careful."

Asuna nodded and quickly checked her own inventory, then stood up with Kirito and proceeded to the door. She really did hope that they found whomever was responsible for the girl, but she was also dreading saying good-bye to her for some reason. They had only found her a day ago, but somehow, in that short time, the girl had monopolized all the tender parts of Asuna's heart.

It was several months since their last visit to the Town of Beginnings on the first floor of Aincrad.

Asuna stepped out of the teleport gate and stopped, staring around with a conflicted heart at the massive square and its buildings.

This was the biggest city in Aincrad, of course, and it had more resources necessary to adventuring than any other place in the game. Prices were cheap and lodging was abundant, which made this the most efficient location for a hometown.

But as far as Asuna knew, none of her high-level acquaintances still hung around the Town of Beginnings. The Army's presence was one reason for that, but the biggest had to be the memory of that moment—when everyone stood in this square, looking up at that stretch of ceiling.

It had all started on a whim.

Asuna Yuuki had been born to a businessman and a scholar, and she grew up with their hopes firmly imprinted on her mind for as long as she could remember. Both her parents were resolute and hard on themselves, and though they were kind to Asuna, she was terrified of how they would react if she disappointed them in any way.

It must have been the same for her brother. Asuna and her older brother went to the private school their parents selected, never got into trouble, and maintained top grades. After her brother left home for college, Asuna dedicated her entire life to fulfilling her family's hopes. She trained in multiple subjects and only spent time with friends her parents accepted. In time, however, Asuna began to feel as though her world was tiny and compressed. It seemed like everything was funneled into one tiny path: the high school her parents chose, the college her parents chose, the marriage partner her parents chose. She grew terrified that she would be stuffed inside an incredibly small and tough shell, never to escape that prison.

Her brother came home and got a job at her father's company. He used his connections to procure a NerveGear and a copy of SAO, his eyes sparkling as he waxed rhapsodic about the world's first VRMMO. Asuna had never so much as touched a video game before, but his descriptions of a mysterious new world sparked something within her.

Of course, if he had simply stashed it away in his room for his own use, she would have forgotten all about the NerveGear. But the timing was poor; he would be overseas for work on the release day of Sword Art Online, so on a sudden whim, Asuna asked to borrow the game for the day. All she wanted to do was see a different world from the one she lived in...

And everything changed.

She could still keenly remember the excitement when she'd gone from Asuna the student to Asuna the adventurer, descending into an unfamiliar town full of unfamiliar people.

But soon after, when the empty god looming over their heads announced that it had become an inescapable game of death, the first thing Asuna thought of was her unfinished math homework.

I have to get back and finish that, or my teacher will scold me tomorrow. It would be an unacceptable blemish on Asuna's life. The true severity of her situation went far beyond that, of course.

One week, two weeks—the days passed mercilessly without any salvation from outside. Asuna holed up in an inn room in the Town of Beginnings, curled up on her bed, wracked with panic. At times she screamed and beat on the walls. It was the winter of her third and final year of middle school. There would be tests soon, and then a new term. Falling off the course now meant the end of her life as she knew it.

Asuna's everyday life was plunged into madness, until she came to one deep, dark certainty:

Her parents would not be worried about the well-being of their daughter; they would be terribly disappointed that she had failed her exams, all over a stupid video game. Her friends would lament her plight, then pity her for her failure, and eventually use her as the butt of a joke.

When these dark emotions had reached their saturation point, Asuna finally came to a firm decision and left her room. She wouldn't wait for rescue. She would escape on her own. She would be the hero who conquered the crisis. It was the only way she could repair the bonds that tied together the people around her.

Asuna arranged her equipment, memorized the entire help manual, and headed into the wilderness. She only slept for two or three hours a day, dedicating the rest of that time to leveling up. She applied all of her intelligence and willpower to the task, and it did not take long until she was among the top players in the game. This was the birth of Asuna the Flash, the mad warrior.

Now, two years later, Asuna was seventeen, and she thought back on her old self with acute discomfort: not just her despondent state right after being trapped in the game, but the painfully compressed life she had led before that. The memories brought a heap of self-pity with them.

She didn't know what "living" really meant. She was sacrificing her present life for some future she thought she was meant to have. To her, "now" was nothing but a step toward that proper future, and once each moment had passed, it turned into nothingness.

The lesson she'd learned from observing SAO was simple: It was pointless to have one without the others.

Those who only strove for the future drove themselves mad advancing through the game, the way she once did. Those who clung to the past hid in their inns on the first floor. Those who only lived in the present sought cheap thrills, sometimes turning to crime.

But even in this world, there were some people who could enjoy the present, remember the past, and work toward an eventual escape. It was a black-haired swordsman who'd taught her that, a year earlier. Once she realized she wanted to live like him, Asuna's life took on real color.

Now she was equipped to break that tough shell the real world held. She felt like she was ready to live for herself—as long as she was by his side...

Asuna leaned closer to Kirito, who she was certain felt his own variety of conflicting emotions at the sight of the city. When she looked up at the baleful stone lid above them again, the pain was only a shadow of what it once was.

Asuna shook her head to clear away the painful cobwebs, then looked to Yui, who was still cradled in Kirito's arms.

"Yui, do you recognize any of these buildings?"

"Umm..."

Yui concentrated on the stone buildings lining the open square, then shook her head.

"I don't know..."

"Well, the Town of Beginnings is a gigantic city," Kirito offered reassuringly, patting her head. "If we keep walking around, maybe she'll remember something. Let's check out the central market for now."

"Good idea."

They nodded together and headed for the main avenue running south.

As they walked, Asuna took a critical look around the square. She was surprised to see how few people there were.

The teleport gate plaza in the Town of Beginnings was enormous, big enough to hold all ten thousand players when the servers opened two years ago. It was a perfect circle of countless fitted paving stones with a large clock tower looming over the center and the rippling blue teleport gate beneath it. Surrounding the tower was a series of narrow, concentric flowerbeds lined with the occasional quaint white bench. It was the perfect place for players to enjoy a brief afternoon respite on such a lovely day, but all the people visible from here were heading to the gate or the plaza's exits, and virtually none were stopping or sitting on the benches.

The teleport squares of the larger towns near the top of Aincrad were always a bustle of player activity. Between the chatters, the party recruiters, the simple street stalls, and the loiterers, it was sometimes difficult to even make your way out into the city.

"Hey, Kirito."

"Hmm?" He turned to look at her.

"How many players do you suppose are here now?"

"Good question...there are about six thousand survivors, and about thirty percent of them are in the Town of Beginnings, including the Army. So maybe just a bit less than two thousand?"

"Don't you think it seems awfully quiet around here for that?"

"Now that you mention it...Maybe they're all in the market?"

But even after they headed down the street from the plaza toward the market area, where shops and stalls lined the path, the town was relatively empty. The energetic cries of the NPC shopkeepers echoed forlornly off the stone walls.

Asuna spotted a man seated beneath a large tree in the middle of the avenue and called out to him.

"Um, excuse me."

He was staring at the branches above with an oddly serious look, and snapped, irritated, from his spot, rather than turn to look at her.

"What do you want?"

"Um...is there any kind of center around here for finding or advertising lost persons?"

The man finally turned his gaze to Asuna. He stared her full in the face, his eyes glinting.

"What are you, an outsider?"

"Y-yes. We're looking for this girl's guardian." She pointed back at Yui, who was dozing lightly in Kirito's arms.

The man wore a simple cloth tunic that made it difficult to discern his class. His eyes went wider when he saw Yui, but they were soon trained on the overhead branches once again.

"Lost kid? Don't see many of those. There's a buncha kids gathered at the church next to the river in sector E-7. Try there."

"Th-thank you."

Asuna bowed briefly, surprised to have actually gleaned some helpful information from the encounter. Suddenly she felt emboldened to ask another question.

"Um...what exactly are you doing? And why is the city so empty?"

He put on a grimace, but his tone of voice suggested that he didn't mind answering.

"Company secret, you might say. But since you're outsiders... why not? See that high branch up there?"

Asuna followed his pointing finger. The branches of the large tree were exploding with autumn leaves, but upon closer examination, there were small golden fruits growing here and there.

"The decorative trees in town are indestructible objects, of course, so even if you climb up there, you can't pick the fruit—or a single leaf, for that matter." He continued. "A few times a day, one of those fruits falls off. It rots and disappears within a few minutes, but if you pick it up before then, you can sell it to the NPCs for a decent chunk. Tastes good, too."

"Oooh."

Asuna had mastered her Cooking skill, so the topic of food ingredients piqued her interest. "How much do they sell for?"

"Promise you won't tell anyone...? Five col a pop."

"..."

Asuna was stunned into silence by the pleased look on his face. She could not believe how meager an amount it was, completely at odds with the amount of work it took to watch this tree all day long.

"Um...that doesn't seem worth it...I mean, just a single worm out in the wilderness will get you thirty col."

Now the man's eyes really went wide. He looked at Asuna as if she had to be insane.

"What, are you serious? If I go out there to fight monsters, I could *die*!"

"..."

Asuna had no response. He was right: Fighting monsters could get you killed. But from her current perspective, he might as well be arguing that one should never walk on the sidewalk, out of the danger of being hit by a car. It was allowing fear to control your life.

Was she just numb to the danger of dying within SAO, or was it that the man was overly fearful? At the moment, Asuna couldn't be sure. Perhaps there wasn't a "correct" answer between the two of them. However, his logic was probably the prevailing opinion here in the Town of Beginnings.

He continued, oblivious to Asuna's inner conflict. "What was the other question again? Why isn't anyone here? They're still here; they're just hanging out in their inn rooms. You might run into the Army's tax collectors during the day, after all."

"T-tax...? What is that?"

"It's a stick-up with a fancy name. Watch out; they won't

hesitate to go after outsiders. Wait, one's about to fall! I'm done talking here..."

He clammed up, concentrating furiously. Asuna bowed in thanks, then realized that Kirito hadn't said a word during the entire conversation.

She turned around to find him focused sharply on the yellow fruit, his eyes narrowed as though preparing for battle. He was clearly ready to snatch the fruit before it fell to the ground.

"Stop that!"

"B-but I'm curious."

Asuna snatched him by the back of his collar and dragged him away.

"Aww...but they look so tasty," he wailed. This time she yanked on his ear to force his gaze away.

"Focus! Where's sector E-7? He said there were a bunch of young players hanging out at the church there, so let's go check that out."

"...All riiight."

Asuna took Yui, now fully conked out, and matched Kirito's pace as he walked off, checking his map. Yui was the size of a ten-year-old, so in the real world, Asuna's arms would give out within a few minutes, but thanks to her strength stat, carrying the girl was like carrying a feather pillow.

They continued southeast down the wide, empty streets for more than ten minutes until they reached a spacious garden-like area. Colorful, leafy trees whistled mournfully in the chilly breeze of early winter.

"According to the map, this is E-7...so where's this church?"

"Is that it over there?"

Asuna tilted her head to indicate a tall spire on the other side of the copse of trees on the right-hand side of the path. A metallic ankh made from a circled cross shone above the blue-gray tiles of the roof. It was definitely a church. There was at least one in every town, and the altar inside offered a few special perks, such as undoing monster-inflicted curses or blessing weapons to do extra damage to the undead. Magic was nearly nonexistent in Sword Art Online, so churches were the most mysterious and supernatural places in the game. With enough regular offerings, some churches allowed you the use of a room, acting as de facto hotels.

"Wait a minute," Asuna called out to Kirito as he started off toward the church.

"Huh? What's up?"

"Umm...I just...want to be sure. If we do find Yui's guardian here, are we...leaving her behind?"

"..."

Kirito's black eyes were soft with concern. He approached and enfolded both Asuna and the sleeping Yui in his arms.

"I don't want to say good-bye to her, either. When she was with us, it was almost like...that little house in the woods was a real home. I felt it, too...But it's not as though we'll never see her again. If Yui gets her memory back, I'm sure she'll come visit us."

"Hmm...I suppose so."

Asuna nodded briefly, rubbed her cheek on Yui, then steeled herself for what had to be done.

The church was small in comparison to the scale of the city itself. It was two floors and had only one steeple. There were multiple churches in the Town of Beginnings, and the one nearest to the teleport square was nearly the size of a small castle manor.

Asuna pushed open one of the large double doors with a free hand. It was a public facility, so it wasn't locked. The interior of the church was dim, with only the light of the candles at the altar ahead weakly glimmering off the stone floor. At first glance, there was no one else inside.

Asuna leaned over the entryway and called out: "Is anyone here?"

Her voice echoed and trailed away, but no one answered.

"I guess it's empty..."

But Kirito disagreed, his voice low. "No, there are people here. Three in the right room, four in the left. A couple upstairs, too."

"How high do you have to get your Search skill before it can detect the number of people behind walls?"

"Once you reach about nine eighty. It's useful; you should get there."

"No way—it's so boring to raise, I'd go crazy...Anyways, why do you suppose they're hiding?"

Asuna cautiously stepped into the church. The building was dead quiet, but she felt like she could hear people holding their breath.

"Um, excuse me! We're searching for someone!" she called out, louder this time. The door on the right opened a crack, and a frail female voice emerged.

"You aren't...from the Army?"

"No, I'm not. I came down from a higher floor."

Asuna and Kirito didn't even have their swords on, much less any battle armor. Army members wore their uniform of heavy armor at all times, so a simple glance would prove to these people that they were unrelated.

Eventually, the door opened all the way, and a single female player reluctantly appeared.

She had short, dark blue hair, and the green eyes behind her large black-framed glasses were wide with fear. She wore a simple navy dress and she clutched a tiny dagger in her hand, still sheathed.

"You're really...not the Army's tax collectors...?"

Asuna smiled and nodded to reassure the woman.

"That's right. We just came here today from up above, because we're looking for someone. We have nothing to do with the Army."

"From above? Does that mean you're real warriors?"

A high-pitched, boyish voice echoed from behind the woman. The door swung wide and several people came rushing out. The door to the left of the altar opened, and more figures emerged.

Asuna and Kirito silently watched, taken aback, as the group of young players, no more than boys and girls, rushed to line up on either side of the bespectacled woman. They appeared to be between the ages of twelve and fourteen and were clearly fascinated by the sight of these new visitors.

"What did I tell you? Stay hidden in the back rooms!" cried the woman, who seemed to be around twenty years old. She tried to push the kids away, but not a single one of them paid any heed to her command.

Almost immediately, one of the first children to appear—a boy with short, spiky hair—voiced his disappointment with the visitors.

"What the heck? You don't even have any swords. Did you really come from above? Don't you have a sword?" He directed the end of his challenge at Kirito.

"W-well, yes, I do, but..." Kirito answered hesitantly, and the children's faces lit up again. "Show us, show us," they demanded.

"Hey! Don't be rude to people you've never met before—I'm sorry, they're not used to visitors like this..."

The woman bowed so apologetically that Asuna had to rush to reassure her. "No, it's all right. You've got a few weapons stashed in your inventory, right, Kirito? Why don't you show them?"

"Um, okay." He nodded and opened his window, fingers flashing. About ten different weapons materialized in turn, piling up on the pew next to him. These were weapons that he'd looted from monsters recently and simply hadn't taken the time to sell for cash yet.

Kirito produced all the extra items in their inventory that weren't pieces of equipment already in use, then allowed the excited children to come closer and see. They picked up swords and maces, exclaiming over the weight and cool factor of each. It was a sight to make any protective parent faint, but in the safe zone of the town, they couldn't hurt themselves with the blades.

"I'm really sorry about this," the woman said with clear concern, but the delight of the children brought a smile to her face. "Please, come this way. I'll prepare some tea..."

She led Asuna and Kirito into the small room on the right side of the chapel and served them each a hot, relaxing cup of tea.

"Now, you said you were searching for someone?" the bespectacled woman inquired, seated in the chair across from them.

"Ah, yes. Um...first of all, I'm Asuna, and this is Kirito."

"Oh! I'm so sorry; I didn't introduce myself. My name is Sasha." They bowed to each other.

"And this is Yui," Asuna continued, stroking Yui's hair as she slept in her lap. "We found her lost on the twenty-second floor. She seems to be...missing her memory..."

"Oh dear." Sasha's deep green eyes went wide behind her glasses.

"She had no equipment or items aside from the clothes she was wearing, and it was hard to imagine that she was living on an upper floor, so we decided to come to the Town of Beginnings to search for her parents or guardian—anyone who might know her. We received word that there were many children living here in this church, so here we are."

"Ah, I see..."

Sasha's glance dropped to the table, her hands cradling her teacup.

"There are around twenty children living in this church, from elementary- to middle-school age. I think it's basically all of the children in this town at the moment. When the game started..."

Her voice was thin, but she spoke firmly.

"Nearly all of the children their age panicked and suffered real mental trauma from the experience. Some of them did venture out of the town to tackle the game, but I think they were an exception to the rule."

Asuna had been in her final year of middle school when it happened, and she'd experienced what Sasha was describing. She knew that in the days of solitude locked inside her inn room, she'd been dangerously close to a total mental collapse.

"It's only natural. They're still at an age where they want to rely on their parents' protection, but then they're told they can't get out and might never return to the real world. These children fell into a state of despondency. Some of them even...severed their connections."

Sasha's mouth twisted sharply.

"For the first month after the game started, I was out in the world, leveling up to help beat the game...but one day, I spotted one of these kids on a street corner in town. I just couldn't leave him to fend for himself, so I brought him to live in my rented inn room with me. Once I'd started that, I couldn't stop thinking about other children in his situation, so I went around the city trying to round up all the kids I could find. Next thing I knew, I was doing this right here. Seeing people like you, who are fighting for all of us up above...I feel ashamed that I dropped out of our quest."

"No...no!"

Asuna shook her head, desperately searching for the right words, but they caught in her throat. Luckily, Kirito finished the thought for her.

"That's not true at all. You're fighting in your own way, Sasha... and much more bravely than I am."

"Thank you. But I'm not doing it out of a feeling of duty. It's quite fun to live with the children." Sasha grinned, then looked at the sleeping Yui with concern.

"Anyway, for the last two years, we've taken a single area of the city each day and looked around every single building there, checking for needy children. I'm certain I would have noticed such a tiny girl. I'm sorry to disappoint you...but I don't think she was living here."

"I see," Asuna murmured, then squeezed Yui again. She pulled herself together to look into Sasha's face. "Um, I don't mean to pry, but how are you making enough money to survive each day?"

"Ah. Well, I'm not the only one. There are some older kids who are working to protect this place, and they're at a high-enough level to be absolutely safe in the fields outside of town. They make sure that we have enough money to eat. It's just not a very extravagant amount."

"That's splendid, though. Based on what we heard earlier, it sounds like people around here consider hunting monsters in the wilderness to be outright suicide," Kirito said.

Sasha nodded. "I believe virtually everyone remaining in the Town of Beginnings feels that way. I can't blame them—it's absolutely true that the risk of death is out there. But in comparison, we're actually earning more than the average player in this city."

She had a point. Permanently renting out the private rooms in this church would likely cost a hundred col per day, well in excess of what that fruit hunter could raise.

"But that just means they've singled us out now…"

"Who has?"

Sasha's gentle eyes turned steely hard. She was about to explain when—

"Miss! Miss Sasha! Come quick!"

The door to the room slammed open, and several children piled inside.

"Hey! Show our guests some respect!"

"This is more important than that!" the feisty red-haired boy from before shouted, tears in his eyes. "Gin and the others have been rounded up by the Army!"

"Where?!"

Sasha bolted to her feet, instantly taking charge.

"In the empty lot behind the item shop in sector E-5. About ten soldiers have the alleyway blocked off. Only Cotta managed to get away."

"All right, I'm coming. I'm sorry about this," Sasha apologized, turning to Asuna and Kirito, "but I've got to help save the children. We'll continue this later, if that's all right…"

"We're going with you, Miss Sasha!" the redhead cried, the other children soon joining in. He raced over to Kirito to plead his case. "Hey mister, let us use your weapons! If we show up with those, the Army will run away!"

"Absolutely not!" Sasha barked. "You will wait *right here!*"

Kirito had been watching the scene unfold in silence, but now he raised his hand to calm the children. He was typically aloof and distant, but at times like these, he always exhibited a sudden presence. The children quieted down.

"I'm sorry to disappoint you," he began calmly, "but those weapons are too powerful for you to equip them. We'll help rescue your friends. Believe it or not, this lady with me is incredibly powerful."

He shot a quick glance to Asuna, who nodded in assent. She stood up and turned to Sasha.

"Please let us help you with this. The more people, the better."

"Thank you. That's very generous of you."

Sasha bowed deeply, then pushed her glasses back up the bridge of her nose.

"We'd better get running, then!"

Sasha burst out of the church doors and took off at a sprint, her dagger swaying at her hip. Kirito and Asuna, still clutching Yui, followed behind her. Asuna looked back to see that a gaggle of children was pursuing in the rear, but it didn't seem like Sasha would waste any energy keeping them in the church.

They wove through the trees into the E-6 sector and then down an alley. Sasha was taking them on a shortcut that would offer the most direct route. They raced past NPC shops and through backyards, until a group of figures blocking a narrow alley came into sight. There were at least ten of them, all wearing equipment colored gray-green and black—the uniform of the Army.

Sasha plunged into the alley before finally skidding to a halt. The Army players noticed her approach and turned around, wicked leers upon their faces.

"Well, well, here comes the nanny."

"Give me back the children," she commanded, her voice steely.

"You make it sound like we've kidnapped them. Don't worry, you'll have them back—after we've taught them a lesson about how society works."

"That's right. Citizens have a duty to pay their taxes."

The men laughed, their voices cruelly high-pitched. Sasha's clenched fists began to tremble.

"Gin! Cain! Mina! Are you there?!" she called out over the men, and a frightened girl's voice came back immediately.

"Help! Please, help us!"

"Forget about the money! Give it all to them right now!"

"But...we can't," wailed a boy this time.

"Kee-hee!" One of the men blocking the alleyway giggled involuntarily. "You've been lagging on your tax payments, I'm afraid...This is going to cost more than just money."

"That's right. We'll need an equipment tribute. Drop your armor and weapons...everything you've got."

As the men cackled gleefully, Asuna understood what was happening behind them in the alley. These armed "tax collectors" were demanding that the trapped children remove everything they owned, right down to their clothes. A bloodthirsty rage swelled inside of her.

Sasha had arrived at the same conclusion, and she tore into the men as though she might start throwing fists.

"Move it...Get out of the way! Or else I'll..."

"Or else you'll *what*, Nanny? You gonna pay the tax for 'em?"

The gloating men showed no signs of moving.

Within the town zone, a program known as the anti-crime code was in effect at all times, which meant that it was impossible to harm another player or force him to move against his will. The flipside of this code was that malicious players could not be dispersed, either. The result was that certain tactics existed for player harassment—there was the "block" formation being employed here, which trapped players in a tight space, or the "box," in which the victims were completely surrounded on all sides.

But this only applied to movement on the ground. Asuna turned to her partner and said, "Ready, Kirito?"

"Yeah."

They nodded to each other and easily leaped into the air. Their agility and strength stats fed directly into the jump height, sending them soaring well over the astonished faces of Sasha and the soldiers and into the blocked-off empty lot.

"Wha—?!" Several of the men leaped backward in shock.

Trapped in a corner of the alley were two boys and one girl in their early teens, huddled together. They'd already removed their equipment and were dressed only in their simple undergarments. Asuna bit her lip, then approached the children and gave them a reassuring smile.

"It's all right now. Put your equipment back on."

The wide-eyed kids nodded and rushed to pick up their armor, fiddling with their menus.

"Hey...no, no, no!" bellowed one of the soldiers, who had finally returned to his senses. "Who do you think you are? You're interfering with Army business!"

"I'll handle this," said a man in heavier-looking armor as he strode forward. He appeared to be their leader.

"I don't recognize you people. Do you understand what it means to defy the Aincrad Liberation Force? We can continue this conversation at our headquarters, if you like."

His narrow eyes glinted dangerously. He drew a large broadsword from his waist, then approached lazily, slapping the flat of the blade against his palm. The face of the sword caught the light of the low west sun; his armor shone dully, with the unique glow of metal that had never been damaged or repaired.

"Or do you want to take this 'outside,' where we can settle it for real? Huh?"

Asuna's teeth ground audibly at that last comment. She'd thought that settling the matter quietly was best, but from the moment she saw the frightened children, her rage had passed its limit.

"Kirito, can you take Yui?"

She handed the sleeping girl to him, and he tossed back her rapier. She caught it, slid it out of its scabbard, and strode over to the leader.

"Uh...uh...?"

The man's face was a blank mask of incomprehension, his mouth half agape. Asuna unleashed a thrust at full power into his dumbfounded mug.

Purple lights. An explosive shock wave. The man's ugly face jerked backward, and he fell onto his rear end, eyes wide with shock.

"If you want a fight, we don't have to take it outside the city."

Asuna closed the distance and her right arm flashed again. Another burst, another explosion. The leader's body shot backward.

"Don't worry, you're not losing any HP. But that just means I can keep doing this as long as I want."

Asuna continued her steady pace. The leader looked up at her, lips trembling. He finally understood what she was doing.

Within the bounds of the city's anti-crime zone, an invisible wall protected every player from weapon attacks and other damage. But that rule had one other consequence to it: Without damage, an attacker would never be identified by the system as a criminal player.

There was a form of training called "zoned battle" that took advantage of this rule. But as the attacker's stats and skills increased, the color and sound of the code's nullifying effect intensified, until sword skills could even knock back the target a little bit. To those unfamiliar with it, the shock was hard to ignore, even if it carried no HP damage.

"A-ah...s-stop..." he wailed each time he was dashed to the ground. "D-don't just watch...Stop her!!"

The other soldiers came to their senses and drew their weapons. They came from both sides of the alley, realizing that something was going terribly wrong.

They formed a semicircle around Asuna, whose eyes were flashing the way they did in the days when she'd been as driven and focused as a berserker. She leaped without a word, attacking the group head-on.

The alley was suddenly full of sound, the roar of explosions and screams.

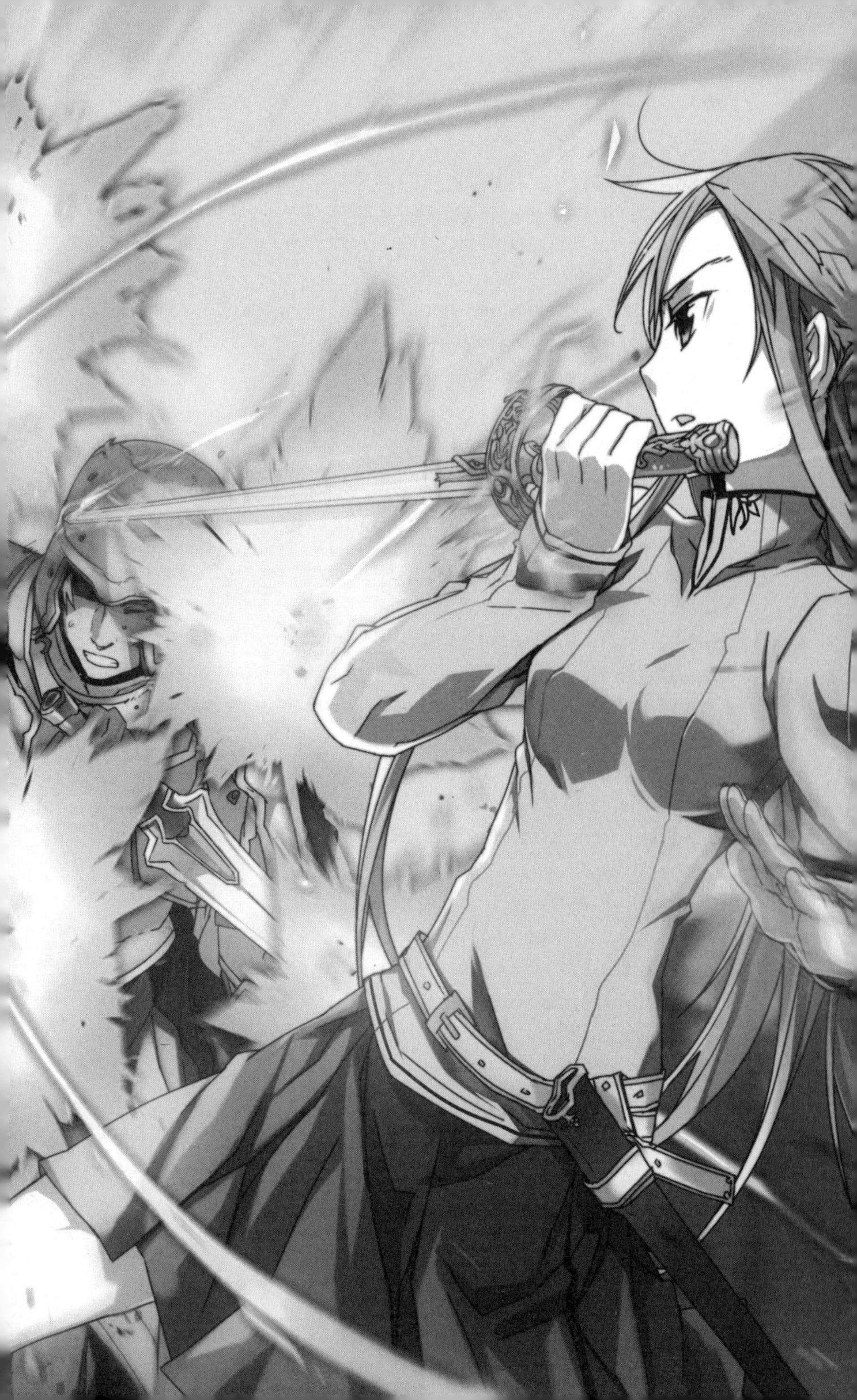

Three minutes later, Asuna regained her wits and lowered her rapier. Only a few soldiers remained in the empty lot, fallen with shock. The rest had abandoned their leader and fled.

"Hahh…"

She sighed and sheathed her weapon, then turned around—and found Sasha and the children from the church standing stock-still in silent shock.

"Oh…"

Asuna gasped and took a step back. She looked down, certain that her fiery, uncontrollable rage must have terrified the children. But the spiky-red-haired boy burst with excitement, his eyes sparkling.

"Wow…that was amazing, lady! I've never seen anything like it!"

"What did I tell you? She's incredibly powerful." Kirito grinned proudly. He was still carrying Yui in his left hand, but he held a sword in his right—he must have taken care of a few soldiers himself.

"Uh…ha-ha."

Asuna laughed uncomfortably, but the kids all cheered and leaped onto her. Sasha clutched her hands to her chest, beaming, tears in her eyes.

That was when it happened.

"Everyone's…hearts," a tiny voiced echoed. Asuna looked up with a start. Yui was now awake in Kirito's arm, looking out into space, her right hand outstretched.

Asuna followed the direction of her gaze, but there was nothing there.

"Everyone's hearts are…one…"

"Yui! What's the matter, Yui?" Kirito cried. She blinked a few times, seemingly bewildered. Asuna rushed over and held Yui's hand.

"Do you remember anything, Yui?"

"I…I…"

She squinted, looked down.

"I wasn't...here...I was in...the deepest deep..."

Yui's face scrunched up as she tried to remember. She bit her lip, and suddenly—

"Aaah...*aaaah!!*"

Her head tilted back and a high-pitched scream ripped from her throat.

"...?!"

Asuna was hit with a noise she hadn't before heard in SAO—a crackle like radio static. Yui's rigid body began to vibrate powerfully, as though it was going to dash into pieces.

"Y-Yui!" Asuna screamed, holding the little body in an attempt to calm it.

"Mama...I'm scared, Mama!" the little girl wailed. Asuna pulled her out of Kirito's arms and squeezed her tightly. Within a few seconds, the strange phenomenon stopped, and Yui's tense body relaxed.

"What was *that* all about...?" Kirito murmured softly. His question echoed through the silent alley.

3

"Pass me a roll, Mina!"
"Pay attention or you'll spill!"
"Hey! Miss Sasha, Jin stole my egg!"
"But I gave you my carrots!"

"This is quite an event..."
"Yeah..."

Asuna and Kirito were watching the battleground that was breakfast at the church unfold before their eyes.

They were in the great hall of said church, in Sector E-7 of the Town of Beginnings. Two long tables were jammed with heaping plates of eggs, sausages, and salad. More than twenty children were squashed onto the benches, eating ravenously.

"It seems really fun, though." Asuna smiled to herself, seated at a separate roundtable with Kirito, Yui, and Sasha. She brought her teacup to her lips.

"It's like this every day. Telling them to quiet down has no effect," Sasha griped, but her eyes crinkled with love as she watched the children eat.

"You really like children, don't you?" Asuna asked. Sasha smiled shyly.

"I was taking elementary education classes in college back in the real world. Remember how big of an issue dysfunctional classrooms used to be? I was so pumped up to be a role model to children. But when I came here and ended up living with these kids, I found out that reality is so much different from what I'd heard...I think I get more support from them than the other way around. But that's fine...or natural, at least."

"I think I understand what you mean."

Asuna nodded and patted Yui, who was concentrating fiercely on the task of moving her spoon to her mouth. Asuna was amazed at how much warmth the girl had brought to her life. It was a different sensation from the painful throb in her chest whenever she touched Kirito. It was a gentle ease, a quiet feeling of being enveloped by invisible feathers.

After Yui's spasms the previous day, it was blessedly few minutes before she'd woken up again. But Asuna didn't want to go trekking long distances and using teleport gates after such a disconcerting incident, so at Sasha's insistence, they spent the night in one of the church's empty rooms.

Yui was feeling well in the morning, much to Asuna's and Kirito's relief, but their situation had not changed at all. The fragment of Yui's memory that had returned made it clear that she'd never been to the Town of Beginnings, and apparently she hadn't even lived with a guardian of any kind. That meant the cause of Yui's memory loss and mental regression was still a mystery, and now they had no clues to follow up.

Despite all that, Asuna was certain of one thing.

They would live together until the day Yui's memory returned. Even once their leave period ended and they returned to the front line, there would be a way to make it work...

Asuna stroked Yui's hair absentmindedly. Kirito put down his cup to speak.

"Sasha..."

"Yes?"

"I wanted to ask you about those soldiers. The Army I remember was pushy and arrogant, but fully dedicated to keeping the peace. Those guys yesterday might as well have been criminal thugs… When did things get like this?"

The corners of her mouth tightened.

"It was about half a year ago that their focus seemed to shift. Some of them started extorting money from people and calling it 'taxes,' and others were trying to crack down on that behavior. I even witnessed Army soldiers fighting over it on occasion. The rumors said there was some factional squabbling in the upper ranks."

"Hmm… well, it is a giant organization with more than a thousand members. You can't expect it to be a singular monolithic entity. But if stuff like what happened yesterday is commonplace, we can't just let that slide. Asuna…"

"What?"

"Does *he* know about this?"

Asuna had to stifle a laugh at the tangible distaste in Kirito's voice at that pronoun.

"I'd suspect that he does… Heathcliff does seem to keep tabs on the Army's activity. The thing is, he doesn't seem to care about anything other than the completion status of the highest-level players. He's asked me all kinds of things over the months about you, Kirito, for instance—but when we raided Laughing Coffin, that criminal guild, he just said it was up to us and left it at that. So I very much doubt that he'll put together a group to force the Army into line."

"Well, I suppose that sounds like him… But that does mean that there's a limit to what we can do about this."

Kirito leaned over to sip his tea, brows furrowed, when he suddenly raised his head and looked to the church's entrance.

"Someone's coming. Just one person."

"Oh? Another guest, I suppose…"

Just as Sasha spoke, there was a rapping at the door that echoed through the chamber.

*   *   *

Sasha strapped her dagger to her waist and Kirito followed, just in case. A few moments later, they returned with a tall woman.

Her long silver hair was tied into a ponytail, and the sky-blue eyes in the middle of her sharp, slender features blazed with a memorable light. She seemed to exude intelligence.

Hairstyle and eye color were customizable in SAO, but given that the facial features of virtually every player were of Japanese ethnicity, few could pull off a look with such striking color choices. Asuna herself had tried out cherry-pink hair for a brief period before she had to ashamedly return to brown. She never brought up that sorry experiment to anyone else.

Asuna's initial reaction was to marvel at the visitor's grace and beauty, but she turned tense when she noticed the woman's armor.

Partially concealed by her steel-gray cape was a deep green tunic and pants with a relaxed upper half, accented by dully gleaming stainless steel armor—the uniform of the Army. There was a short sword on her right hip and a coiled black leather whip on her left.

The children all fell silent as they noticed her clothes, their gazes wary. Sasha gave them a reassuring smile. "She's all right, children. Continue your breakfast."

At a glance, Sasha didn't seem like the most dependable person, but the children had absolute trust in her. They relaxed and returned to their noisy eating. Sasha showed the woman over to the small table and pointed out a chair. She bowed and sat down.

Asuna was unsure of what was happening, and she shot a questioning look at Kirito. He answered as he returned to his seat.

"Um, this is Yuriel. She wants to speak to us."

The silver-haired woman called Yuriel turned her gaze on Asuna and bowed.

"It's nice to meet you. I'm Yuriel, and I belong to the ALF."

"ALF?"

Asuna had never heard this designation. The woman nodded.

"Oh, I'm sorry. It's short for 'Aincrad Liberation Force.' It's a wordy title to say in full, so..."

Yuriel's voice was a luscious, relaxed alto. Asuna had always felt her own voice was too squeaky and childish, so this only added to her envy.

"It's nice to meet you, too. My name is Asuna, and I'm from the Knights of the Blood—well, I'm actually on temporary leave at the moment. This is Yui."

Yui had taken her time emptying out the soup bowl and was now working on her fruit juice. She looked up and concentrated on the newcomer. She tilted her head a bit, then smiled and returned to her task.

Yuriel's sky-blue eyes had gone wide when she heard the name of the guild.

"The KoB...No wonder you were able to dispatch them so easily."

Asuna realized that she was referring to the thugs from yesterday, and her hackles raised anew.

"Does that mean...you're here to take issue with what we did?"

"No, not at all. The opposite, in fact—I want to thank you."

"..."

Asuna and Kirito sat in silent confusion. Yuriel turned to them and straightened herself formally.

"I came to make a request of you two."

"A...request?"

She nodded, her silver hair waving. "That's right. Allow me to explain. The Army did not always have this title. The current Army moniker, the ALF, wasn't official until a former sub-leader of the guild, a man named Kibaou, seized the reins. Our original name was the MTD guild...Have you heard of that?"

Asuna hadn't, but Kirito answered immediately. "That's short for MMO Today. It was the biggest website in Japan covering online games. And the manager of the site organized that guild. But I thought his name was—"

"Thinker." Yuriel's face blanched slightly as she spoke the

name. "And he did not want to create the heavy-fisted organization that the Army is today. He only wanted to share resources such as food and information equally, among all players."

Asuna had heard stories about the Army's ideals and subsequent collapse. The idea was good: fighting monsters in safe groups for stable income, then sharing that money equally. But at heart, MMORPGs are a battle over system resources, and just because SAO put players in an extreme situation did not change that fundamental truth. In fact, it only accentuated it.

To make good on that ideal required the organization to have a realistic size and considerable leadership, and the guild was simply too large for that to happen. Looted items were kept off the ledgers, players were purged, others fought back, and the guild's leader slowly lost control.

"And that's when a man named Kibaou emerged," Yuriel said, her voice pained. "He took advantage of Thinker's hands-off approach to gather likeminded officers in his push to strengthen the organization. That's when the guild's name was changed to the Aincrad Liberation Force. Their first step was to make it policy to hunt criminals and control the most efficient fields in the wilderness. Until that point, we'd played nice with other guilds and observed proper farming manners, but with the power of numbers, we could control areas for long periods of time, increasing our income dramatically. As a result, Kibaou's faction only gained more influence. These days, Thinker is more of a figurehead than anything else... Now Kibaou's people are getting carried away and undertaking extortion inside the town under the guise of a 'tax.' Those were their foot soldiers you stopped yesterday."

Yuriel paused to take a sip of Sasha's tea. "But Kibaou's faction had a weakness of their own. They focused so much on accumulating resources that they completely ignored the progress of the game. They'd put the cart before the horse. The average player within our guild began to point out the fallacy of this strategy... so Kibaou took a wild gamble to quell the unrest. He organized a group of a dozen or so of the highest-level players in the guild and sent them to raid the latest boss."

Asuna couldn't help but glance at Kirito. The memory of fateful Corvatz and his Army team's ill-prepared attempt at Gleameyes, the boss of the seventy-fourth floor, was still fresh in their minds.

"High-level or not, it's undeniable that our best fighters do not match up to you advanced clearers. Ultimately, our party was defeated, the captain was killed, and Kibaou was excoriated for his reckless gamble. We might have succeeded in kicking him out of the guild, but…"

The narrow bridge of Yuriel's nose wrinkled, and she bit her lip. "Three days ago, his back to the wall, Kibaou set a trap for Thinker. He set up a corridor crystal to exit deep in a powerful dungeon and succeeded in getting Thinker to walk through it. Thinker went in unarmed, believing he and Kibaou were simply going to have a man-to-man discussion, and as a result, he was stranded in the deepest part of the dungeon with no means to fight his way free, nor any teleport crystals…"

"Th-three days ago…? Then he's…?" Asuna asked reflexively. Yuriel gave a slight nod.

"His name has not appeared on the Monument of Life yet, so we think he managed to reach a safe haven. But it's a very high-level dungeon, and he apparently can't work his way free. As you know, there's no way to send him a message within the dungeon, and he cannot access the guild's item storage from there, either. There's no way to get a teleport crystal to him."

Arranging a corridor crystal to exit into certain death was a tried-and-true method of murder known as "Portal PKing," and Thinker must have been aware of the practice. They might have been at odds, but he'd never expect another officer in his own guild would go to such lengths. Or perhaps he just didn't want to think his comrade capable of such a thing.

As though reading Asuna's mind, Yuriel muttered, "He was always too nice for his own good."

She continued, "The Contract Scroll is an item that signifies the guild leader. Only Thinker and Kibaou can control it, so if Thinker never comes back, the guild personnel list and finances will be entirely under Kibaou's control. As Thinker's aide, it is my fault that I could not prevent him from falling into that trap and my responsibility to rescue him. But the dungeon he is trapped inside is too difficult for me to conquer at my current level, and I cannot rely on the help of other Army members."

She bit her lip hard, looking straight into Kirito and Asuna's eyes.

"When I heard that an incredibly powerful pair of fighters had just come to the city, I couldn't resist the temptation to call upon you. Mr. Kirito…Miss Asuna."

Yuriel bowed deeply, formally, to both of them.

"I fully understand how presumptuous this must sound of me, but could I ask that you assist me in rescuing Thinker?"

She stopped, her lengthy story concluded. Asuna gave Yuriel a scrutinizing look.

It was sad to say that within SAO, trusting the word of others was impossible. Even now, they couldn't deny that this might be a plot to draw Kirito and Asuna out of the safety of town to do them harm. Normally, if one maintains an adequate knowledge of the game they're playing, a con artist's story will eventually tip its hand, but Asuna and Kirito were far too ignorant of the Army's inner workings to know if this tale was true or not.

After a quick glance at Kirito, Asuna reluctantly spoke up.

"I'd like to help you, if there's anything we can do. But for us to commit to that, we'll need to do a minimum of research to back up your story."

"That is…natural, of course." Yuriel nodded. "I'm aware that I'm asking the impossible of you. But the thought of Thinker's name being crossed out on the Monument of Life in Blackiron Palace at any moment is driving me to my wits' end."

When Asuna saw the silver-haired woman's proud eyes mist up, her suspicion was shaken. *I want to believe her,* she realized.

But at the same time, two years of experience in this virtual world were blaring a warning alarm not to let emotion cloud her judgment.

She glanced at Kirito, who seemed to be conflicted as well. His pensive black eyes reflected a heart that was torn between the desire to help Yuriel and a concern for Asuna's well-being.

At that moment, Yui, who had been keeping silent, raised her face from her cup and said, "It's okay, Mama. She's not lying."

Asuna was taken aback. Not just at the content of Yui's statement but at the proper form and structure of it, in comparison to the halting pidgin of the previous days.

"Y-you can tell, Yui?" Asuna inquired closely. Yui nodded.

"Yeah. I can't... explain, but I can tell."

Kirito shot out a hand to scrunch Yui's hair affectionately. He looked to Asuna and grinned.

"I'd rather trust and regret than doubt and regret. Let's do it. I'm sure it'll work out."

"You never have a care in the world, do you?" Asuna shook her head in exasperation but added her hand to Yui's head.

"I'm sorry, Yui. We're going to have to put off finding your friends for a day. Hope you don't mind," she murmured. Asuna wasn't sure if Yui really understood it, but the little girl beamed and nodded happily. She stroked that smooth black hair once more and turned to smile at Yuriel.

"We'd love to lend you our aid, meager as it is. I certainly understand the feeling of wanting to save someone who means a lot to you..."

Yuriel bowed deeply, her blue eyes brimming with tears.

"Thank you... Thank you so much..."

"Let's save the thanks for *after* we've rescued Thinker." Asuna grinned again. Sasha had been watching the entire conversation in silence, but now she clapped her hands together.

"Well! Now that that's settled, it's time to eat up! There's plenty left; don't be shy. You too, Yuriel!"

*   *   *

The weak light of early winter filtered through the deeply colored branches of the town's trees, to cast pale shadows on the cobblestones. Very few people passed through the back alleys of the Town of Beginnings, which, in contrast to its massive size, only made it seem colder.

The group was fully armed now. Asuna and Kirito, who was on Yui-carrying duty, followed Yuriel's brisk lead through the town.

Asuna had naturally wanted to leave Yui with Sasha while they handled this business, but Yui stubbornly insisted on going along, so they had no choice. Their pockets were stuffed with teleport crystals, of course. If it came down to it—cruel as it might be to Yuriel—they were prepared to cut their losses and flee at any moment.

"Oh, now that you mention it, I forgot to ask about the most important thing," Kirito called out to Yuriel. "What floor is the dungeon on?"

"This one," she responded flatly.

"...?" Asuna was perplexed. "This...one?"

"There's a large dungeon here...beneath the center of the Town of Beginnings. I suspect that Thinker is trapped down at the bottom of it."

"You're kidding," Kirito groaned. "There was nothing like that during the beta test. I can't believe I missed it..."

"The entrance to the dungeon is in the basement of Blackiron Palace—the headquarters of the Army. I believe it's the kind of dungeon that only becomes available once a certain stage has been reached in the upper floors. We only discovered it after Kibaou had seized control, and he plotted to have his faction monopolize its resources. He kept it a secret from Thinker and me for quite a while..."

"I see. Fresh dungeons always have rare items that only pop once, then never again. They must have made quite a tidy profit from that."

"Actually, it seems that wasn't the case," Yuriel said, slightly pained. "For a dungeon on the starting floor, it's extremely difficult and dangerous. The average monster in there is on par with foes from at least the sixtieth floor and up. Kibaou's advance party was badly overmatched, and they needed an emergency teleportation just to make it out alive. They used so many crystals that the cost of the expedition far outweighed the reward."

"Ha-ha, serves them right."

Yuriel returned Kirito's chuckle with a smile, but her expression darkened again right away.

"But that just means that saving Thinker will be that much harder. Kibaou set the marker for that corridor crystal's destination deep in the dungeon when he was running for his life. That's where Thinker ended up when he traveled through the corridor. In terms of level, I can barely manage to beat the monsters in a one-on-one fight, so a series of them is out of the question. If you don't mind my asking, are you two capable of...?"

"Well, if it's equivalent to the sixtieth floor..."

"I think we can handle ourselves." Asuna finished Kirito's sentence. Delving into the sixtieth-floor dungeon with a proper safety margin meant being at least Level 70. Asuna was presently at Level 87, and Kirito was more than 90. They would probably be able to clear the dungeon while protecting Yui at the same time, a thought that relieved her. But Yuriel still showed concern.

"All right, but...there's one other thing that worries me. According to one of the members of that advance party, there was a giant monster deep in the dungeon...A boss-level encounter."

"..."

Asuna and Kirito shared a look.

"Do you suppose the boss is also equivalent to the sixtieth floor? What was the boss on that one?"

"I think...that was the armored samurai guy made out of stone."

"Oh, that one...It wasn't too tough, was it?"

They turned to Yuriel and nodded.

"I think we'll be able to handle it."

"Oh, that's wonderful to hear!"

Yuriel finally allowed herself a smile, her eyes squinting as though staring into something bright.

"So you've actually been through boss fights before...I'm so sorry to have taken your valuable time like this..."

"It's okay, we're on leave now," Asuna hastily clarified.

As their conversation went on, a massive, gleaming black structure came into view ahead. It was Blackiron Palace, the largest building in the Town of Beginnings. Right inside the front door was a chamber containing the Monument of Life, the epitaph that contained the names of all the players inside the game. Anyone was free to visit this entry chamber, but the Army had complete control of everything beyond it.

Yuriel guided them not into the front entrance of the palace but around the back. The tall castle walls and deep moat that kept out intruders were uniform around the length of the perimeter. Not a single soul passed them on the street.

After several minutes of walking, Yuriel stopped at a staircase that ran from the street down to the surface of the moat water. Peering over, they saw that the stairs led not to the water's edge but down into a dark hallway cut into the stone slope.

"This leads to the sewers beneath the palace, which is where we'll find the entrance to the dungeon. I'm afraid it's rather dark and cramped..." She trailed off, glancing with concern at Yui, still in Kirito's arms. Yui grimaced and piped up, affronted.

"I'm not scared!"

Asuna couldn't help but giggle.

The only thing they'd told Yuriel about Yui was that she was "living with them." Yuriel didn't pry any further, but she was clearly uncertain about bringing the girl into a dangerous dungeon.

Asuna hastened to reassure her. "Don't worry. She's much tougher than she seems."

"Yep. She'll be a great warrior one day," Kirito added, laughing as he met Asuna's glance. Yuriel nodded in satisfaction.

"Let's get going, then!"

*   *   *

"Nwaaaah!"

The sword in his right hand slashed straight through the monster.

"Ryaaaa!"

The sword in his left knocked it flying.

In his first use of Dual Blades in quite some time, Kirito was unleashing on their hapless foes all the pent-up energy that had accumulated during his vacation time. There was no room for Asuna, who was holding Yui's hand, or Yuriel and her metal whip. Each time they met a group of giant frogs with slimy skin or crayfish with massive gleaming pincers, Kirito rushed forward with reckless abandon, his swirling limbs creating a gale of destruction that decimated everything in its path.

Asuna could only sigh in exasperation, but Yuriel's eyes and mouth were gaping as she witnessed Kirito's berserk performance. It must have been a sight completely beyond her experience in battle. Yui's cheerful chants of "Good luck, Papa" only made the scene more comical.

A few dozen minutes had passed since they'd entered the black stone dungeon from the dark, dank sewers. It was larger, deeper, and more populated with monsters than they'd expected, but thanks to Kirito's game-breaking Dual Blades, the two women weren't tired in the least.

"I...I'm sorry. Now it feels like I'm just having you do all the dirty work," Yuriel muttered apologetically. Asuna grinned weakly.

"No, trust me, he's just...sick. Let him get it out of his system."

"Wow, that was mean." Kirito's ears pricked up as he returned from slaughtering his latest batch of victims. "Want to switch places, then?"

"In a little bit."

Asuna and Yuriel looked at each other, grinning.

The silver-haired whipmaster waved a hand to bring up her map and pointed out the flashing friend marker that indicated Thinker's location. Because they didn't have the map for the dungeon, the space between them and Thinker was blank, but they'd already covered at least 70 percent of the distance.

"Thinker's location has not moved for several days. I believe he's inside a safe area. If we can just reach him, we'll be able to teleport him out...Thanks for your help. We're almost there."

Kirito hurriedly waved his hands in supplication when Yuriel bowed to him.

"N-no, really, I'm doing it for the fun of it. Plus there are the items..."

"Oh?" Asuna spoke up. "Find anything worthwhile?"

"Yep."

Kirito quickly zipped through his menu and soon, a reddish-black chunk of meat appeared with a *splat*. Asuna pulled away from the grotesque blob.

"Ugh...what is that?"

"Frog meat! They say the grossest stuff can be the tastiest sometimes. Can you cook it for me?"

"Eww! No way!!" she screamed, opening her own window. She and Kirito shared an inventory, and she quickly scanned it until she found an entry labeled SCAVENGE TOAD MEAT x24, then dragged it into the trash icon.

"What? Nooooo..."

Kirito's piteous wail sent Yuriel doubling over, clutching her stomach with laughter. Yui piped up in that instant, beaming happily. "She finally laughed!"

Asuna thought back and realized it was true. Yui's spasms yesterday had happened just after they'd driven off the Army soldiers and brought the children to laughs and cheers. It was as though the little girl was especially sensitive to laughter somehow. Did it have something to do with her original personality, or had her trauma done this to her? Asuna lifted Yui up and hugged her tightly. She swore that she would give the girl as many laughs as she could take.

"Let's keep moving!"

And farther into the depths they went.

When they'd first entered the dungeon, most of the monsters they had encountered were aquatic creatures, but the deeper they delved, the more undead they ran across: zombies, ghosts, and the like. Those sent a chill through Asuna's chest, but Kirito's two swords instantly sent the spirits to an eternal rest.

Normally it was considered poor behavior for a player to rampage freely through an area below his or her recommended level, but with no one around to offend, they were free to do as they pleased. If time had permitted, Asuna might have suggested allowing Yuriel to play a supporting role so that she could gain valuable experience and level up, but Thinker's rescue was their primary goal.

Two hours passed in a blink, and in that time the distance between their location and the potential safe area where they would find Thinker was closing slowly but steadily. After the umpteenth black skeleton warrior had fallen to Kirito's blades, they spotted a corridor filled with warm, inviting light.

"A-ha! The safety zone!" Asuna cried. Kirito ran a Search skill check and nodded.

"There's one player inside. It's green."

"Thinker!"

Yuriel leaped forward, her metal armor clanking, unable to hold herself back. Kirito and Asuna hurried after her, swords and scion still clutched in their hands.

They ran down the hallway toward the source of the light, curving to the right until they reached a large intersection. A small room was visible on the other end of it.

The room's light was nearly blinding after their eyes had been so accustomed to the gloom of the dungeon, but they could see a man standing inside it. The backlight prevented them from seeing his face, but he was waving his arms at them wildly.

"Yurieeeel!!"

He shouted as soon as he recognized her. Yuriel returned his wave and began running faster.

"Thinkerrr!!"

The tears were audible in her voice, but his next scream drowned her out.

"Stay back!! The corridor is—!"

Asuna warily slowed her pace, but Yuriel did not hear him. She was racing directly for the lit room.

The next instant—

A single yellow cursor appeared from the right side of the blind intersection, just a few meters before the safe room. Asuna quickly checked the name that appeared: THE FATAL SCYTHE.

It was a unique name with a definitive "the" before it—the mark of a boss monster.

"Yuriel, stop! Come back!!" she screamed. The yellow cursor slid left, approaching the intersection. It was going to collide with the woman. They had only a few seconds left.

"*Ksh!!*"

Suddenly, Kirito, who had been running ahead at Asuna's left, vanished…or so it seemed. But he'd actually sped forward with blinding speed, a shock wave rattling off the walls.

He practically blinked across the remaining meters, grabbing Yuriel from behind with his right hand and plunging his left-hand sword into the paving stones. There was an enormous metal screech. Sparks flew. They'd stopped just before the open intersection so quickly that the air practically burned. In the next instant, a massive black shadow rumbling past crossed that empty space.

The yellow cursor shot about ten meters down the left corridor before stopping. The unseen creature slowly turned around and appeared to ready itself for another charge.

Kirito let go of Yuriel and pulled his sword from the stones before taking off down that left branch. Asuna hurried after him.

She helped the dazed Yuriel to her feet and pushed her across the intersection, then plopped Yui into Yuriel's arms.

"Take her into the safe area with you!"

The whipmaster nodded, her face pale, then picked up Yui and headed for the light. Satisfied, Asuna drew her rapier and turned back to the left corridor.

Before her was Kirito's back, his two swords drawn. Beyond him was a large, vaguely human silhouette in a tattered black robe, hovering two and a half meters tall.

The inside of the hood and the arms extended from the sleeves were squirming with a dense darkness. Two bulging, bloodshot eyes were visible within a sunken, darkened face, and they were trained directly on the humans below. The creature clutched a large black scythe in its right hand. Viscous red drops hung from the vicious curve of the weapon. It was the very image of the Grim Reaper.

The reaper's eyeballs swiveled to stare at Asuna. A dread chill ran through her entire body, as though her heart had been gripped by terror's hand.

It can't be that dangerous from a statistical perspective, she told herself. But as she readied her rapier, Kirito's ragged voice sounded from up front.

"Asuna, go back to the others in the safe area and teleport them out of here at once."

"Huh...?"

"This one's bad news. I can't even see its data with my Identification skill. I think it has to be ranked for the ninetieth floor or above..."

"...?!"

Asuna swallowed hard, her body stiffening. As they talked, the reaper began weaving its way through the air toward them.

"I'll buy us time; now go!!"

"N-no, you have to come with us..."

"I'll be right behind you! Hurry!!"

Even a teleport crystal, the last line of defense, is not an infallible tool. The process takes several seconds, from holding the crystal to indicating a destination to the completion of the teleportation. If a monster hits the player before it finishes, the process is canceled. This inability to complete teleportation is a common cause of death when a party's discipline breaks down and members attempt an emergency escape.

Asuna was torn. If she turned back and helped the others escape, Kirito's legs were fast enough that he might be able to find an opportunity to turn and reach the safe area on his own. But the monster's initial charge was frightfully quick. What if she made it out, and he never reappeared? The thought was unbearable.

Asuna glanced quickly down the right-hand corridor.

I'm sorry, Yui. I promised we'd stick together…

"Yuriel, take Yui and teleport out of here!" she shouted. Yuriel shook her head, her face frozen in horror.

"No…I can't…"

"Hurry!!"

In the next moment, the reaper, its scythe held at the ready, plunged forward with terrible speed, dark miasma spilling from its sleeves.

Kirito crossed his swords before him, standing tall in front of Asuna. She clung desperately to his back, adding her rapier to his Dual Blades. The reaper gave no thought to their weapons, swinging its massive scythe down at their heads.

A red flash. A shock wave.

Asuna felt herself spinning round and round. She struck the floor, bounced up to smack against the ceiling, then crashed to the stones again. Her breath stopped. Her vision darkened.

In her daze, she checked their HP and saw that both had been knocked to less than half by that single hit. The unfeeling yellow bar told her that she wouldn't survive the next such attack. *I have to stand, but my body won't move…*

But the next instant—

She heard little tapping footsteps. Asuna glanced toward them with a start and saw someone running toward them like a clumsy kitten unaware of the peril it approached.

Fragile limbs. Long black hair. But Yui was supposed to be back in the safe area. She looked up at the giant reaper without an ounce of fear in her eyes.

"No! Get out of the way!!" Kirito screamed, desperately trying to raise himself off the ground. The creature was slowly raising its heavy scythe again. If Yui was caught in its wide swing path, her HP would certainly be wiped out entirely. Asuna tried to shout, to call out a warning, but her mouth was frozen.

In the next moment, however, something impossible happened.

"It's all right, Papa, Mama."

Yui's body floated up into midair.

She didn't jump. It was a graceful motion, as though she were beating invisible wings, until she came to a stop two meters off the ground. Her right hand, so very tiny, was raised up high.

"No…No, Yui! You have to get out of here!"

But Asuna's scream was drowned out by the reaper's massive scythe, which came mercilessly downward with a visible trail of reddish-black light. As the wickedly sharp point came into contact with Yui's pure white palm—

It met a brilliant purple barrier and bounced back with a massive blast. Asuna stared with astonishment at the system tag that floated around Yui's hand.

IMMORTAL OBJECT. A designation for in-game elements that could not be killed—an impossible status for a player.

The black reaper's eyes bulged and swiveled as though baffled by this unexpected outcome. The next moment, something even more shocking occurred.

With a *fwoom!*, crimson flames swirled around Yui's outstretched hand. They burst outward for a moment before contracting into an elongated rectangular shape. Within moments, the shape had refined itself into a massive blade. A gleaming edge materialized within the flames, extending, extending…

The sword in Yui's little hand easily eclipsed her own height. The dank corridor was lit by the gleam of the blade, like a metal just before it melted. Yui's thick winter clothes burned away in an instant, as though enveloped in the blade's fire. Beneath those charred remains, she was wearing her original white one-piece dress. Mysteriously enough, both the dress and her long black hair showed no signs of being affected by the flame.

The giant sword, longer than she was tall, rotated once…

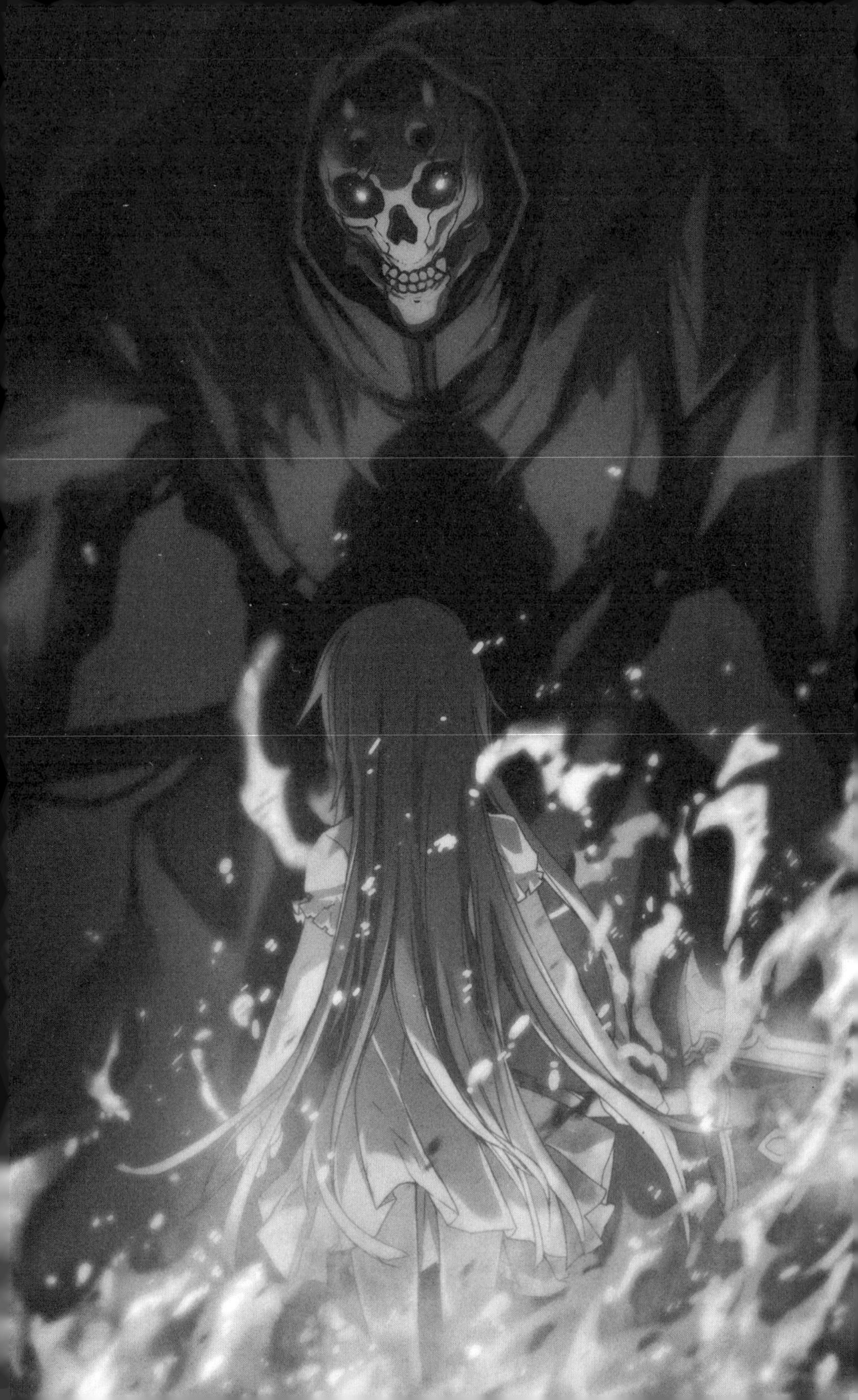

And without a moment of hesitation, Yui plunged toward the black reaper, her blade tracing a path of fire.

The boss monster was only a system procedure, acting on simple algorithms, but it seemed as though those bulging, bloodshot eyes were filled with fear.

Yui rocketed through the air, clad in a vortex of flames. The reaper held its scythe in front of itself, taking a defensive posture as though it feared the tiny girl. Yui met it head-on, swinging her enormous, blazing sword.

The fiery blade connected with the horizontal hilt of the scythe. For an instant, both figures stopped.

But Yui's sword immediately returned to life. As though cutting through solid metal with impossible heat, the glowing weapon slowly bit through the scythe. Yui's hair and dress and the reaper's robe were blown backward so powerfully they threatened to rip away. Occasional spark clouds, bursting to life, lit the dim dungeon in harsh orange light.

Eventually, the reaper's scythe went *bwoom* and split cleanly in two. An instant later, the pillar of fire that was Yui's weapon smashed directly into the boss's face, unleashing all of its pent-up energy.

"*Hng…!!*"

Asuna and Kirito had to narrow their eyes and cover their faces at the power of the ensuing fireball. At the same time that Yui brought down the blade vertically, the fireball burst, enveloping the massive creature in a crimson whirlpool that carried it down the hallway. Behind the roar of the blast was the dying screech of the monster.

When they opened their eyes again, the boss was gone. Tiny flames licked the stones here and there, sputtering remnants of the prior inferno. In the midst of all that stood Yui, head down. Her blade was resting on the ground, point down, melting back into flames the way it had materialized.

Asuna finally found the strength to lift herself up, getting to her feet with the aid of her sword. Moments later, Kirito stood as well. They took a few wobbling steps to the little girl's side.

"Yui..." Asuna croaked. Yui turned to her without a sound. The tiny lips were smiling, but those big black eyes were brimming with tears.

Yui looked up at Asuna and Kirito and softly spoke:

"Papa, Mama...I remember everything."

The safe haven in the deepest stretch of the dungeon beneath Blackiron Palace was a perfect square. There was only one entrance, and a polished black cube pedestal sat in the middle of the room.

Asuna and Kirito silently stared at Yui, who was seated on top of the stone. Yuriel and Thinker had already teleported out, so it was just the three of them.

Yui was silent for several minutes after announcing that her memory had returned. She looked sad for some reason. After a long while, Asuna overcame her hesitation and spoke up.

"So, Yui...you remember everything? About what happened to you...?"

She was still facedown, but the little girl eventually nodded. Her tiny lips opened, her face still caught between a smile and tears.

"Yes...Kirito, Asuna—I will explain all of it."

As soon as she heard those formal words, Asuna felt a terrible foreboding in her chest: the knowledge that something had come to an end.

Yui's words slowly trailed through the square room.

"The world of Sword Art Online is controlled by an enormous computer system. That system is named Cardinal. Cardinal tweaks the balance of the game world of its own accord. It was designed in such a way that it doesn't need human maintenance. Two core programs work together to correct errors, and countless sub-programs maintain every little thing in the world. Monster and NPC AI routines, drop balance of items and currency—everything is undertaken by programs under Cardinal's supervision. But there was one area that had to be left to human hands: trouble stemming from the player's mental health. Such issues could only be solved by another human being, and to that end, several dozen staff members were supposedly hired to address this issue."

"GMs," Kirito muttered. "Yui, are you saying you're a game master? An Argus employee...?"

Yui was silent for several seconds, then shook her head.

"But Cardinal's developers created another program, one that would allow the system to even address players' mental care. A program that would closely monitor the players' emotions through the NerveGear, then pay a visit to those who were experiencing severe problems... The Mental Health Counseling Program, MHCP001, codenamed 'Yui.' That was me."

Asuna held her breath in shock. She couldn't immediately process what she'd heard.

"A program...? You're... an AI?" she gasped. Yui nodded, still smiling sadly.

"I've been given emotion simulation processes in order to make me more acceptable to human players. It's all false... even these tears. Forgive me, Asuna..."

Large drops spilled from Yui's eyes and evaporated into points of light. Asuna took a step toward Yui. She reached out to touch her, but Yui shook her head. As though saying she wasn't worthy of Asuna's comfort.

Asuna squeezed out more words, still disbelieving.

"But... why didn't you have any memories? Is that even possible for an AI...?"

"Two years ago, on the day this game began..."

Yui looked downward and began to explain.

"Even I do not know exactly what happened. Cardinal gave me an order I wasn't expecting. It told me not to interfere with any players whatsoever. Forbidden to interact directly, I had no choice but to sit back and monitor the players' mental health, nothing more."

Asuna instantly understood that the "unexpected order" was a directive from Akihiko Kayaba, SAO's supreme GM, but Yui would likely not possess any information about him. Even so, her young face was fraught with silent pain.

"The situation was about as bad as I could have expected... Nearly the entire player population was ruled by negative emotions: fear, desperation, rage. Some even fell into madness. And all I could do was watch them. My duty was to attend to their emotional issues as soon as possible... but I was prevented from doing so. Trapped in the contradiction of duties without rights, I self-destructed, errors piling up in infinite loops..."

In the quiet dungeon, Yui's frail voice was like the plucking of delicate silver threads. Asuna and Kirito listened in silence.

"One day, in the midst of my usual monitoring, I noticed two players with vastly different mental parameters from the average values. Your brain waves were different than anything I'd detected before. Joy...Peace...Not only that, but something I could not identify. I had to keep monitoring you. Every time I came into contact with your conversations, a strange type of desire was formed within me...When such a routine should have been impossible: 'I want to be near them. I want to meet them. I want to speak with them...' So I took a physical form at the system console nearest to your home and wandered in search of you. I was most likely in a shattered and fragmented state at the time, though..."

"And that was within the forest on the twenty-second floor...?"

Yui nodded slowly.

"Yes. Kirito, Asuna, I've always wanted to meet you. You can't understand how happy I was...when I saw you in the forest... It's strange, isn't it? I shouldn't be able to think this way—I'm only a program..."

More tears spilled out, and her mouth clamped shut. Asuna was struck with an indescribable emotion. She clutched her hands to her chest.

"Yui...you really are an AI. You have true intelligence," she whispered.

The little girl's tiny head inclined slightly. "I don't...understand...what happened to me..."

Kirito had been silent the entire time, but he stepped forward now.

"You're not just a program being manipulated by the system anymore, Yui. That's why you can put your desires into words," he said gently. "What *is* your desire?"

" I want…I want…"

She stretched her thin arms out wide to the both of them. "I want to be with you forever…Papa, Mama!"

Asuna didn't even bother to wipe away the tears. She rushed over to Yui and clutched her little body tight.

"We *will* be together forever, Yui!"

A moment later, Kirito's arms enveloped the both of them.

"That's right…you're our daughter. Let's go home and live as a family forever…"

But within Asuna's arms, Yui shook her head.

"Huh…?"

"It's too late," she said.

Kirito pressed her for more information, confused. "What do you mean, too late?"

"It was touching that stone that allowed me to regain my memory."

She turned and pointed to the black cube that sat in the center of the room.

"When you sent me into this safe haven, I just happened to brush past the stone, and that's when I learned everything. It's not just a decorative object…that's a command console designed to give the GMs emergency access to the system."

As though Yui's words contained some kind of command, several paths of light suddenly traced their way across the surface of the black stone. A soft hum sounded, and a pale holo-keyboard appeared, floating above the stone.

"I believe the boss monster was placed here to keep players away from this console. I was able to access the system through this terminal and generate an Object Eraser to delete the monster. When I made contact, the speech abilities that Cardinal's error-correcting processes had destroyed were restored in full…

but it also means that after being ignored for so long, Cardinal is finally aware of me again. The core system is searching for my program at this very moment. It will consider me a foreign process and delete me, I suspect. I do not have much time left…"

"But…no!"

"Isn't there anything we can do? Maybe if we leave this area…"

Yui simply smiled softly at their exclamations. Tears dripped down her pale cheeks once again.

"Papa, Mama…thank you. We must part ways here."

"No! This can't happen!" Asuna screamed, desperate. "This is where it all starts! We're supposed to live together…as a family…"

"All that time in the darkness and pain, never knowing when the end might come…it was you two who kept me together," Yui said, staring right at Asuna. It was then that her body began to glow with a faint light.

"Yui, don't go!"

Kirito gripped her hand. Her tiny fingers softly squeezed his.

"But being with you meant that everyone had a smile…That was enough to make me happy. Please, take on my role…and help others be happy, too…"

Yui's hair and dress began trailing frail little drops of light, delicate as morning dew. They were slowly disappearing. Her smile grew transparent, her weight vanishing.

"No, Yui! You can't go! I'll never be able to smile without you there!"

Yui smiled, wreathed in overflowing lights. Just before she disappeared, she reached out and traced Asuna's cheek.

Smile, Mama…

Asuna heard the voice inside her head, just as the lights pulsed and burst outward. In the next moment, her arms were empty.

"Aaaaahh!!"

Asuna slumped to her knees, unable to hold back the sobs. She crumpled over the stone floor, wailing like a child. The teardrops she shed spilled onto the floor, mixing with the remains of Yui's light before they evaporated.

4

As though the cold snap from yesterday had never happened, a warm breeze brushed the grass. Drawn by the pleasant warmth, several birds were perched in the garden trees, watching the humans below with apparent interest.

They'd moved a large table out into the spacious front yard of Sasha's church for an unseasonal garden party. Each time food was produced from the grill—as though by magic—the children cheered with delight.

"To think there was food in this world that could actually taste so good…"

Thinker, the highest-ranking officer of the Army, was tearing into Asuna's special barbecue with a look of sheer bliss. Yuriel sat next to him, beaming. On first meeting, she'd appeared to be an icy lady warrior, but seated next to Thinker, she had transformed into the image of a cheerful young wife.

They hadn't had time to sit around and get a good look at Thinker with all the commotion yesterday. Now that he was seated across the table, they saw a gentle, good-natured man quite at odds with his position leading a massive military guild.

He was just a tad taller than Asuna but quite a bit shorter than Yuriel. His slightly pudgy build was clad in drab clothing, and he wore no armor at all. Yuriel was not in her Army uniform today, either.

Thinker held up his empty glass to accept Kirito's offer of more wine and inclined his head to indicate thanks.

"Asuna, Kirito, you've done me an incredible favor here. I don't even know how to thank you…"

"Trust me, I've gotten plenty of help from *MMO Today* over the years." Kirito grinned.

"There's a name I haven't heard in ages." Thinker's round face beamed widely. "At the time, those daily updates were a huge burden. I used to think to myself, 'Doing a news site ain't what it's cracked up to be'—but I'd take it in a second now over running a guild. I should have just gotten into the SAO newspaper business."

The table echoed with laughter.

"So…what happened with the Army?" Asuna asked. Thinker's smile vanished.

"Kibaou and his followers have been expelled, something I should have done a long time ago…My distaste for confrontation let the situation grow out of hand. I'm actually thinking of disbanding the Army entirely."

Asuna's and Kirito's eyes widened. "That would be quite a bold move."

"The Army just got much too large for its own good. I'm thinking of dissolving it so I can build a more peaceful, cooperative organization. After all, it would be irresponsible to get rid of it and just abandon everything we worked for."

Yuriel squeezed Thinker's hand and continued for him.

"We're thinking of redistributing the Army's resources not just among the members but among all the people here in this town. They've suffered because of us, after all…I'm so sorry about what happened to you, Sasha."

Sasha's large, bespectacled eyes blinked in surprise at their sudden apology. She hurriedly waved her hands in protest.

"N-no, not at all. The good people in the Army have helped out some of the children in the field, too."

Her easy acceptance brought the warmth back to the table.

"By the way," Yuriel asked hesitantly, "what about the girl from yesterday—Yui, was it...?"

Asuna shared a look with Kirito, then smiled reassuringly. "Yui is...back home."

She brought her right hand to her chest. A thin necklace was sparkling around her neck, one that hadn't been there the day before. A silver pendant hung in the center of delicate silver links, and in the center of that pendant was a large, translucent stone. When she traced the teardrop shape, she felt as though a slight warmth flowed into her fingertips.

After Yui had vanished amid those tiny lights and Asuna wailed against the cold stone floor, Kirito suddenly shouted at her side.

"Cardinal!!"

She raised her teary face to find him screaming at the ceiling.

"Don't assume you'll keep getting away with everything!"

Kirito gritted his teeth and leaped onto the black console at the center of the room, tapping at the holo-keyboard that was still visible above the stone. For an instant, the shock made her forget her grief.

"K-Kirito...what are you—?"

"I might still be able to crack into the system using the GM account," he muttered, his fingers flailing wildly. A large window popped open, and the room was lit by the glow of text rapidly scrolling past. Asuna watched silently as Kirito attempted several different commands. A small progress bar appeared, filling from left to right. Just as it was about to finish—

The entire stone console flashed a cold white, and Kirito was blasted backward as an explosion ripped the air.

"K-Kirito!!"

She rushed to help him up.

Kirito sat up shaking his head, but there was a faint smile on his exhausted face. He held out his right fist to her, clutched tight. Confused, she extended her open palm.

When he opened his fist, a large crystal in the shape of a teardrop fell into Asuna's hand. A white light beat steadily in the center of the complex, glittering jewel.

"What is it...?"

"Before the access privileges that Yui used to start up the console expired, I was able to separate Yui's program files from the system and materialize them as an in-game object. It's Yui's heart...She's right in there."

And as though his willpower were entirely drained, Kirito flopped back down on the floor and closed his eyes. Asuna peered closely at the jewel in her hand.

"I know you're in there, Yui...my sweet little Yui..."

The tears rushed forth again. As though to answer Asuna's call, the soft light at the center of the crystal beat once, brighter than usual.

After waving a mournful good-bye to Sasha, Yuriel, Thinker, and the children, Asuna and Kirito walked through the teleport gate to the twenty-second floor, where they were greeted by a chilly wind carrying the scent of the forest. Their journey had only lasted three days, but as Asuna sucked in a deep breath, it seemed like they'd been gone for much longer.

What a great, wide world...

She pondered the mysteries of this strange floating realm. Each of the virtually countless floors had its own residents, laughing and crying and carrying on with their lives. Well, to be fair, the majority of them were probably suffering more than enjoying themselves. And yet they still continued their own personal battles.

And where do I belong?

Asuna looked up at the base of the floor above as they trudged down the path to their home.

I have to return to the front line, she suddenly realized. *Very soon, I'll have to take up my sword again and return to battle. I don't know how long it will take, but I have to keep fighting until*

I've ended this world and brought back a smile to every living person in this game. I have to bring them joy...It's what Yui wanted.

"Hey, Kirito."

"Hmm?"

"If we beat the game and this world goes away, what happens to Yui?"

"Good question...I'm probably cutting it close on memory space. I have my NerveGear's local memory set up to cache a portion of the client program's environment data within the unit. It'll probably be tricky to extract it in a form that's recognizable as Yui, but...I think it'll work out."

"Great."

Asuna leaned over and squeezed Kirito.

"Then we'll be able to see Yui again in the real world. Our very first child."

"Yeah. I'm sure we will."

Asuna looked down at the crystal that sparkled between them. *Good luck, Mama,* she thought she heard faintly.

(The End)

002-04

Red-Nosed Reindeer

§ 46th floor of Aincrad
December 2023

1

The bloodred Vorpal Strike split the darkness and reduced the two giant insects' HP to zero.

I caught the bursting of their polygon shells out of the corner of my eye, and as soon as the post-skill cooldown had worn off, I spun around to deflect the jaws that had been bearing down on my back. The giant ant flipped backward with a hideous, ear-rending screech, and I dispatched it with the same move.

Just three days ago, I'd learned this single heavy attack when my One-Handed Sword skill reached 950, and I was amazed at its versatility. The pause after the move was a bit on the long side, but that shortcoming was made up for by the skill's reach, twice as long as the blade itself, and power rivaling that of a two-handed lance. Spamming it like this against another player would allow him to read your timing pretty easily, but there was no issue with the simple monster AI routines. I used it over and over, carving an easy crimson path through the oncoming horde of foes.

But I knew that running through waves and waves of monsters by simple torchlight for nearly an hour was wearing on my concentration. The mandible bites and acidic saliva projectiles were a very simple attack pattern, but my reflexes were wearing down. There were gobs of these giant ants, and they weren't pushovers.

They dwelt just three floors below the current frontier, the forty-ninth floor, which made them significantly powerful. The situation was still within my level safety margin, but if I let them surround me and attack undefended for a few seconds, my HP bar would certainly fall into the yellow zone.

There was only one reason to go solo adventuring in an already-cleared floor: This was a popular grinding spot that offered an excellent experience-point rate. The giant ants that spilled out of the many holes in the surrounding cliffs had high attack values but weak defense and HP. As long as you avoided their lunges, it was possible to rack up huge kill numbers in a short period of time. On the other hand, this wasn't a good solo hunting ground, because as mentioned earlier, getting surrounded and losing your composure was a sure way to get crushed. Yet, as a popular grinding spot, there was a gentleman's agreement that each party waiting to hunt had to trade off after an hour. I was the only one waiting by myself. At this very moment, familiar guilds were waiting at the entrance of the canyon for my return, their faces no doubt stamped with looks of exasperation. Actually, exasperation was probably a best-case scenario. Most of the players in the big guilds took cooperation and teamwork for granted and called me a "power-crazed lunatic" or "the lone beater." Not that I cared what they thought.

I checked the timer on the left side of my vision and saw that I'd reached fifty-seven minutes, so I made a mental note to retreat the next time there was a break in the waves of ants. I took a deep breath and tried to summon the last of my concentration for this final spurt.

Ants closed in on the right and left. I froze the right ant with a deftly aimed throwing pick, then dispatched the left one with a clean three-part attack called Sharp Nail. I spun around and finished off the first ant with a Vorpal Strike right into the center of its gaping mandibles. While I waited for the cooldown to wear off, I blocked a flying green glob of acid with my left glove, clicking my tongue in irritation at the slight loss of HP as the leather hissed and smoked. Leaping skyward, I split open the attacking ant's soft belly while still in the air, then landed and finished off the final two ants with the longest combo I'd currently mastered, a six-attack maelstrom. With all the ants gone for now, I took off running before more could spill out of their nest.

It took me less than five seconds to race through the thirty-meter-long ant canyon, and only when I'd spilled out of the narrow entrance did I breathe again. Gasping for fresh air like that made me wonder if the lack of oxygen was only inside my head or if my flesh-and-blood body back in the real world was also starved for air. Before I could guess at an answer, my stomach convulsed and I heaved several times before falling to the cold midwinter ground.

Several footsteps approached as I lay there. I knew the people around here, but I wasn't in the mood for greetings. I wearily waved them away, but then there came a heavy sigh and a rusty, rasping voice.

"I've opened up a bit of a head start on you guys, so I'll sit this one out today. Remember, don't break the circle formation, and always be ready to cover the guy next to you. If you're in danger at any time, just call out. If the queen appears, clear out at once."

Six or seven voices responded in the affirmative to those leaderly directions, and the footsteps clomped away through the grass. Once I'd finally regained my breath for more than a few moments, I pushed myself up with a hand and slumped against a nearby tree branch.

"Here."

I gratefully caught the tossed restorative potion and flipped the cork out with my thumb before downing it greedily. The bitter, lemony taste was the most delicious beverage my lips had ever tasted. When it was emptied, I lobbed the bottle aside. A few seconds later, it glowed faintly and disappeared.

I'd known Klein, the leader of the guild Furinkazan, since the very start of SAO. He still sported that same ugly bandanna and lazy stubble he liked to call facial hair.

"You don't think you might be pushin' your luck a bit, Kirito? How long have you been here?"

"Since about...eight o'clock at night," I said wearily. Klein grimaced outlandishly.

"Oh, come on. It's two in the morning now. You've been at this for six straight hours? If you lose your edge in this hunting ground, it'll cost you your life, man."

"I'm fine. When others come and line up, I take an hour or two off."

"And if no one showed up, you'd just keep going."

"That's why I do this in the dead of night. You might have to wait five or six hours in the middle of the day."

Klein tsked in obvious disgust, then removed the rare katana from his belt and sat down in front of me.

"Look...ever since the very first day of SAO, I've known about your strength. How high is your level now?"

A player's level and other statistics were his lifeline, so it was an unwritten rule within SAO that one never asked or offered those details, but there was no point being so standoffish with Klein. I slumped my shoulders and answered honestly.

"I just went up today. Sixty-nine now."

Klein stopped rubbing his chin, his half-hidden eyes suddenly wide.

"Are you kidding me? When did you get a whole ten levels higher than me? In that case, this makes even less sense. Your level-raising activities are off-the-charts bonkers, man. Let me guess: You spend your afternoons looking for empty hunting grounds to farm, too, right? I don't understand what drives you to these lengths, and don't give me that crap about beating the game faster. You getting tougher on your own means nothing when it's the big guilds like the KoB that determine the pace of our boss conquests."

"Gimme a break. I'm a levelaholic. It just feels good gaining EXP."

I gave him a self-deprecating grin, but Klein brushed it aside, dead serious.

"You can't fool me with that lame excuse. Even I know how hard it is when you run yourself ragged farming levels. Working solo really takes it outta you. Working a hunting ground like this one without a single partner, even close to Level-70, you might as well not have a safety margin at all. You're walking a tightrope, and what I wanna know is what you're getting out of something so reckless."

Furinkazan was a guild made of friends that Klein had known from before SAO. They were a group of regular vagabonds who detested meddling, and as their leader, Klein was no exception.

He was a good guy, but I suspected that he felt some unspoken pressure to exhibit such concern for a wandering beater like me. I had a feeling I knew why, and I didn't want to force him to go through this routine, so I let him off the hook.

"It's all right, you don't have to make a show of worrying for my sake. You want to know if I'm hunting flag mobs, don't you?"

Flag mobs were in-game monsters that possessed a programming flag—a switch that would trigger or advance a quest or event of some kind. Most of them appeared intermittently, just once every few hours or days, but some also existed like boss monsters, and thus could only be summoned once and never again. As you might expect, such foes were terribly powerful, and common sense stated that they must be tackled with a full raiding party.

Klein's face stiffened in guilt, then he turned away, rubbing his chin.

"I...I didn't mean nothin' like that..."

"Let's be honest. You bought some intel from Algo that I'd bought intel about a Christmas event boss...and I bought that intel about you in exchange."

"What?" Klein's eyes widened in surprise and confusion, then he clicked his tongue loudly. "Damn Algo...I guess they don't call her 'The Rat' for nothing."

"She'd sell her own status info for the right price. So now we both know that we're gunning for this Christmas boss. And we've also bought all the hints the NPCs have provided to this point. Which means you should know full well why I'm engaging in this insane grinding, and why I'd ignore all the warnings directed at me."

"Yeah, sorry...I shouldn't have tried to trick you." He removed the hand from his chin and scratched the back of his head with embarrassment. "It's only five days left until the evening of the twenty-fourth...Every guild wants to squeeze in productive last-minute preparations for the boss fight, but I don't think many of them are stupid enough to do it in the middle of the night when it's freezing like this. Anyway, listen...we've got nearly ten members. This is a boss fight we feel like we can win. A flag mob for a once-a-year event isn't gonna be doable for a solo, and you know it."

"..."

I looked down at the dried brown grass, unable to deny it.

An entire year had passed within Aincrad. Now that we were facing our second Christmas within the game, rumors were racing throughout the populace. About a month earlier, NPCs on various floors had started divulging information on the same quest.

They claimed that in the Month of Holly—at the stroke of midnight on December 24, to be precise—deep in a forest somewhere in the game, a monster named Nicholas the Renegade would appear at the foot of a massive fir tree. Whoever defeated it would receive the equally massive riches contained in the giant sack slung over its back.

Even the powerful guilds, which never spared their attention for anything other than conquering the latest labyrinth, salivated at the prospect. This treasure, whether it was a giant mound of col or a bundle of rare weapons, would greatly assist their primary goal, it was clear. Sword Art Online had done nothing but take from its players so far, so who were we to ignore this rare reversal of the trend in the form of a Christmas present?

But as a solo player, I wasn't drawn to the rumors at first.

Klein was right: It probably wasn't the kind of monster I could hunt down on my own, and through my adventures, I'd earned enough money to buy my own residence if I wanted. Most of all, I didn't need the notoriety that would accompany my participation in this hotly contested flag-mob hunt.

Until about two weeks ago, that is, when I'd stumbled across some NPC information that changed my perspective 180 degrees. Ever since then, I'd attended the most popular hunting grounds and suffered the chuckles of the crowds in a last-ditch attempt to squeeze in every last level I could.

Klein joined me in silence for a while, but eventually his low rumble returned.

"It's that other thing, isn't it? The stories of a resurrection item…"

"…Yeah."

If he knew that much, there was no use hiding it anymore. I confirmed his suspicions, and the katana-wielder let out yet another long sigh.

"I know how you feel… It's an item out of our wildest dreams. 'Inside his sack there is a holy tool that can bring back the souls of the departed.' But… I agree with the crowd on this one, man. That part's bound to be fake. Or to be more accurate, it probably *was* true at the time SAO was developed as an honest VRMMO… but not anymore. I bet it was supposed to be an item that would let you revive a dead player without suffering an experience penalty. But that's not possible anymore. The 'penalty' for dying now is death, period. Remember what that son of a bitch Kayaba said on the very first day?"

In my ears echoed the words from the hooded GM claiming to be Akihiko Kayaba on that tutorial day. When my hit points reached zero, my consciousness would disappear from this world and never return to my physical body.

I couldn't imagine that he was lying. And yet…

"Not a single person here knows exactly what happens after you die in this world," I said, as though fighting the possibility. Klein's nose wrinkled, and he spat cynically.

"What, you think if you die, you'll just return to your body totally alive, and Kayaba will pop out and go, 'Psych'? You gotta be kidding me. We resolved that debate a year ago. If this were all a stupid joke like that, the people who died already would have spread the word, and people would have ripped all our Nerve-Gears off. The fact that hasn't happened is proof the stakes of death are real. The moment our HP hits zero, the NerveGear turns into a microwave and boils our brains from the inside out. Because if that's not true, then what does that mean for those of us who got wiped out by these damn monsters? The ones who cried out in fear, saying they didn't wanna—"

"Shut up."

I cut him off, surprised at the hoarseness in my own voice.

"If you really think I don't know all of that, we have nothing more to talk about. Yeah, I know Kayaba said that. But you remember what Heathcliff from the KoB said when we worked together on the most recent floor boss: If there's even a one-percent chance you can save the lives of your partners, you chase that possibility with all you've got, and anyone who can't summon that dedication isn't worth being in your party. I don't really like the guy, but he's right. I'm just talking potential scenarios here. What if dying here means your mind never comes back, but it also doesn't just go away? What if you get placed in some kind of holding area, waiting and waiting to find out what becomes of the fate of the game? That theory leaves open the possibility of this resurrection item."

It was a rare speech for me. Once I'd laid bare the slim possibility I clung to, Klein's anger abated and he looked at me with something resembling pity. When he finally spoke again, it was calm and quiet.

"I see... You still can't get over your old guild, can you, Kirito? Even though it's been more than half a year..."

I turned away and mumbled an excuse.

"It's *only* been half a year. Of course I can't forget them. The entire guild was wiped out... except for me."

"What was it called, the Moonlit Black Cats? They weren't a front-line guild, yet they ventured damn close to the frontier. Then the thief, of all people, trips an alarm trap. It wasn't your fault, man. If anyone says anything, it'll be to praise you for what you did, not bash you."

"That's not the point. They were my responsibility. I could have kept them from going up to that floor, could have told them to ignore that chest, could have sprung everyone out of there after the trap went off…"

If only I hadn't kept my level and skills hidden from them. That was the cruel truth of the matter that I kept a secret from Klein. I kept talking before he could offer some clumsy consolation.

"So maybe there isn't even a one-percent chance of this working. Maybe the chance that I can find this Christmas boss, the chance that I can beat it all on my own, the chance that this item actually exists, and the chance that the game really does hold on to its victims, all added together…are so miniscule that I might as well be searching for a single grain of sand in the middle of a desert. But…it's still not zero. As long as it's greater than zero, I have a duty to seek out that possibility to the best of my ability. Besides, Klein…I know you're not hurting for money, either. Doesn't that mean your reasons for hunting the boss are the same as mine?"

Klein snorted and reached down to pick up the katana's scabbard off the ground. "I'm not a dreaming idealist like you, Kirito. But yeah…I've lost a friend to this game, too. If I don't do what I can for him, I won't sleep well at night…"

He stood up. I grinned wryly.

"It *is* the same."

"Nope. That's just a fringe benefit of all the loot we stand to gain from this…Well, anyway, I'm worried about how the others will manage if one of those bigger ants shows up. I'd better go back there."

"Sure."

I hung heavily off the tree branch with my eyes closed. His last words trailed off as he walked away.

"Also, my concern for you wasn't just part of a mind trick to get that info outta you. If you push yourself too hard and die doing this, I ain't usin' that revival item on ya."

2

"Thank you for your concern. If you don't mind, I'd like to take you up on your offer to guide us to the exit."

Those had been the first words I heard from Keita, leader of the Moonlit Black Cats.

It had been a spring evening, about five months since the start of the game of Russian Roulette that was Sword Art Online, and I was romping around a labyrinth about ten floors below the current front line, collecting ingredients for a new weapon.

As a beater—a former beta-tester whose knowledge of the game allowed me to burst out of the gate, earn experience efficiently, and handle the toughest monsters on my own—the task was yawningly boring. I'd carefully avoided any other adventurers and reached my quota of items in just two hours. As I prepared to leave, I came across a party running the other direction as they were chased by a swarm of larger monsters.

Even a solo player like me could tell this was a poorly balanced party. Out of the five, only one man bearing a shield and mace was equipped to man the front line. The others were a thief with daggers, one person with a quarterstaff, and two spearmen. The one with the mace was losing HP, but without any partners to alternate with and block blows, it was all he could do to continue backing away from the enemy.

I looked at each of them in turn to check their HP. They had enough to make it to the exit, but if they pulled in another group of monsters along the way, there was no guarantee of their safety. After a moment of hesitation, I leaped out of the hidden pathway and called out to the man with the staff, who I gauged to be their leader.

"Want some help up there?"

He goggled wide-eyed at me for a moment but quickly acquiesced.

"Yes, please. If you feel in danger at any time, go ahead and run for it."

I pulled the sword from my back and called out to the mace-wielder to switch, then forced my way to the front of the horde of monsters.

It was a pack of armed goblins, the same enemies I'd just been farming repeatedly for the past few hours. If I unleashed my sword skills, I could wipe them out in an instant, and even if I just stood there unresisting, my Battle Healing ability would ensure that I could take a hail of blows without danger for quite some time.

But for an instant, I felt fear—not of the goblins but of the watchful eyes of the people behind me.

Ordinarily speaking, it was poor form for a high-level player to strut around a lower hunting ground as though he owned the place. Do it for long enough, and someone would hire the big-time guilds to get rid of you, and after they'd hung you out to dry, you were placed on the "bad player" lists in the game's newspapers. As this was an emergency, it seemed like my transgression could be overlooked, but I was still afraid of that moment when the gratitude in their eyes turned to disgust at a beater like me.

I limited my sword skills to the most basic I had, taking my time against the goblins. But I had no idea what a horrendous mistake this would lead to much, much later.

*   *   *

After a few potions for the mace-wielder and several switches, we'd defeated the band of goblins at last. I was surprised at the ferocity of the cheer that arose from the five strangers. They exchanged high fives and shared in the joy of victory.

On the inside I was uncomfortable, but I tried on an awkward smile and shook the hands they offered me. The last to approach was one of the spear-users, the sole woman of the group, her eyes filled with tears as she gripped my hand with both of hers. She shook my hand so hard her black hair shivered.

"Thank you... Thank you so much. I was so, so scared... It was amazing the way you saved us. Thank you."

When I heard those words and saw the wavering tears, I felt an emotion that I still can't put a name to today. All I can remember is that I was glad I'd saved them and glad I'd been strong enough to do so.

I'd been a solo player since the start of the game, but this wasn't the first time I'd ever stepped in to help a party. Among advanced players, however, it was an unspoken rule to help one another when in need. They lived in dangerous circumstances where one might easily find oneself in need of assistance, so it wasn't necessary to seek out thanks, and when offered, it was accepted with a curt nod and nothing more. After a brief post-fight readjustment, you silently headed off to the next battle. It was a purely logical system, suited to the sole purpose of being in that environment: strengthening oneself.

But these people, the Moonlit Black Cats, were different. They heartily celebrated this single victory and praised one another's bravery. The scene might as well have been accompanied by a victory fanfare from a single-player RPG. Perhaps I was swayed by their camaraderie when I offered to guide them to the exit of the labyrinth. Perhaps I was struck by the sudden thought that maybe these people understood the concept of "conquering" this insane game better than anyone else playing it.

"I was running low on my stock of potions, too. Would you like me to accompany you to the exit?"

Keita's face split into a wide grin at my bald-faced lie. "Thanks for your concern."

No. Now that it's been half a year since the Moonlit Black Cats were wiped out, I can be honest. I felt good. I'd built up my status for selfish reasons playing solo, and I had finally used that strength to help those who were weaker than me. I'd felt the pleasure of being needed—that was all.

After we left the labyrinth and returned to town, Keita offered to buy me a drink at a pub, which I accepted at once. Once we'd had a toast of wine—which had to be expensive for them—and finished our introductions, Keita pulled me aside and hesitantly inquired about my level in a low voice.

I'd been expecting this question. In preparation for it, I'd decided on a suitable number to tell him that wouldn't give away my actual strength. I told him the number I suspected was about three levels higher than their average as a guild—and twenty lower than my actual total.

"Wow, you can actually solo that dungeon at your level?" he marveled. I looked sheepish.

"Well, all I'm really doing is sneaking around and looking for solitary monsters I can handle on my own. It's actually not very efficient."

"Oh…I see. Well, Kirito…this is kind of awkward to ask, but I just have a feeling that some other guild will come knocking at your door soon enough. Would you want to join our group?"

"What?" I pretended not to understand. Keita continued his pitch, the blood rushing to his round head.

"Well, level-wise, we're actually able to handle that dungeon. The problem is our skill variety. As you saw earlier, Tetsuo's the only one who can handle the front line. He doesn't have time to recover all by himself, and we tend to wind up on our heels a lot. You'd be a huge help in that regard, and also…Hey, Sachi, c'mere!"

The woman Keita beckoned over was the small black-haired spear-wielder. The woman named Sachi came, wineglass in hand, and nodded to me shyly. Keita placed a hand atop her head as he explained.

"As you can tell, her weapon is a two-handed longspear, but her skill numbers are lower than our other spearman. So I want to switch her to a sword and shield now, while we have the chance. But it's hard to find the time to train something like that, and she's having trouble getting the hang of the sword. Do you think you might be able to coach her a bit?"

"Oh, don't treat me like such a child!" Sachi retorted, then stuck out her tongue and laughed. "I always liked standing in the back and poking the bad guys with a long pole. It's scary switching to the front and getting up close and personal!"

"How many times do I have to tell you, that's why you get to hide behind the shield! Seriously, you've always been such a scaredy-cat."

Until now, I'd lived a Spartan life on the frontier of SAO and was used to MMORPGs being nothing but a competition over limited resources. This friendly bickering was a pleasant and radiant scene to behold. When Keita noticed the way I was watching them, he chuckled and explained with a touch of embarrassment.

"See, all of us used to be in the same computer club in high school. She and I lived pretty close to each other, in fact... Oh, but don't worry. They're all really nice, and I'm sure you'll fit in right away, Kirito."

I'd already seen proof of their friendly nature on the trip out of the labyrinth. The fact that I was lying to them sent a prickle of guilt down my spine, but I smiled and nodded anyway.

"In that case... I guess I'm in. It's nice to be here."

The Moonlit Black Cats' party balance was vastly improved just from adding a second fighter to the front rank.

If any of them had bothered to glance at my HP bar with just

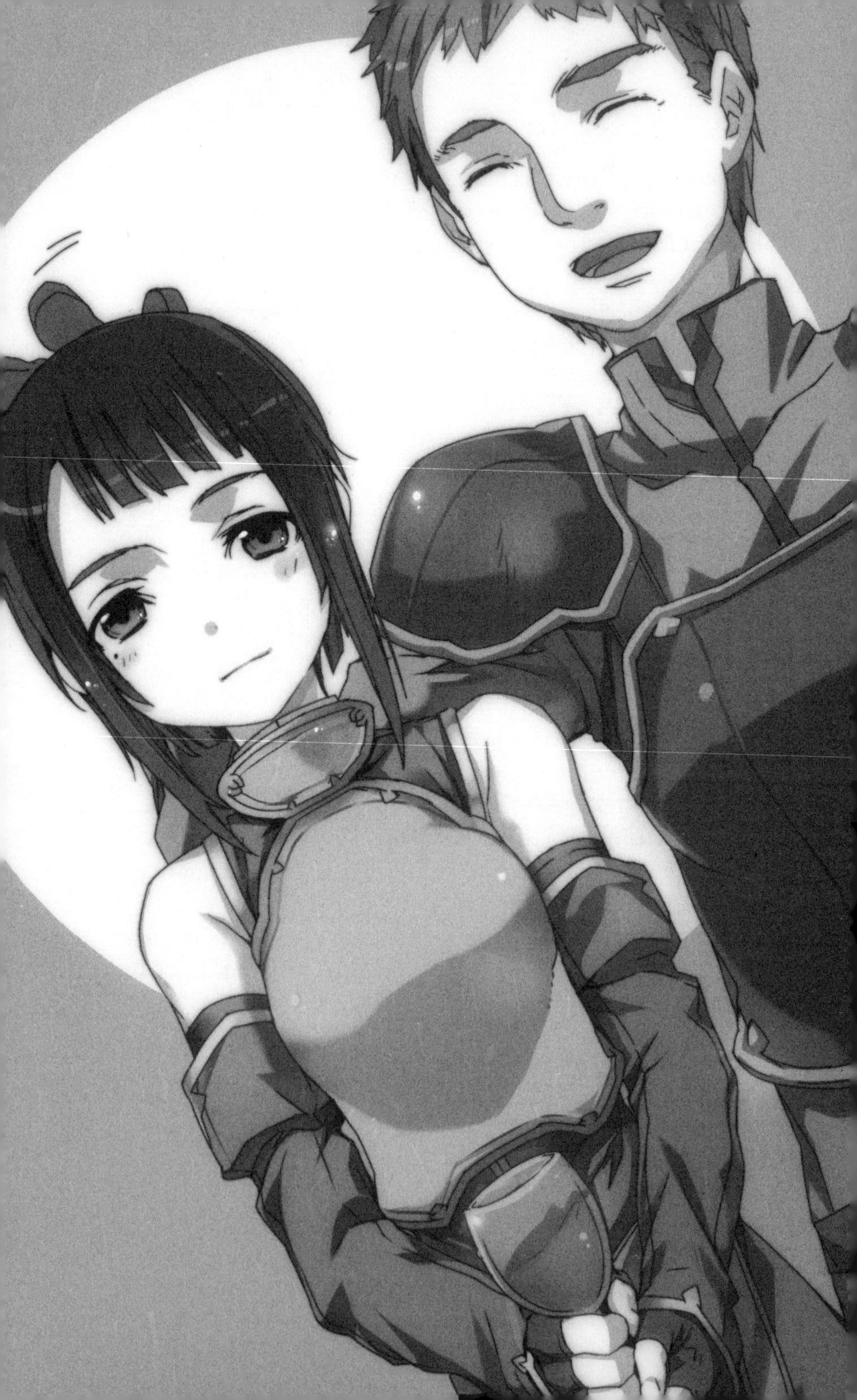

a smidgen of suspicion, they would have noticed that it mysteriously never seemed to diminish. But when I told my trusting guildmates that my coat was made of a special material—this, at least, was not a lie—they took it at face value.

When we fought as a party, I focused solely on defense, allowing the rear members to do the killing blows that gave them experience bonuses. Keita's group was leveling quickly now, and just a week after I joined, we were hunting on the next floor up.

We were sitting in a circle in the dungeon's safe haven, chowing down on Sachi's homemade sandwiches, as Keita eagerly told me about his personal dreams.

"Of course, the safety of the group comes first…but if safety is all you want, we could be sitting on our hands back in the Town of Beginnings, right? I'm hoping that if we keep leveling up like this, eventually we'll be good enough to join the clearers in advancing the game. Right now, top guilds like the Knights of the Blood and the Divine Dragon Alliance are doing all the heavy lifting up above. What do you suppose separates them from us, Kirito?"

"Umm…information, maybe? They seem to have a stranglehold on where the most efficient hunting grounds are and how to get the best weapons."

This was a fact I'd learned from being one of those heavy lifters myself, but Keita wasn't satisfied with that answer.

"Well…I'm sure that's part of it. But I think it's willpower. Like they have the strength of will not just to protect one another but all the players in the game. It's that source of strength that helps them keep beating bosses, one after the other. We're still on the side that's being protected, but I think our will to help is just as strong as theirs. That's why I think that if we keep trying our hardest, we'll catch up to them someday."

"I see…Let's hope so."

I reassured him, but inwardly, I knew it wasn't anything so noble. The motivation that drove the clearers to be what they were was simple: the obsession with being the very strongest swordsman who stood atop all the thousands in the game. Consider this: If the clearers of SAO truly wanted to protect the entire gaming populace, they would take their hard-earned information and items and share them as evenly as possible with all the mid-level players. Doing so would both raise the floor of all players and vastly increase the number of fighters available to tackle the latest bosses.

The reason they didn't share any of that was because they wanted to stay on top. I was no exception. At the time, I was slipping out of the inn late at night and teleporting to the latest floor to keep leveling up. Doing so only increased the level gap between the rest of the Moonlit Black Cats and me. I was betraying their trust, I knew it, and I kept doing it.

But at the time, I actually believed him a bit. I thought that just maybe, if I helped power-level the guild up to reach the top echelon of players, Keita and his ideals might just break through the closed circle of the clearers and change them for the better.

The Moonlit Black Cats' advancement was truly startling. The places they were adventuring I'd conquered long before, so I knew the danger spots to avoid and the lucrative spots to hit. With my careful guidance through the ideal paths, the average level of the guild shot upward, well ahead of the pack. They'd been ten floors below the current front line when I met them, and in short order they'd closed that gap to five. The guild's coffers were positively bulging, and the purchase of our own guild home was becoming a realistic goal.

The one thing that wasn't going perfectly for the guild was the plan to turn Sachi into a shield-bearing swordswoman.

I couldn't blame her for having trouble. More than statistical prowess, in order to tackle the challenge of close-range combat, you needed the steadfast courage to overcome the fear of SAO's terrifying beasts. Many players had lost their lives just after the start of the game because they panicked in close combat. Sachi was the gentle and timid type, which made her particularly unsuited for that kind of battle.

I wasn't in any particular rush to advance her training as a shield-user, knowing full well that I was powerful enough to be all the defense the group needed, but our guildmates did not agree. In fact, they seemed to be upset that despite being the new member, I was "forced" to take on much of the stressful front-line duty. Because the group was so close-knit, they didn't speak their minds openly, but the pressure on Sachi was intensifying.

And then, one night, Sachi disappeared from the inn.

The inability to check her location in the guild registry was likely a sign that she was inside a labyrinth all by herself. Keita and the others flew into a panic and decided to go searching for her.

I was the only one who insisted on searching outside of the labyrinth. I told them there were a few places out in the wilderness that had similar cloaking qualities, but that was only a bluff. In fact, I was certain I could find her because I had the Track skill, a high-level offshoot of the Search skill, but I couldn't let the others know that.

After they raced off toward the floor's labyrinth, I stood in front of Sachi's room and activated my Track skill, then followed the trail of light green footsteps that appeared.

To my surprise, the little footprints disappeared into a waterway on the outskirts of town. I peered inside, and amidst the echoing drips in the darkness, I saw Sachi, huddled in the corner beneath a concealing cloak she'd recently acquired.

"Sachi…"

Her shoulder-length hair draped over her face as she looked up, startled.

"Kirito…how did you know I'd be here?"

I paused, trying to think of an answer.

"Call it a hunch."

"Oh…"

She smiled weakly, then placed her head back on top of her knees. I resumed my rapid contemplation, searching for the least suspicious words I could offer.

"Everyone's worried about you. They went looking in the labyrinth. Let's go back."

She didn't respond for quite a while. A minute passed, maybe two. Just as I was about to repeat myself, I heard her mutter, face still down.

"Will you run away with me, Kirito?"

"Run away? What from?" I asked automatically.

"From this town. From the Black Cats. From the monsters… From Sword Art Online."

I didn't know enough about girls—about people in general—to have an immediate answer for this. After another long period of thinking, I hesitantly asked a question.

"What, like…a suicide pact?"

After a moment of silence, Sachi let out a humorless chuckle.

"Ha-ha…Yeah, maybe…Sorry, no. If I had the guts to die, I wouldn't be hiding in town like this. Sit down; don't just stand there."

Still unsure of what to do, I sat down on the cobblestones, slightly apart from Sachi. The lights of the town filtered faintly through the crescent-shaped waterway exit, like starlight.

"I'm scared to die. I'm so scared, I can barely sleep anymore," she murmured. "Why did this happen to us? Why can't we leave the game? If it's just a game, why do we have to die when we lose? What does that Kayaba person stand to gain from this? What's the meaning of it all…?"

I could have given a separate answer to each of these five questions. But even I knew that those weren't the answers Sachi was asking for. I considered her words and found my voice.

"I don't think there is a meaning…and no one's getting anything. All the important things were finished from the moment this world was built."

I'd told a horrible lie to the girl who sat next to me crying so hard the tears had stopped. I was getting something out of this—I was deriving pleasure from slipping into the Black Cats and hiding the truth of my own strength, of feeling superior to them.

I should have told her everything at that point. If I had even an ounce of sincerity in my body, I would have laid bare my own hideous ego right there and then. At the very least, that might have taken some of the pressure off Sachi—maybe even given her a little peace of mind.

Instead, I sold her pure fiction.

"...You're not going to die."

"How can you be sure?"

"The Black Cats are plenty strong as they are now. We're well within the margin of safety. As long as you're in this guild, you'll be safe. And there's no reason to force yourself to become a swordswoman."

Sachi looked up at me, her eyes pleading. I turned away, unable to face her stare.

"Really...? You're sure I won't die? I'll get back to my real life?"

"Yeah...you won't die. Not before we beat this game and get out of here."

They were the cheapest words I could have possibly said, without a shred of conviction or believability. But Sachi inched over to my side anyway, put her head on my shoulder, and cried.

A few minutes later, I sent a message to Keita's group and escorted Sachi back to the inn. I sent her up to her room, then waited in the pub on the first floor for the group's return. When they got back, I explained the situation to them: that it would take time to teach Sachi the shield, that she should remain a spear-fighter for now, that I wasn't bothered at all by staying on the forward line.

They seemed to be a bit suspicious of whatever had happened between the two of us, but they graciously accepted my proposal.

I was relieved at that, but it hadn't actually addressed the fundamental problem, of course.

Starting the next night, Sachi came to lie in my bed and was finally able to sleep again. She claimed that lying next to me while I told her she wouldn't die was the only way she could relax enough to sleep. This meant that I could no longer slip out late at night to farm more experience, but it didn't ease the feeling of guilt over deceiving Sachi and her friends.

My memories of that time are as tightly packed as a snowball, and it's difficult to recall the details. If there's anything I can say, it's that there was no romance between the two of us. We slept in the same bed, but there was no touching, no whispering words of love, no long stares into each other's eyes.

We were like two alley cats finding solace in licking each other's wounds. Hearing my words, Sachi was able to forget her fear, and by providing for her, I was able to assuage my guilt at being a dirty beater.

That's right—by observing Sachi's anguish, I think I was finally able to see the true nature of SAO. Until that point, I'd never truly felt the dread of knowing that this game could kill me. I'd blazed through the lower floors, mechanically slaying the monsters I'd known inside out since the beta test, then used that level buffer to maintain my place among the top clearers in the game. I was no Heathcliff, but thinking back on it, my HP bar had basically never fallen into the danger zone...

I'd been lounging atop a mountain of resources I'd won without any trouble, while countless players around me trembled in terror at the very real possibility of death. By facing and recognizing this injustice, I felt like I had finally found a way to assuage my own guilt: protecting Sachi and the rest of the Moonlit Black Cats.

I forced myself to forget that I'd joined their guild and concealed my level for the purpose of feeling better about myself, and I told myself that my lies were protecting them and raising them into a first-class guild. I was trying to change my own memory to support my ego. Every night, Sachi curled into a ball next to me, and I repeated, *You won't die; you won't die; you will survive* like a magic charm. When I did so, Sachi would look up at me underneath the blanket, smile just a little bit, and fall into a light sleep.

But Sachi died in the end.

Not even a month from that night in the underground sewer, she was cut down by monsters right before my eyes, her body and soul scattering into nothingness.

That day, Keita was off visiting a real-estate dealer to inquire about a one-story house to use as our guild base—we'd finally scraped together the amount we'd set as our goal. Sachi and I and the three other members sat around the inn waiting for Keita's return, laughing at the miserable amount of col remaining in our shared guild inventory. Eventually, Tetsuo the macer spoke up with an idea.

"Hey, let's go make some money in the labyrinth and buy a set of furniture for the new house. Keita'll freak out when he sees it."

We decided to go to the labyrinth just three floors below the current frontier, a dungeon we'd never visited as a group before. I'd been there before, of course, and I knew that it was a lucrative destination full of dangerous traps. But I didn't tell them that.

Level-wise, we were relatively safe within the dungeon, and our hunting was fruitful. We raised our expected quota within an hour and were turning around to leave and shop for our furniture when the guild's thief found a treasure chest.

I told him that we should ignore the chest. But when he asked why, I couldn't tell him that I knew the traps were noticeably more dangerous on this floor. I only gave him a vague excuse, saying I got a bad feeling from it.

When he opened the chest anyway, an alarm trap clanged noisily, and monsters stormed through the three doorways into the room. I immediately sensed that we were in trouble and commanded everyone to use crystals to teleport out. But when it became apparent that we were also standing in an anti-crystal zone and there was no escape, the entire group fell into a panic—myself included.

The first to die was the thief who'd set off the trap. Next was Tetsuo the macer, then the spearman.

I was terrified, and I unleashed a storm of the high-level skills I'd been hiding this entire time, desperately trying to stem the tide of monsters. But there were too many. I didn't even have enough time to turn around and destroy the ringing alarm that was summoning them.

Just as Sachi was about to be swallowed by the wave of monsters, she stretched out a hand and opened her mouth, as if to say something to me. All I saw in her eyes was a heartrending, pleading trust, the same light she shone on me every night.

I don't remember how I survived. The next thing I knew, the storm of monsters and my four guildmates were gone. And even after all of that, my HP bar was barely less than halfway full.

I returned to the inn alone, my mind a blank slate.

Keita was sitting there waiting, the key to our new guild house on the table. He listened to my story—why the others died, why I survived—and when I was done, he looked at me with eyes devoid of all emotion and said just one thing. *You're a beater. You didn't have the right to get involved with us.*

He stood up and marched his way to the outer perimeter of Aincrad, and before my very eyes, he vaulted over the fence with no hesitation and flung himself into the infinite void.

Keita had spoken the absolute truth. There was no doubt that my pride, my arrogance, had killed the four—no, five—members of the Moonlit Black Cats. If I hadn't gotten involved with them, they'd have stayed down in the safe middle zone. They'd never have rashly attempted to disarm a trap far beyond their means.

The key to survival in Sword Art Online isn't reflexes, or stats, or weapons—it's adequate knowledge. I'd given them a quick step up, an advanced course in power-leveling, but I didn't give them information. That was a tragedy waiting to happen. I swore to Sachi that I'd protect her life, and I ended up killing her.

I needed to accept whatever word she was going to say in that final moment, even if it was the worst curse she could possibly hurl at me. That was the reason I clung to the slim possibility of that item of resurrection. I had to hear that word.

3

In the four days leading up to Christmas, I managed to squeeze in one more level, putting me at 70.

I literally didn't sleep a wink during that period. At times I was plagued by headaches that felt as though nails were being driven into my brain. It was probably what I deserved, but I don't think I could have slept if I'd tried, anyway.

Klein and the rest of Furinkazan didn't show up at the ant canyon spot again. I kept lining up between the parties from the major guilds, mechanically slaying ants over and over. With time, the looks I got turned from mocking to hateful. I think some of them might have called out to me, but whenever I met those gazes, I turned away and left.

The biggest debate among the many hopeful adventurers looking to seize Nicholas the Renegade's Christmas presents was where exactly to find the giant fir tree he was said to appear beneath. As a matter of fact, between my grinding sessions with the ants, I had arrived at an answer I was certain was correct.

I'd bought the locations of several major trees from informants and gone to inspect them all in turn. What I found was that they all had the look of a classic Christmas tree, but they were all cedars—not firs. Unlike the spiky-pointed leaves of a cedar tree, fir tree needles are rounded at the end like little ellipses. I knew the difference because we had trees of both types in my backyard growing up.

Several months earlier, I'd been exploring a random-teleporting dungeon called the Forest of Wandering on the thirty-fifth floor, where I found one giant, gnarled tree. It was so strange and distinct that it had to have a purpose, and I'd investigated the possibility that it might be involved in a quest of some kind, but to no avail. Thinking back on it now, I know the tree had been a fir. I was absolutely certain that on this very night, the flag mob named Nicholas the Renegade was going to appear at the foot of that tree.

I continued wiping up the ants around me while the fanfare celebrating my level-up to 70 played. When both were finished, I pulled a teleport crystal out of my pouch, then immediately jumped to the town on the forty-ninth floor without bothering to inform any of the waiting players.

Once in the teleport square, I checked the clock tower to see that barely three hours remained until midnight. The rest of the plaza was filled with people walking in pairs, hand-in-hand or around the shoulder, strolling leisurely. I weaved my way past them and hurried to the inn.

Inside the building, I raced to the room I'd been using for weeks. First I opened the storage chest and pulled all of the healing and antidote crystals and potions from the item window that appeared and transferred them to my inventory. They represented a fortune in monetary terms, but I was prepared to use every last one of them if necessary.

I also removed the rare sword I'd been saving for a special occasion, made sure it was in good condition, then switched it out with the sword on my back, which was damn ragged after all the ant-hunting. My leather coat and other pieces of armor were quickly replaced as well.

I was about to close the window when all my preparations were complete, but my hand stopped when I looked at the top of the item list.

There was a tab labeled SELF that contained all of my personal items and another tab titled SACHI next to it.

This was a shared inventory, a setting that players could enable when they were close but not going to get married. Unlike marriage, in which all items and money were shared, only the things either of us placed in this space were accessible to both of us.

Sachi had never wanted words of love or even a hand to hold, but she had suggested creating this space shortly before she died. When I'd asked her why, she said it would make sharing potions easier—a weak excuse, given that we had a shared guild tab for that very purpose already. But I agreed and set up a tab for us.

Even after Sachi died, the window remained. Her name was still on my friends list, of course, but now it was grayed out and inaccessible. The potions and crystals left in our shared inventory could no longer be used.

After half a year, I still couldn't bring myself to remove that tab, even though I'd mechanically eliminated the guild tab without a second thought. It wasn't even because I thought there was any way to bring her back. I just couldn't allow myself to erase that reminder of my guilt.

I stared at Sachi's name, lost in thought for nearly ten minutes before I came back to my senses and closed the window. Two hours until midnight.

On the way from my room to the teleport square, I thought back to the look on Sachi's face in that final moment, over and over, wondering what it was she was about to say.

When I walked through the teleporter and onto the thirty-fifth floor, the town was far quieter than on the front line. It wasn't quite at the epicenter of the mid-level players' hunting range, and the town itself was a rather unremarkable rural village. Still, there were players here and there, so I flipped up the collar of my coat to avoid their gazes as I sped out of town.

I had neither the time nor the peace of mind to bother with

monsters on the way. I turned around to make sure no one was trailing me, then took off at full speed. The past months' insane leveling had given a big boost to my agility, so my legs felt light as feathers as I tore across the fields of snow. The usual dull pain throbbed in my temples, but at least that kept sleep from overwhelming my brain.

After a ten-minute sprint, I reached the entrance to the Forest of Wandering. This dungeon was split into countless square areas, the connecting exits of which jumped about at random, making it virtually impossible to manage without a special map.

I opened mine and took a hard look at the sector I'd marked beforehand, tracing the route back to the entrance. I burned the directions into my brain, then headed into the black night of the forest.

I reached the fir tree's area with a minimum of trouble, only needing to stop for two fights I couldn't run past. I had thirty minutes left.

I could easily lose my life doing this; I was going to fight one-on-one against a boss monster that could almost certainly kill me, but I didn't feel even the slightest hint of fear. In fact, I almost felt as though I would welcome that outcome. If there was one way I was allowed to die, it would be in a quest to bring Sachi back to life...

I didn't think of it in heroic terms—that I was "searching for my place to die." I wasn't allowed to seek a meaning in my own death. Not when I'd let Sachi and our four friends die without purpose.

What does it mean? Sachi had asked me. *There is no meaning,* I'd responded.

Now I had the chance to make those words reality. Sachi had died a meaningless death within a meaningless death game, created by a meaningless mad genius named Akihiko Kayaba. Now, just like her, I was going to die alone, forgotten by all, bereft of any meaning.

If I somehow survived and defeated this boss, the rumors of the resurrection item would certainly turn out to be true. I had no proof, but I was certain. Sachi's soul would come back from the Land of the Dead or the River Lethe or wherever she was, and I would be able to hear her final words at last. Finally, finally, the time had come…

Just as I began to close the last several meters to the tree, I sensed several players emerging from the warp point behind me. I held my breath and put a hand on my sword, leaping away from them.

They numbered around ten. Standing at the lead was a man like a samurai, outfitted with light armor, a lengthy blade, and a bandanna tied around his head—Klein.

The members of Furinkazan looked around nervously as they approached. I stared straight at Klein and growled.

"You followed me?"

He nodded, scratching the hair that was splayed upward by his bandanna. "That's right. We've got an expert in Tracking."

"Why me?"

"Because I caught a tip that you'd been buying intel on tree coordinates. I had one of us planted in the forty-ninth-floor square watching for you, and he saw you take off for a floor without any of those publicly known coordinates. Listen, I think your talent for battle and your game instincts are off the charts. In my opinion, you're the best player among the clearers…even better than Heathcliff. Which is exactly why I refuse to see you throw away your life like this, Kirito!"

He reached out and jabbed a finger right at my face.

"Forget about tackling this monster on your own! You're joining our party for this. Whoever gets the resurrection item to drop keeps it, and no hard feelings!"

"But then…" I couldn't even believe that Klein's words stemmed from friendship and honest concern at this point. "Then there's no *point*…I have to do it alone…"

I still clutched the hilt of my sword. My mind was racing, feverish.

I have to kill them all.

When this game of death began, I'd abandoned Klein as an utter newb and headed for the next town on my own, an act I deeply regretted for a very long time. When Klein survived the game's trials and had grown into a powerful warrior in his own right, I was profoundly relieved.

In this moment, I was honestly considering killing one of the precious few people I could call a friend—sinking to the depths of a criminal to achieve my goal. A tiny voice in my brain cried, *Don't do it, it's pointless!,* but a much louder one drowned it out, bellowing, *A meaningless death is exactly what you want.*

If I drew my sword out even an inch, I knew I wouldn't be able to stop myself. I was sure of it. My right hand trembled as the two conflicting urges fought for control over me. Klein just looked on, pity in his eyes.

That was the exact moment that a third party entered the opening.

And this party was not a mere ten strong. Just at a glance, they had to be at least three times that size. I stared at the throng in astonishment, then muttered to the equally stunned Klein next to me.

"Guess you guys got followed, too, Klein."

"...Guess we did..."

The newcomers stood at the edge of the clearing about five meters away, staring at Furinkazan and me. I recognized several of their faces from the ant canyon. The Furinkazan swordsman standing closest to Klein leaned over and murmured softly.

"That's the Divine Dragon Alliance. They're not afraid to go orange for the sake of a flag boss."

I knew that name. They were the largest of the clearer guilds, just as famous as the Knights of the Blood. Their average level was likely lower than mine, but even I didn't think I could win against so many.

But wasn't that really the same thing, when you got down to it?

Whether killed by the boss or killed by a guild, I was dying an ignoble death either way, I realized. And it had to be a better way than fighting Klein, right?

This time, I was going to draw my sword. I was tired of thinking. Better to turn myself into a machine. I swing my sword with all of my being, kill everything in sight, and eventually I'll wear down and break.

But Klein's bellow stayed my hand.

"Shit! Goddammit!" He'd drawn his weapon even before I did, and he called out to me with his back turned. "Go, Kirito! We'll hold 'em off! Go and kill that boss! Just make sure you don't die in the process! You're not permitted to die before I do! Is that understood?!"

"..."

There was hardly any time left. I turned my back on Klein as well, then headed off toward the final warp point without a word of thanks.

The fir tree was just where I remembered it, and just as gnarled and twisted, too. It stood in the center of the almost empty clearing, sparkling bone-white from piles of snow. It was like a meadow barren of all life.

When the clock readout in the corner of my vision hit midnight, the air was filled with the sound of jingling bells. I looked up to the top of the tree.

Amid the black of the night sky—technically, just the bottom of the floor above—two lines of light appeared. When I focused harder, I saw that it was a giant sled being drawn by hideous monsters.

When it reached the top of the fir tree, a black shadow leaped from the sled, and I stumbled backward several steps.

The monster that landed in the snow with an impressive splash had to be at least three times my height. It was humanoid, but its arms were freakishly long, and it hunched over in a way that made it appear to drag along the ground. In the darkness beneath its jutting brow, two small red eyes glowed, and scraggly gray whiskers drooped down from the bottom of its head to dangle at its legs.

What was truly grotesque about it, however, were the red-and-white jacket and pointed cap it wore, and the ax and sack it carried. The designer of this creature likely figured that players would see this twisted caricature of the familiar Santa Claus and either quake in fear and revulsion, or laugh out loud. But facing Nicholas the Renegade alone, the creative intention behind the beast was the last thing on my mind.

Nicholas opened its mouth, the twisted beard wriggling as it readied to speak its dramatic line of quest dialogue.

"Shut up," I muttered, drawing my sword and leaping forward through the snow.

4

For the first time in an entire year of play in Sword Art Online, my HP fell into the red zone and stayed there.

When the boss finally fell and exploded, leaving only his sack behind, I didn't have a single recovery crystal left. I'd been closer to death than ever before, but despite my slim survival, I felt no joy of victory or relief. It was almost a sense of disappointment. *Oh, I'm still alive.*

The sack of presents followed by shattering into fragments of light as I slowly returned my sword to its sheath. All the items the boss dropped would have automatically been added to my inventory. I sighed heavily and raised a trembling hand to call up the window.

There was an almost disgusting number of new items in the display: weapons and armor, various jewels and crystals, even food ingredients. I carefully scrolled through the extensive list, looking for only one thing.

A few seconds later, it popped into my view, so matter-of-factly that it caught me off-guard.

It was labeled the SACRED STONE OF REBIRTH. My heart instantly leaped to life—it felt as though the paralysis that had afflicted it for the past days and months was finally wearing off, and blood was flowing through it again.

Would I really, truly be able to bring Sachi back? Was it possible that Keita and Tetsuo and everyone else who'd died in SAO might not have lost their souls after all...?

I might be able to see Sachi again. The thought set my heart trembling. No matter the insults she might hurl at me, no matter the lies she might rightfully accuse me of, this time I would hold her in my arms and tell her. Not that she wouldn't die, but that I would protect her. That I'd made myself so much stronger just for that purpose.

My trembling fingers stumbling several times, I finally got the Sacred Stone out of my inventory. The egg-sized jewel hung radiant above my status window, sparkling beautifully with the colors of the rainbow.

"Sachi...Sachi..."

I called out her name as I clicked the jewel and hit the HELP button. A simple description appeared in that familiar system font.

"By selecting the Use command from this pop-up window or calling out the command 'Revive: (Player Name)' with it held in your hand, the target player can be brought back to life during the brief period (roughly ten seconds) between death and the conclusion of the disintegration visual effect."

Roughly ten seconds.

That tiny little phrase told me in the clearest, cruelest terms that Sachi was dead, and she would never come back.

Roughly ten seconds. That was the amount of time that the NerveGear took to microwave the player's actual brain after her HP dropped to zero and her avatar shattered into pieces.

I couldn't help but imagine it. When Sachi's body disappeared, just ten seconds later, the NerveGear on her head killed its wearer. Did Sachi suffer? What did she think in those final ten seconds? Did she curse me to her final moment...?

"Aaah...aaaahhh..."

It burst out of me like an animal screech. I grabbed the Sacred Stone floating above my window and hurled it with all my strength against the snow.

"Aaaaaaahhh!!"

I stomped it with my boots repeatedly as I screamed, but the jewel kept gleaming, expressionless. It didn't break in half; it didn't even crack. I roared with all of my being, got down on my hands and scrabbled through the snow wildly, rolled back and forth as though possessed.

It was meaningless. It had all been for nothing. Sachi's fear and pain and death, my insane fight against the Christmas boss, even the birth of this world and the imprisonment of ten thousand innocent people inside of it. There was no meaning to any of it. In this moment, I understood entirely that this was the one absolute truth of SAO.

How long did I go on? No matter how much I screamed and wailed, it never felt like I was going to cry. My avatar must not even have had that function. Eventually I dragged myself onto my feet, picked the stone out of the snow, and headed back to the warp point that led to the previous area.

Only Klein and the rest of Furinkazan were left in the clearing. The Divine Dragon Alliance was gone. I mechanically counted Klein's group to confirm that none of them had died as I walked up to their seated leader.

Klein appeared to be just as terribly exhausted as I was. I guessed that he had decided to settle the matter with the DDA through a one-on-one duel, but no emotion rose in my chest at the thought.

He looked up at my approach, and relief crossed his face for a moment. But he must have noticed my expression, because his mouth tightened immediately.

"…Kirito…"

He muttered it, his voice hoarse. I tossed the crystal onto his knees.

"That's the resurrection item. You can't use it on someone who died in the past. Next time someone dies in your presence, use that on them."

I had nothing more to say. I turned to leave, but Klein grabbed my coat.

"Kirito…Kirito, man…"

I watched with curiosity the two trails of tears run down his stubbled cheeks, as though they were some rare and unfamiliar phenomenon.

"Kirito…you gotta promise…that you'll survive…Even if everyone else dies, you gotta keep going, man…Live on until the end…"

I pulled my coat from Klein's fingers as he continued bawling and repeating himself.

"So long," I said, and walked off into the Forest of Wandering.

The next thing I remembered, I was back in my inn room on the forty-ninth floor.

It was after three o'clock in the morning.

I wondered what I would do next. My reason for living over the past month, the resurrection stone, had been real, after all—but not what I wanted. Over that time, I'd turned myself into a laughingstock, a fool starved for experience points. I'd even lost the last remaining friendship I had at the end.

After long, embattled thought, I decided to challenge the boss of this floor's labyrinth in the morning. If I won, I'd go straight up against the boss of the fiftieth floor. Then the fifty-first.

It was the only fitting ending to such a pitiful clown. I felt much better once I made up my mind to do it, and I sat in my chair waiting for the dawn, unseeing and unthinking.

The moonlight streaming through the window slowly changed position bit by bit, then faded, replaced by the dim gray light of dawn. I had no idea how long it'd been since I'd last slept, but for it being my final morning after the worst night ever, I felt surprisingly good.

The clock on the wall pointed to seven, and I was just standing up from the chair when an unfamiliar alarm reached my ears.

I looked around the room but could not identify the source of the sound. Eventually, I noticed in the corner of my vision that a purple marker alerting me to open my main menu was flashing. I waved my fingers to bring it up.

Inside the menu, the tab for my shared inventory with Sachi was glowing. There was some kind of timed alarm item inside of it. I scrolled through the items, confused, until I found an audio message crystal that was timed to go off today.

I removed it from the menu and placed it on top of the table.

When I clicked the crystal, I heard the familiar sound of Sachi's voice.

Merry Christmas, Kirito.

By the time you hear this, I will likely already be dead. If I were alive, I would have taken this crystal out and told you this on Christmas Eve myself.

Well…first, I should probably explain why I decided to record this message.

I don't think I'm going to survive for very long. Of course, I don't mean this in the sense that I think you or anyone in the Black Cats isn't strong enough. You're an incredibly good player, and I can tell that everyone else is getting better by the day.

Umm, how should I explain…? Recently, a good friend of mine died, someone from another guild. That friend was just as big a scaredy-cat as me, and never hunted anywhere that wasn't supposed to be absolutely safe, but that didn't matter when a monster attacked her all alone at the worst possible time. This really made me think for a long time, and I realized something. If you want to survive throughout this entire game, it doesn't matter how strong your friends are. If you yourself don't have the will to live, the determination to survive, you won't make it.

I'll be honest—I was scared from the moment I first set foot in the wilderness. I never wanted to leave the Town of Beginnings. I was friends with everyone in the Moonlit Black Cats in real life, and it was fun being around them, but I never wanted to go out and hunt. And with that kind of attitude, I was bound to die someday. It's not anyone else's fault. That's all me.

Ever since that one time, you've told me I'll be all right, every single night. That I'd never die. So if I die, I have a feeling that you'll blame yourself terribly. You'll never want to forgive yourself. That's why I decided to record this message: to tell you that it's not your fault. I wanted to tell you that it's my fault. I set the timer on this message to next Christmas because I wanted to try lasting until that long, at least. I want to walk through town with you while the snow is out.

To tell the truth…I know how strong you are. Once, when I was in your bed, I woke up and saw your window open over your shoulder.

I tried my hardest to think of why you would work with us but hide your real level, and I still don't understand. But I figured you would tell me eventually, so I stayed quiet about it. I…I was really happy to know how strong you are. Once I knew that, I was finally able to sleep at your side without any fear. And the idea that you might actually need to be around me made me really happy. That meant that there was even a meaning to a scaredy-cat like me reaching the upper floors.

Um…um, so what I want to say is that even if I die, I want you to keep going. Stay alive until the end of the game and find the reason why this world was created, the reason why a wimp like me came here, and the reason that we met. That's my only wish.

Umm…there's a whole lot of time left here. These things can really hold a lot of storage. Well, since it's Christmas, I'll sing you a song. I'm actually a pretty good singer. I'll sing you "Rudolph the Red-Nosed Reindeer." Normally I'd pick something a bit cooler, like "Winter Wonderland" or "White Christmas," but this is the only one I remember the lyrics to.

Why do I remember the lyrics to "Rudolph"? The other night, you said that everyone has a role to fill. That there was a reason everyone was here, even me. That made me really happy, and it reminded me of this song. It was almost like I was the reindeer and you were Santa. Okay, to be honest…it was more like you were my dad. My dad left when I was little, so every night, I've wondered if this is what it's like to sleep next to your dad. Okay, here goes.

Rudolph the Red-Nosed Reindeer / Had a very shiny nose
And if you ever saw it / You would even say it glows

All of the other reindeer / Used to laugh and call him names
They never let poor Rudolph / Join in any reindeer games

Then one foggy Christmas Eve / Santa came to say
Rudolph with your nose so bright / Won't you guide my sleigh
    tonight?

Then how the reindeer loved him / As they shouted out with
    glee
Rudolph the Red-Nosed Reindeer / You'll go down in history!

You were like the stars, shining and illuminating the dark
path in the middle of the night for me. So long, Kirito. I'm glad
I met you and got to be with you.

Thank you.
Good-bye.

(The End)

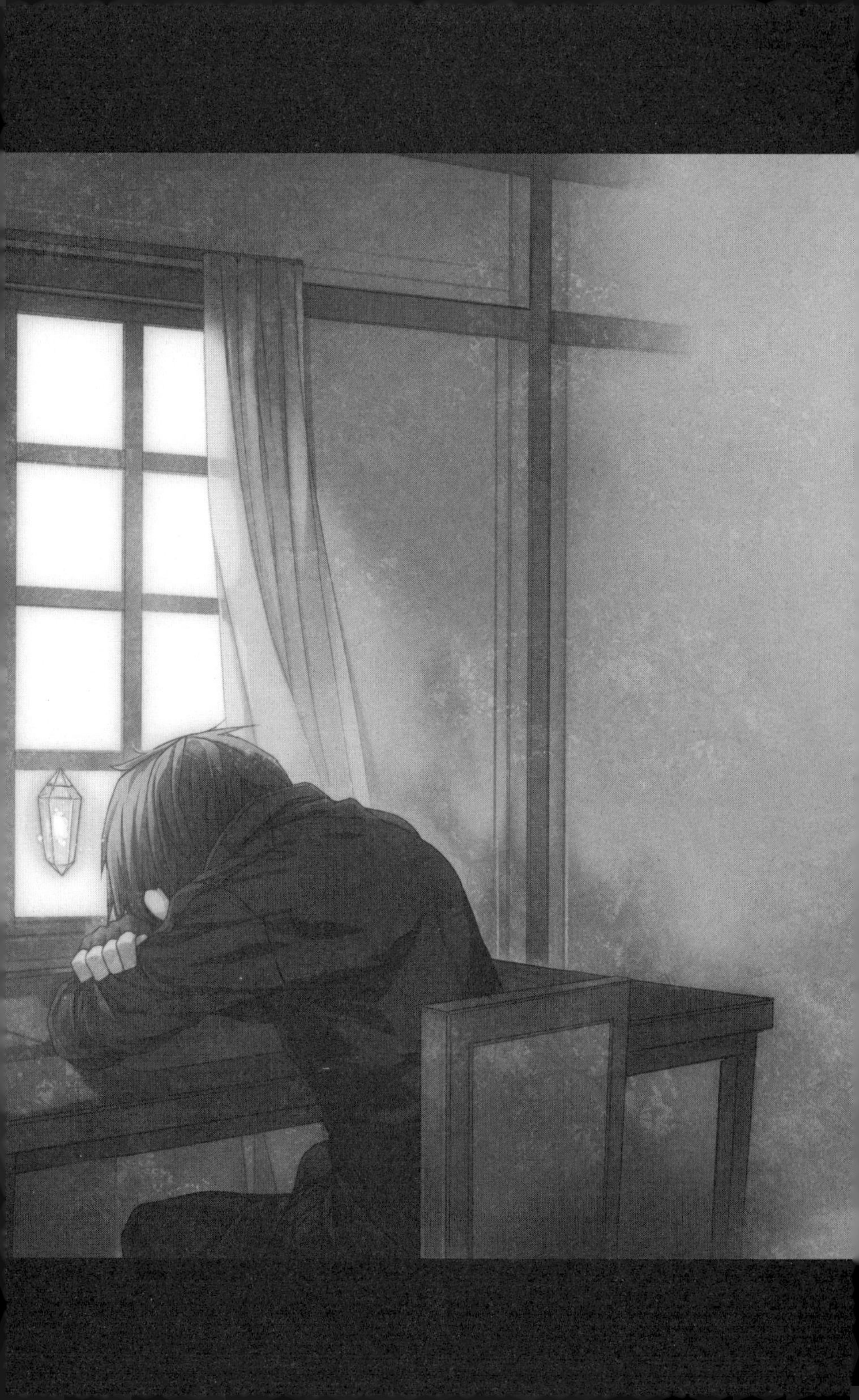

AFTERWORD

It's good to see you again—or for the first time, whichever the case may be. I'm Reki Kawahara. Thank you for reading Volume 2 of *Sword Art Online*.

After publishing the first volume, I received a great many responses wondering how the story could continue after an ending like that. After all, the game was beaten and the world came crashing down. I myself realized that there were virtually no elements of the story that might continue from there.

So here's the follow-up: a retread back in time. And not only that, a collection of sub-stories. I'm truly sorry for this...

I've played a number of online games in the past, and I never succeeded in joining the top echelon of players in any of them. I spent all of my days watching other players with rare weapons and elite stats crush hordes of monsters and marveling at their feats.

So while the first volume focused on Kirito and Asuna, two of the game's "clearers" (top players), I really wanted to write more about the normal, mid-level folks who don't get much of the spotlight. That's the angle I was going for with the four stories contained in Volume 2. Each story features Master Kirito kicking ass and taking names, but the admiration and wonder of the characters who watch him, like Silica and Lisbeth, are an expression of my long-held emotion toward such bad-asses in real life.

One of these days, I'd like to go around showing off a rare sword that only has three copies on the entire server, just to see what it's like.

One more apology. The heroine in each of the four stories in this volume is a different woman, but the male lead across from them is always Kirito. I realize there's no possible excuse for this blatant favoritism, but if I might attempt to rationalize it, think of a mystery series, in which the killer and victim are always different, but the detective is always the same, and you'll see that it's quite natural and normal to...Okay, you're right, sorry, sorry.

I'd like to end with enormous thanks to both abec, who provided charming and unique illustrations for each of the heroines in these stories, and to my editor, Mr. Miki, who was never intimidated by the weird and complicated background of my stories and still found the wherewithal to add his own suggestions and ideas.

But most of all, thanks to you for following along, dear reader.

Reki Kawahara—May 26th, 2009

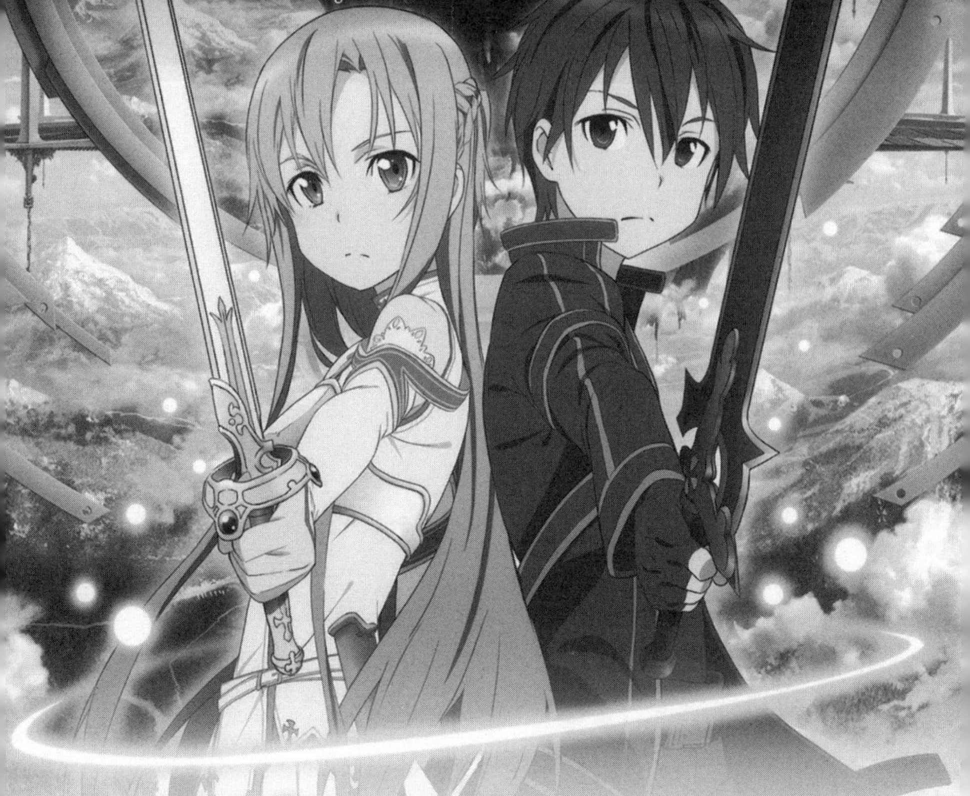

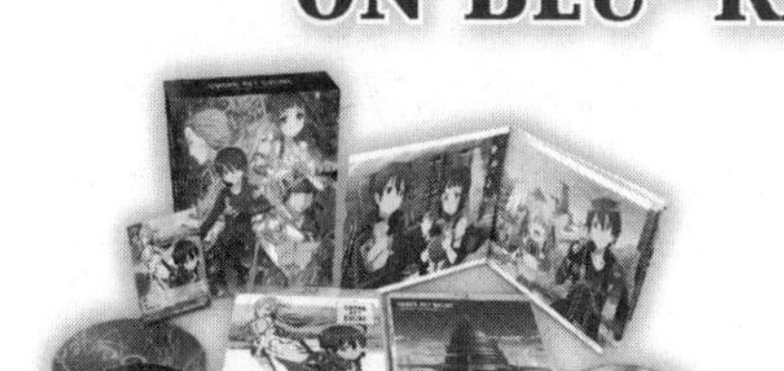

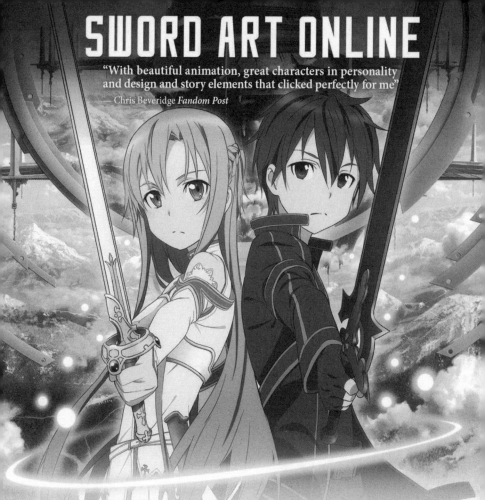

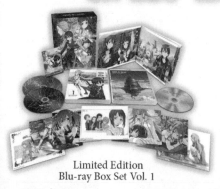